LOVE PAINTED IN LIES

A Maida Vale Tale

Holly Denham

Cover design by Nada Orlic
Interior layout by Penny Brucker

ISBN: 978-1738564811

A WARM THANK YOU TO:

Everyone in Maida Vale & Mayfield for your support. Especially those in The Rose & Crown & The Middle House

All our extended family from the FOHM Forum and all the wonderfully kind candidates from the world of corporate reception who have helped spread the word.

Michael for his valuable guidance on art-related matters and to Jo for encouragement and for helping us with her memories.

Also to our talented artistic cousins for, well, for just being them.

To our talented Editor (and mother) Jeanette, who worked on this so patiently (not patently –we got this right now x).

To Bonnie for her first Hurrah!

And finally, to Margaret & Barry, for their love.

Holly Denham

CONTENTS

Chapter One 9

MAIDA VALE, JULY 9

Chapter Two 31

A POLICEMAN CALLS 31

Chapter Three 59

WHAT HAPPENED 59

Chapter Four 81

DEVON 81

Chapter Five 95

TIME TO TELL 95

Chapter Six 115

THE INVITATION 115

Chapter Seven 129

THE PARTY 129

Chapter Eight 143

THE METROPOLITAN POLICE ART AND ANTIQUES UNIT 143

Chapter Nine 155

THINGS HEAT UP 155

Chapter Ten 169

EVERYONE KNOWS 169

Chapter Eleven 179

DATING DEVON 179

Chapter Twelve 197

INTO THE DARKNESS 197

Chapter Thirteen 211

THE NET CLOSES 211

Chapter Fourteen 217

CONFRONTATION 217

Chapter Fifteen 233

RUNNING AWAY 233

Chapter Sixteen 245

THE FESTIVAL 245

Chapter Seventeen 261

THE CHASE 261

Chapter Eighteen 281

THE PLAN 281

Chapter Nineteen 297

THE FINAL STRAW 297

Chapter Twenty 315

SIX MONTHS LATER 315

Chapter One

MAIDA VALE, JULY

~NOW~

Cool in the summer but drafty in the winter, my parents' Victorian basement conversion flat had been their home since before I was born, and now I had moved back in with them.

"I can make us all breakfast," Mum suggested from the kitchen doorway, unaware of our breathless panic. "And we have something in a tin here, I can put it in the oven or in the toaster?"

Dad mouthed her last words to himself, whilst his old eyes searched the walls, seemingly in the hope their meaning might be written there somewhere.

"No need. Thanks, Mum," I replied, snatching the tin of beans from her as I passed and placing it back on the kitchen bin-lid to stop it from springing open.

We had watched *Mamma Mia* the night before, while sharing a bottle of wine or two, which had left me feeling rather tender. "Has anyone fed the dogs yet?"

"I haven't," Dad uttered to himself.

I gave his arm a squeeze as I passed. With Dad's bad hip, he was really the only person I hadn't been asking.

"Mum, I can't find my schedule," Harriet whined.

The twins' bedroom was its usual bric-a-brac jumble of hidden secrets and lost dreams. Or just horribly messy, depending on your view.

Since having children, I had developed a range of new skills like saying, 'Show me the money,' when I wanted to scream 'Shit!'

"What is peace negotiation?" an impatient young recruiter had once asked, whilst studying my CV.

"If you had met the two Harries you would know," I had replied. He hadn't met them. They were told to wait outside. Which was a shame because when the twins were with me, I felt less awkward.

"Well, you can't put that on your CV," the recruiter had concluded. He was wrong, of course, because I did. 'Finding things' was another one he hadn't liked.

After a few minutes of kneeling down, my arms flailing around under her bed, I gave up and shuffled in on my front, and there, tucked in at the back, was Harriet's class schedule.

"Pah!" I said smugly.

The noises from the flat were softened underneath, and my cheek dropped onto the cold laminate floor.

"This would have been too much for you," I commented to my now-dead husband.

If you'd known how to cook a roast, my little Mk1, at least I'd have had a choice, he replied stiffly.

He often replied stiffly. But then not being alive would do that to you, wouldn't it?

It was peaceful under there, and I could have stayed, only

there were footsteps, shuffling, and Harriet's head appeared next to mine, her frizzy blonde mop partly stuck over her face.

"Mummy, who are you talking to?"

"I'm playing a game, shall we lie here all day?"

Harriet regarded me curiously. "No, Mummy, I have school and you have..."

"What?" I was interested.

She thought. "A lot of pets to look after."

"Your shirt will be covered in dust now."

"Dust and cat hair," she replied confidently. We inched our way back out and brushed ourselves off.

"Does anyone at school have this many animals?"

Harriet fixed me with her serious look. "Mummy, we have a zoo."

I checked my watch again. "Show me the money!" Taking her hand I led her through to the bathroom, snatching a hairbrush on the way. I began attacking her tangled tufts.

"OUCH! Mummy, that hurts!" Harriet squealed as the plastic prongs fought bravely against her curls.

It was my children's first week at a new junior school – we had joined at the end of the summer term, year five – and we had been late once already. And all the other girls there seemed to be on time, and immaculate, but I could never get Harriet's blonde frizz to stay in one place, whether tied back, bunches or plaits. Imagine the typical mad-scientist look – that was how she woke each day. It was basically untameable. And with mine and Harry's hair, with our mild espresso-toned waves, she had taken hers directly from her father. Walking back into my bedroom, my bare foot trod in something squishy. "What's that from?" I asked myself, inspecting the sole.

Harry answered for me. "A cat, Mum. It's cat sick."

"I know what it is, I mean what have they eaten that's been bad?"

"A rat from your cupboard? Because London is full of them," he taunted. "By the way, we forgot to tell you…"

"Oh my God! Why are you both still in pyjamas?!" I almost screamed.

"Because today," he flicked his wedge of dark chocolate hair away from those blue eyes, enjoying my pain, "is take-a-bottle-to-school-go-in-your-pyjamas-day."

"Right, and I'm a pickled walnut," I responded.

"It's true!" Harry shouted defensively.

Harriet joined in. "I know it sounds like he just made it up, Mummy, but it really is the truth."

"How is this even a thing?" I began making the bed.

Harry spoke slowly, as if it should be patently obvious to anyone with a brain. "If-you-donate-a-bottle-of-wine-for-the-raffle, we-can-go-to-school-in-our-pyjamas."

My mornings had often been filled with exciting surprises like this one. They usually started with the sentence, "We forgot to tell you today we need…" and at that point it could be anything at all. Seriously, like we need to take to school a frog that has a slight cough, or a box of blue ants, or a talking geranium. It was always information they should have shared with me weeks before that day. "So, it's pyjamas… OR…" I began hopefully, but I already knew the answer.

They replied together, "WE DO NOT LIKE 'ORs!'"

I gave in.

No time to wash. I threw on some jogging pants, fed the dogs and cats, emptied the compost bin, checked Dad's blood pressure, gave him his pills and his eye drops, topped up the water bowls and we were off.

Pouring out of our basement flat in a tish-tosh tumble of half-closed bags and unkempt hair, the Harries and I raced up our stone steps to the pavement above. The sun was just making its way along the buildings on the far side, not yet hitting the pavement, but you could feel it was going to be a scorcher of a day. Elgin Food & Wine was our local corner shop. Rummaging in the alcohol aisle in my grubby sweatpants, hair in a mess, smelling rather pungent from the previous night's wine, two children next to me in their pyjamas, I didn't realise we were being scrutinised by other shoppers.

"Get the cheapest bottle you can find, Harry!" I urged.

"There's wine here for a fiver, Mum?" he cried gaily.

"Too expensive," I replied. "There must be a cheaper bottle we can have?!"

"£3.99!" Harriet screamed joyfully.

"Bingo! That'll do us nicely," I cheered.

The three of us joined the back of a queue of people waiting to be served. A couple of heads turned, taking in our appearance.

Harry grumbled, as we approached the front, "Mum, we're going to be late for school again!"

"How is that my fault?" I fretted, plonking my wine on the counter in front of the shocked assistant. "When I have to buy this first."

Behind me, a hawkish woman with a hardened face said,

"Drinking at this time, and she can't even be bothered to dress the poor lambs."

"It's not for me," I explained, patting down my tangled hair. "It's for them." I threw her a big helpful grin, before we were outside and running up the street, while a nagging thought surfaced; my last comment probably hadn't helped matters.

Up the road, we rounded St Dunstan's gates.

"I've always thought schools look particularly eerie when empty," I noted.

"It's not empty, Mum," Harry said bitterly. "Everyone's in lessons."

A walk of shame through the playground, faces staring at us through windows.

We were given another late mark.

On the way back, I passed Shane the Caretaker (or scare-taker, as Harriet liked to call him), a jovial Irishman who it seemed always had time to offer words of wisdom. "Look at the state of you. Want to borrow a comb, Minty?" he chuckled.

Back at home, my sister Tamsin was waiting for me, standing outside in our basement patio, smoking and agitated. "He… he's back," she stuttered. Her tanned, slender figure was accentuated by a perfectly tailored orange summer trouser suit. She looked even more fashionably emaciated than usual. Her balayage hair fell in loose waves. She wore understated jewellery, oversized sunglasses, and lots of lipstick.

"Are you eating properly?" I asked.

She took a long drag on her cigarette, then whipped off her glasses to reveal dark, watery, fearful eyes. "Not eaten, not slept either, because he's back."

"You keep saying that, but who is, Tammy?"

Now, some words, if you see them written down or hear them, instil an instant emotional response, like 'anxiety' – horrible word, 'fear' – evil word, 'calm' – soothing, 'disgust' – yucky, 'Trump' – (as in ex-president) that word makes me cross. However, when Harry joyfully screams 'he's done a Trumpy,' it brings his giggles but also a bad smell. I'm not sure how to feel about that one. Anyway, the word I was about to hear gave me an uneasy feeling.

"Quinn." She shuddered.

My heart began pounding, and my stomach dropped into a void. ***Get-out-never-doubt-BOLT!***

"Your eyes have gone," Tamsin reminded me.

I brought them back and focused on her. "Sorry. I was just calming things down."

She tutted. "Anyway, he's here, in London."

"Are you positive?"

Quinn was a huge mammoth of a man with an evil temper. He got his start in Glasgow, working as a bouncer for some of their roughest clubs, later running his own group of doormen who were good at stopping trouble, but could also cause trouble if you didn't use their firm on your club door. It was a simple business model which developed over time into a large security company with the same marketing technique of intimidation, bullying, extortion and violence, spreading across all the major cities in the UK. That's when we'd first met him.

"Oh yeah," she breathed, her face drawn and haunted as she reflected. "He was in the crowd at yesterday's ECO exhibition."

"Really?" I tried to picture it. "I'm sure he's too busy breaking people's arms and legs to worry about saving the planet, Tam."

"Why do you have to say that?"

"Because let's be honest, that's what he does," I reasoned, "and he does it really well."

"Stop it. Just…" She shook her head.

I'd upset her already. I seemed to do that a lot.

"He was there in the crowd…to watch… me." The last word almost toppled from her mouth, unwillingly.

I scrunched up my face, imagining it all. "You think he went all the way there to hear your speech?"

"No, Minty! Not for my fucking speech! I don't know why he was there."

"You sure? It's been a while, maybe it wasn't him."

"How many people do you think would look like they wanted to kill me with those dead angry eyes?"

"Waitrose shop assistants, Uber drivers and Gail's Bakery baristas to name a few."

"Gail's Bakery…?"

"You had a hissy fit last week when you burnt your mouth on a skinny latte."

"Okay, but none of them are seven feet tall and 22 stone."

"To be honest, I think Quinn was six-six and closer to 25 stone."

She stared at me blankly, as she often did. "It was him. But what does he want with us after all these years?" she snapped. "And why do you think he looked so angry?"

I worked on an expression that would cover this situation, as

I did know exactly why he would be angry.

She studied my face, her eyes narrowing. "What is it, Minty? Do you know something?"

"Honestly, nothing at all…" I was a useless liar.

And at that moment, the door next to us was yanked open. My dogs ran out, wagging their tails as if I'd been gone for a week. Mum appeared, her face weathered by years of gardening and long walks, a testament to her love for the outdoors. She looked upset. "Minty! Where have you been?!"

Tamsin sighed. "She's been feeding Oprah Winfrey's chickens, Mum."

"Really?" my mother gasped.

"No," Tamsin said, resigned, kissing Mum's cheek. "Check the board."

Mum's short-term memory was fading quickly, and information no longer seemed to stick. To spare her the need to ask Dad every few minutes, I started writing on a series of large whiteboards whenever I went out, hanging them around the flat, including on the back of our front door.

"Oh!" She moved the door so she could read it, then reappeared. "At school…oh thank goodness!" And her kind hazel eyes brightened with the excitement the day could bring. "Where are we off to now?"

Tamsin tried to grab my hand, but I slipped past her. Today was not the day to talk about Quinn.

Years into my parents' retirement, Mum was still eager to be busy. Dad, on the other hand, would have been happy in his armchair, pawing through books on the latest artists 'making a name for themselves', or sitting outside on the steps, smoking a 'ciggie' and quietly listening to passers-by as they talked on their phones, unaware he was beneath them.

"Minty, while you were gone," he said, "I heard a woman up there arguing with a man…"

"Her husband?" I enquired.

"Could be." He smiled, always liking it when I'd help colour in a story. He went on, "Her husband's gone, and she's sat on our wall above on her phone, asking if she can stay at someone else's."

"Gosh," I said. "Do you think it was her lover?"

"Without a doubt." He beamed, elated by this pocket of mischievousness we may have uncovered, finally erupting into a coughing-laughing fit.

"I thought you'd given up smoking?" Mum scolded him.

"I have, Margie!" he replied crossly, continuing the charade, and beneath his silver-streaked hair, he winked at me, those eyes twinkling as ever.

"Where are we off to now then?" my mother repeated.

"The park, Mum," I answered, and I took her hand.

~ THEN ~ AGE 4

"We are depending on you. The world is depending on you."

The licence in my hand was different to the one Mum carried in her handbag, because mine had been stamped with the words '*LICENCE TO KILL*'. The small, folded card had the shaded-in outline of a girl that kept her face a secret, and on the front, a coat of arms with the words 'Minty – Double Agent.' "But why me?" I asked my sister.

She bent down until our eyes were level. "Because you're the only one who can do this, and they won't know you're working for the other side."

"What do you want me to do, Tammy?"

"We need to know what they're planning."

Her two friends, sitting on her bed, backs against the wall, nodded, and although I had yet to start at school, I knew the importance of this mission.

Outside in the hall, on my own, I studied the licence my sister had made me, with that impressive red stamp. I imagined other less trusted agents only had theirs marked '*LICENCE TO PULL HAIR AND SAY MEAN THINGS.*' I folded the card and tucked it carefully into my dungarees, edging all the time towards the door with 'RUPERT'S BEDROOM' painted on it, to find out what they were planning.

Inside, my brother and his friend didn't seem to be planning anything, just eating paper, fighting and making bad smells.

Ten minutes later, I was back, clutching the remains of the licence in my hands along with a fading Chinese burn on one wrist.

"If you're good and quiet," Tamsin said lovingly, "you can stay with us and listen to my Walkman in the corner," and she handed me her favourite pencil case.

Lying on the floor, I pieced together the cardboard licence which Rupert had torn up and drew another identical to the first, even down to the strength of the scribble lines.

It attracted gasps of admiration from the older girls and filled my heart with pride.

That was the beginning.

A year or so later, another memory.

My parents liked to park their caravan at the bottom of a Welsh mountain, then make us walk up it. When I ran out of steam, I got to sit high up on Dad's shoulders, looking down at my brother and sister, enjoying the smell of Old Spice and tobacco coming from his hair and holding on tight.

"Leave the ears, Minty," he'd say, but his chin was all stubbly, and his ears were nice and soft to grab.

Mum filled our backpacks with carefully wrapped sandwiches, a carrot and apple each, some Kendal Mint Cake, and strapped our junior art easels to our packs. At lunch time we would stop, eat and paint, arranging ourselves next to our father while Mum sat nearby on a rug, reading a book or planning the next day's walk.

"Just paint what you see," Dad advised us one day, a cigarette clasped between his teeth as usual, taking a wide bristled brush and making arcs across his paper with nothing but water, then dabbing in with light grey patches of paint, which dispersed, making heavy rain-filled clouds. "Develop your own style, and don't be afraid to go for it." And go for it we did. When Dad reached for the yellow ochre or the cerulean blue, so did we. "Minty, you're still painting what's on my paper," Dad noted, "not what's in front of you. Look at the view, feel the movement in those mountains like your sister is doing… and… Rupert, what is that?!" He pointed to Rupert's picture, tight-lipped, nostrils betraying mounting frustration.

"It's a tree," Rupert retorted innocently.

"It's black." Dad's breathing was becoming pronounced. "Point to a tree, any tree you can see that looks like the black splodge you've painted."

Rupert glanced over at Mum, who hid her face behind her book.

"Don't look at your mother, she doesn't find this funny. Come on, point to this tree!"

His young eyes scanned the Welsh countryside, nodding sincerely. "There aren't any, Dad," he said, as if he understood the valuable lesson he was being taught.

"Correct," my father thundered. "I said build the picture slowly, start light and get darker. What is darker than black, Rupert?"

"I…"

"Nothing is darker than black, is it, Rupert?"

"But I'm trying," my brother insisted.

Dad took a closer look. "And what's that meant to be, in the middle of the field?"

Rupert shrugged. "A penis, Dad."

A large hand flew out to clip the side of Rupert's head but missed. Rupert may not have liked painting, but he liked ducking, and was good at it.

Three years went by. After church on Christmas Day, before we opened our presents, Grandpa (my father's father) sat on a chair, and we lined up with all our cousins, one by one, stepping forward to tell him what we had created or achieved that year. Grandpa was a fearsome man, so staunch, red-faced, and difficult to please, that most of the children nervously shook, and voices trembled. All the parents watched on, hoping their offspring impressed, and because Dad's two sisters' children were all so incredibly talented, going after them was even scarier.

"What did you do during the holidays, Jacob?" Grandpa asked my eldest cousin, who was 19.

Jacob replied, "I built a motorbike and drove it through France before I ran out of petrol on the coast of Italy, where I drew customers' portraits in cafés for money, and when I had earned enough, I bought some materials, built a small floating craft and sailed three hours to the island of Capri."

"Good boy," Grandpa said. And we all moved along. "Now Rupert, you're my son's only boy," he threw Dad a disapproving look, "so you'll be the one carrying the family name. What did you do this summer?"

Rupert took a breath. "I learnt how to do this," he announced, before putting his hand under his armpit to make a series of squelching sounds, which were the only noises audible in the silent, shocked room.

To stop Rupert from being clouted, I quickly held out my picture.

"Barry!" Grandpa barked, his face now red as a radish. "Why is your youngest waving one of your old paintings at me?!"

"That's not mine," Dad pointed out.

Grandpa glared at him then back at me, and lastly down at the hardboard painting held between my fingers. "Yes, it is." His mouth twitched. "That's the oil painting you did at college."

"No," Dad replied, "Minty did this herself, it's a copy."

Grandpa took it from me with one hand. With the other, he fumbled to find the magnifying glass he always kept on a cord around his neck, finally bringing it up to study my picture more closely, his eyes widening, a look of joy spreading across his face and to my parents, radiating pride. A chair was brought up and placed next to him, and he patted it. "You sit next to your old grandpa, and let's judge the rest together, shall we?" And each time a cousin came forward, much to everyone's amusement he'd say, "I need to check with my assistant, because one day, my granddaughter here will make our family name famous."

I did, but not quite in the way he'd hoped.

~NOW~

So, Quinn was back.

That thought would have to stay in its cupboard.

But things would certainly need to be organised. And quickly.

We saddled up the dogs (put them on leads) and went to Maida Vale Park.

After Dustin died, things were even quieter than before, so I'd acquired two Old English sheepdogs, Muffin and Paddington, to keep me company. But taking them for a walk often ended in drama because although still puppies at eleven months old, they were playful and huge. Their very long white hair was either down over their faces, so you could only see their black noses, or it was tied up with colourful ribbons or hair bobbles, depending on whether Harriet had been creative that day. Old English sheepdogs herd, and ours liked to herd the twins to bed at night, or herd other dogs to me in the park, which was why I spent my time apologising to small dog owners. Paddington also liked to chase cyclists, seg-boards, skateboarders and scooters and his tongue was too big for his mouth, so the end was always hanging out. Because of this he drank lots of water, which had to go somewhere – another reason we weren't popular as he tended to relieve himself on objects, like yoga mats, exercise balls, or once inside a lady's handbag. Since our arrival a week ago, on any given day, I could be found running across the green, chasing a huge carpet of fluff and screaming "Paddington!"

I set my parents up with their usual coffees in the park café, while 'The Krays,' as they were recently named by the Maida Vale Doggy Facebook Page, went about getting their exercise by causing mischief. During a break in the mayhem, I joined Cynthia on a park bench. She was our 80-year-old neighbour, who babysat us when we were young, and who still lived in the basement flat next door. Cynthia never shied away from the direct questions. "Did you love Dustin?" she asked.

"Of course."

"What was he like?"

"He was very passionate about his cars – he liked restoring old ones."

"Did he love you?" she asked.

"I'd like to think so."

Cynthia studied me with something close to irritation. "He didn't tell you?"

"He was a man of very few words."

She sighed. "We would tell each other all the time, Kenny and I. You know it's nearly a year that he's been gone, but of course you know that."

Her husband had died not long after mine had.

I gave her hand a squeeze and she dabbed at her eyes.

We sat in silence for a bit, with only the sound of Paddington herding a Chihuahua, and its owner bellowing at me from a distance. The soft floral aroma of Cynthia's fragrance filled the air, and I was about to speak when she said…

"I still talk to him, you know."

"And I still talk to Dustin," I admitted. "I even imagine he replies."

"Kenny really does reply to me."

"Oh," I said, wondering where this was going.

"You remember we buried him under the flowerbed?"

"I do," I answered, turning to face her. "You got special permission from the council."

"Well, he likes to pop up sometimes."

"Pop up?"

"From the earth."

"Oh." I gave this some thought. "And – you've seen him?"

"No, just occasional footprints, which appear by the roses outside the back doors." And, as if that wasn't endearing enough, she added, "Just knowing he's there watching over me, while I sleep, is everything."

What could I say? That this wasn't Kenny, but possibly a would-be thief or stalker?

I was about to suggest this when she winked.

"I leave him messages on a chalkboard, and once in a while I get a reply." With that she stood and strolled off along the path, leaving me utterly baffled.

Back home, Tamsin was still fretting. "Let's not tell Rupert about Quinn yet, and obviously don't mention this to anyone else, especially not Thomas." Thomas Francis Junior, Tamsin's husband, knew nothing of her involvement in our mutually dark past. She put a finger to her lips and glared at me, before heading into my parents' bedroom, where Thomas was lying on his back, on their bed, looking at his mobile.

My sister had been by every other day to check up on us and see how I was taking care of Mum, and she enjoyed marching around the flat, sighing a lot.

"Why?" Tamsin tutted, slamming one of their drawers.

"Why what?"

"Why is Mum's dress in Dad's sock drawer?" she demanded, slamming another drawer to accentuate just how upset this made her.

"It's like someone's going through their things and mixing it all up."

"Someone is. Mum."

"I get that, but come on, Minty, it only takes a few minutes to nip around and put them in the right places."

Thomas raised a disapproving eyebrow towards me.

My sister wasn't finished. "And why have her favourite leather gloves had the fingers cut off?"

"Mum did it herself." I took them from her, suppressing a smile. "She said they were getting in her way."

"But why did you let her? It's embarrassing, she looks like an elderly middle-class biker."

I mumbled, "Which is kind of cool."

Tamsin shook her head and picked up my cardigan, and I followed her through to my room, where she plonked herself down on the edge of my bed with a huge sigh and glanced over at a tray, on which a 1,000-piece puzzle I'd been making with Mum was nearly completed.

"Minty…" she said. "Thomas and I were wondering…" She bit her lip to let me know she was about to broach a tough subject.

"What?"

"If Mum and Dad wouldn't be happier if they sold their flat and lived with us in RTW."

My sister meant Royal Tunbridge Wells (or simply 'Tunbridge Wells' to everyone else).

"Please don't move them," I pleaded, "all their friends are here."

"Let's monitor the situation and see how we get on, shall we?" Tamsin waited for me to say something, blowing out some air and making lip-smacking noises while scanning the room. "Getting so stressed about this Edinburgh thing." Tamsin had been invited to exhibit her eco-house designs at the prestigious Edinburgh Art Festival.

"I'm sure it'll be a big hit."

"But on top of that, this," she said. "Quinn showing up! Why now?" When she spoke again, her words were barely above a whisper. "You still think about everything we all did?"

"Of course," I replied. "You?"

"All the time. I guess, though, it affects you less, because of the way you are."

~ THEN ~

My childhood was punctuated by instances like this. At one

moment, I was surrounded by people, and the next, I was alone. This, I had decided, was because I had gone through a time-warp, and it made me special.

"You're not special," Rupert assured me, "you're an arse-wipe."

The three of us were sitting outside the manager's office for the Scouts and Girl Guides.

Tamsin was kinder. "Don't listen to him."

Mrs Tomkins, in her strange brown uniform, beckoned me in. I stood in front of her desk while she made the call, and with one hand over the receiver, she whispered to me. "Who do I ask for?"

"My mum," I replied.

Her eyes blinked large behind her circular glasses, making her look more like an owl than ever. "I meant, what's her name?"

"Margaret," I answered.

There was a click from her phone.

"Hello, Margaret," she boomed. "This is Brown Owl. We've had an issue here at the New Forest Campsite."

On the second day during a woodland trip, we had stopped to eat our packed lunches. Thirty children, all chatting and munching. After I had finished mine, I had noticed a cocoon under some bark, and the sounds of the forest went in an instant. *I was transformed inside the cocoon, felt my new strong legs kick out the cocoon walls, desperate to use my wings, rolling free, into the twigs outside, the sun on my face, spreading my wings and…*

And when I looked up again, all the other children and teachers had gone. Two hours had passed. I was completely alone, in the forest by myself. At first, you're scared because you think you'll get told off, but soon that fear becomes one for your own safety. They found me as it was getting dark.

Mrs Tomkins tried to explain herself. "I'm sorry, Margaret, but we didn't want to worry you…" And having only known her to give orders, it was strange to see her now receiving them. "Err, yes, Margaret, I certainly will do, that's right, but you never mentioned a medical condition—"

The receiver was handed to me, and I pushed it tightly against my ear, getting as close as possible to the comforting sound of my mother's voice.

"Minty darling?" she said.

"Yes, Mum?"

"Don't worry, I'm on my way."

That incident was the tipping point for my parents. My distraught mother took me to various doctors, and after lots of tests, the specialist confirmed my mother's suspicions when he announced: "I'm afraid your daughter is partially deaf, and one ear is particularly bad, and she will need to wear a hearing aid for the rest of her life." My mother burst into tears of relief, that they had found something that could be fixed.

But of course, there was nothing wrong with my hearing. Mum wanted a reason for my behaviour, and I wanted to help her, so I invented a reason – I was deaf. A few months later, I messed up the tests, forgot which one was meant to be worse and both ears were deemed healthy. My hearing aid was removed. The specialist proudly announced, "It's a miracle, your daughter is cured!" My mother cried with joy once more.

The drifting off problem persisted though, which meant

school life became awkward, mainly for Tamsin.

"Why don't you stand up for yourself!" she demanded, when she had had to step in once more, finding me cornered in the playground. But it didn't actually get to me. When I was scared, or very anxious, I had learned to zone out at will, which left me in a happy-safe emotional vacuum. It was just like boxing up bad news and keeping it hidden. The only negative was for a few seconds, I would giggle nervously, while my eyes flittered about in the back of my head like I was possessed, which did tend to scare other children.

My report card was just full of comments like, "Doesn't listen, won't concentrate, drifts off, isn't in the classroom with us."

On the day I was offered a place to study at St Martin's College of Art, I was tootling along a country road in my Morris Minor, imagining what college life would be like, *smells of wooden easels, turps, excited chatter, my new teacher's voice, kind, she liked me, told everyone else to calm down, explaining our first assignment, she winked, I felt warm, connected, clever.* Whilst picturing this I drove the wrong way around a roundabout, over a bank, through a pub garden, smashed through tables of angry drinkers and finished by ploughing my car into a village pond, missing everyone by a whisker. They certainly didn't think I was very clever. College life was nearly no-life, and I never drove again.

CHAPTER TWO

A POLICEMAN CALLS

~NOW~

We were trying to remember where we had parked. And Dad wasn't happy about it. "Why aren't there ever any available parking spaces outside our flat?" he ranted. "I'll tell you why. Because of people like them! Look at those two in that car, they've been there all morning. I have a good mind to knock on their window—"

"Please don't, Dad," I begged. "They don't look very chirpy."

We located Dad's old Saab in the end, and he drove us to a DIY store on Shirland Road so I could buy some butane for my blowtorch, then on to my parents' favourite canal restaurant in Little Venice, for our weekly brunch treat.

Amidst the gentle hum of quiet conversations from other diners, I supported my father on one side as we navigated through the decking area. The soft clinks of cutlery and the subtle aroma of freshly prepared food filled the air, creating a warm, inviting ambiance whilst we searched for the perfect table. Mum's Alzheimer's gave her good days, when you would barely notice anything was wrong, and bad days, when she'd be rude, which she had never been before, or ones when the world was full of danger – today would be one of those days.

"Let's not sit near the edge, Barry," Mum insisted, "it scares me," she said.

"Trumpers-Pumpers, Margie." Which meant 'okay' in Dad-speak. But he sounded disappointed not to be closer to the water, where we could see the canal moving slowly beneath.

I attempted to reassure her. "It has a safety-rail Mum."

"That's no use," she replied dismissively. "I nearly fell in there once."

"Did you?" Dad considered this, scratching his head.

"Yes," she replied, arranging her auburn hair with those grey roots, which we would need to dye soon. "And it's just lucky that waiter was there to catch one of my legs or I would have been gone for good!"

Dad nodded without conviction. "Godfathers!" he concluded.

An image of the quick-thinking waiter holding onto one of my mother's legs as she hung upside-down hovered awkwardly between us, until I said, "I hope you gave him a tip?"

"Or a kiss?" Dad added.

"Certainly not!" Mum said. "You're the only man I've ever kissed, Barry." And she leant over, putting both arms around his neck, and planted one on his cheek.

Dad made a funny little shuffle in his seat, as if he had got the winning bingo numbers. "And this is a good news scene," Dad said, surveying his surroundings. "Hey, Minty, is there a George on the horizon yet?" George was Dad's go-to name for a man. He struggled with names, so all men were called 'George'.

"Not yet, Dad," I answered. "But I'm fine without one."

He patted my arm. "I know you are, but there will be one along soon. Mark my words."

Once a year, Inspector Michael. T. James from the Arts & Antiquities unit of the Metropolitan Police Service would reappear.

In Sussex, I could be walking up a country lane, or creating a steel sculpture in the garden, and there he suddenly was. Once he even sat down next to me on the beach. Always in a slightly scruffy dark suit, always very pleasant, but as the years passed, with less hair.

Tamsin thought he had a bit of a thing for me. I doubted that. He just liked to pass by to keep tabs on me.

His car slowed next to us as we left the restaurant, the passenger window opened, and his deep voice boomed from within. "Hey, Minty, just keeping tabs on you."

You see?

Bending closer to get a better look, I replied, "I know, and it's very kind of you, Inspector, isn't it, Mum?"

"Oh yes," my mother agreed, waving her hand toward the car. "But he's not a policeman, is he?"

"I think he is, Mum." Supporting myself with one hand on the roof of his car, I peered inside. The passenger seat was classically untidy, with empty water bottles, crisp packets and mess.

He smiled. "You sold any new pictures recently?" That was his little joke he said, every year.

"You know I've stopped painting, I'm only doing metalwork

these days."

"I know." He nodded looking away, and when he turned back his eyes had darkened. "But you want to know what I find strange?"

"What is that, Michael?"

"A woman, at the drop of a hat, pulls her children out of school, gives up her cottage in the country, and moves back to London to live with her parents."

"You're talking about me, aren't you?" I smiled proudly.

"Yes, Minty. And this all happened so very, very quickly."

"I guess it was a bit of a rush," I admitted.

"And with your children starting a new school… right at the end of a term. Seems strange to me."

"Does it?"

"Right at the end of the summer term?" He scratched his greying cheek-stubble.

"Nothing strange about it at all, Inspector. I was worried about my mother's health," I replied.

His voice hardened. "And last week an old friend of yours, Quinn, arrived off a flight from Glasgow, did you know that? Bit of a coincidence."

"I didn't know," I lied. Tamsin had been right. That beast of a man with a nearly indecipherable Glaswegian accent was back.

"He was drunk," the Inspector said with venom, "and broke an airline seat."

"Because of his size?" I offered.

"No, it just got in his way," the Inspector growled, glancing up at me before carrying on. "He was abusive to their staff, got escorted off the plane at Gatwick. Questioned and released, but maybe he was still upset with seats, because at 9 p.m. he put someone's head through a park bench in Billericay."

"Really?"

"Yup."

"Actually – through the bench?"

He shrugged. "I think the wood was rotten. But this was an innocent man taking a romantic stroll with his wife in the park, before a chance encounter with Quinn left him kneeling on a bench with his bleeding head stuck through the seat's wooden slats until his wife could get him an ambulance."

"That's not good," I said helpfully, shaking my head and trying to picture the poor man's awful predicament.

"No. It is not good," he agreed.

"Is the man okay?"

"Fine, but I imagine romance in the park will be off the table for that couple for a while. You think Quinn's here for you?"

"I hope not," I said.

The Inspector was evaluating my responses. "And a famous piece of art, which was worth much more," he waved his hand casually, "than the football team I support…"

"Which team is that, Michael?"

"Queens Park Rangers, although that's not saying much these days."

"Sorry, I know nothing about football."

He ignored me and forged ahead. "This iconic painting had been hanging on the wall of some Russian's mansion for years, and was recently valued, and it turns out, it is no longer the painting—" and in one smooth movement his head tilted toward mine "—it once was."

"What do you mean?"

"It's now a FAKE!" he said.

Panic rose up inside.

Hide-and-sickle-mrs-pickle-SHUT!

My eyes cleared and my view was of the sky. I straightened my neck, bringing the Inspector's baffled face back into my vision.

He was frowning. "You did that thing again. It's hard talking to you when you do that."

"Does this bit of art have a name?" I asked.

"It was by Rousseau, named *The Doctor*." His eyes attempted to burrow their way into my mind.

My mother's head appeared next to mine, rescuing me for the second time that day, her voice shrill and demanding. "When will you sort out the traffic lights on Widley Road?" A rush of relief swept over me.

He looked confused. "Sorry, that's not my type of police work," he began, trying to get the moment back.

But Mum wasn't letting go. "Well, it's right by the school gates, and it's simply not safe!"

"I'll get someone to look into it."

"See that you do. Come along, Minty." And she dragged me back from the window. "Why don't they leave you alone?"

"I don't know, Mum, but thank you." I gave her cheek a grateful kiss. "And if you can help Dad into the car, I need to make a call."

I left a message for Maxi to call me back. My one surviving friend from school and the only other person who knew what had really happened the week Quinn had arranged for me to meet the Russian.

"Insects have brains, and they feel hunger and pain," I pointed out, as we drove back along Warwick Avenue.

My mother's face had been frozen in concentration with her tissue hovering above the spider's head as it crawled along their dashboard.

She withdrew her hand, and offered Dad, who was driving, the same look she gave him when I said I wanted to keep the scrap metal I'd hoarded beneath their outside steps.

We stopped at Faith's Trinket Trove to buy a lovely wooden owl for Mum (she had developed a fixation with them recently). Then home for a quick change, and we were outside. My parents in their swim costumes for sunbathing on deckchairs at the end of our 10-metre-long triangular garden. Me in my overalls and welding helmet.

Creating had always helped me focus my mind and organise things into drawers in my head, which was needed, because I had begun to feel a little swamped.

Maximus was a rescued-metal cyborg stallion, and a resplendent mix of stainless steel (shiny) and carbon steel (dull), which stretched out across six feet of lawn. I'd begun making him in Sussex and much to my parents' horror he'd come with me, taking up residence in their garden. His flowing mane was a lightweight row of chains, which had been soaked in acid to remove the rust, and then I'd polished them into a gleaming silver.

I put on my gloves and chose a lovely vintage hubcap, which I'd polished on the buffing wheel until it was gleaming. Then, I fired up my torch; the low hiss of the blue flame transformed into a sharp sizzle as the torch touched the metal. I adjusted the short blue flame and began welding the hubcap onto Maximus' flank.

How will my pair of munchkins survive their new school? It would be my fault if things went wrong. And Mum's mind was getting worse; there were patches when things seemed okay, and there were other times like this morning with the toaster. And Dad must know, surely? What was he thinking? Should I say something?

And the police. They were back again, and presumably going through everything I did many years ago.

I needed a time machine, to change a few things I'd got up to.

And we had a dead man walking, cat sick, the cost-of-living crisis, and now Quinn was down here somewhere.

That's a lot to cope with.

Cost-of-living and cat sick could fit in one mind-drawer together.

The hubcap was firmly in place, so I cut the gas and lifted my shield to take a breath.

The garishly colourful stripey deckchairs were highlighted by the sun, the dark shapes of my parents in them, with the top of Dad's wispy white hair fluttering in the breeze.

"All okey-dokey?" I asked from behind them.

"We're okey-dokey, if you are," Mum replied, nudging Dad.

I dug out a softer piece of metal, salvaged from a scrap-metal dealer, and slid it onto my workbench. Took a pair of crimpers and began twisting it to the shape I needed.

Prioritise, Minty, I thought, *which problem needs urgent attention?*

"I do worry about her," Mum said.

"What?" Dad asked.

"I said I worry about her!"

Dad answered, "So do I."

"Hmmm…I am here, you know," I called.

"Your sculpture," Dad shouted back, over his shoulder, "I imagine it's thirsty work?"

I checked my watch. "Not gin time yet, Dad, we haven't even had lunch." Although maybe today we could start slightly earlier. "You want to take a look, Mum?" I asked.

She was up and making her way around to my creation. "Oh wonderful, it's lovely, dear," she exclaimed.

"How about me?" Dad called.

"One more day, and I'll show you." I covered it up with a cloth.

Dad had never appreciated my love for reproducing a style or piece. Never in my life had he ever looked at something I'd drawn, painted or sculpted, and said, "Yes, Minty that's amazing, I love it!"

There was always a comment about where I'd found the idea. "Originality is the key," he would say. "Express yourself, not someone else."

"Ah-hum." Mum cleared her throat to get my attention. "What are we doing next?" She smiled sweetly.

"We'll take the dogs to pick up the twins from school, and we'll have spaghetti Bolognese for dinner."

Dad's eyes lit up. "Good-oh, vegetable or meat?"

"Dad, if everyone on the planet ate meat only once a week,

there'd be no more deforestation and we'd save 10 million lives."

"Okay, dear," Mum said politely but with humour, "so what does that mean for today?"

"We're having a meat Bolognese."

"Hurray!" they cheered.

I cooked us meat once a week. And if anyone moaned, I suggested we follow my cousin Nathaniel's way of life, which kept them quiet. Nathaniel and his wife lived in a converted barn, grew their own vegetables and made an income by selling arts and crafts, and only ate meat if it was roadkill; in that case they would park up and lift the unfortunate animal into the cooler to cook later. But you were NOT allowed (as Rupert had suggested hopefully one Christmas) to go out looking for things to run over.

"Is that it for today?" asked Mum, disappointed.

"No, there's one more thing…" I replied.

And with music playing from my bedroom and the double patio doors open, I held my mother's hands, and we boogied away in the garden to her favourite songs, while Dad tapped his leg to the beat. And that's how things were at first.

~ THEN ~

I met my first boyfriend, Jude, at St Martin's College of Art. He had skin paler than snow, only ever ate marmite and crackers, and had somehow managed to stretch the piercing of his left earlobe enough to fit a plastic doll's arm through the hole, so whenever we kissed, I always had this tiny hand reaching toward me.

My tutors, although happy with the technical aspect of my paintings, were always disappointed with my great love for reproducing other famous works.

After university, I continued replicating an artist's approach, character and ideas, enjoying this much more than finding my own identity.

After Jude left me, I dated an independent film director who smoked so much weed he often argued with his own shadow on set.

Tamsin, Rupert and I were living together in Willesden Green, not far from our parents. Tamsin had graduated with a 1st from UCL in architecture and was working her way up in an architectural design firm. Rupert was on his third business bankruptcy.

After being let go after my second year at an apprenticeship for an art forensics firm, I had failed to hold down a few other art or design related jobs, and I was at a low point, feeling lost, when it happened once more.

"Sacked again? Minty, why!" We were in our shared flat, and I'd been waiting for Tamsin to come home, to give her my bad news. She took off her raincoat, threw it over a chair and dumped her briefcase on the kitchen table. "That gallery could have led to something better, tell me you didn't go missing?"

Getting to work on time had been a fiddly affair, and that was what she was referring to. I'd be on the busy Underground during rush hour, a few stops from Bond Street, where I needed to get off. I'd begin thinking about something, slip into my own world, look up again and see the carriage was empty and we were at the end of the line.

"No, I swear I didn't," I said.

She glared at Rupert, who ran an agitated hand through his wavy blond locks. "Don't look at me," he answered defensively in his gravelly public-school-boy accent, "I only just found out myself."

"Then what happened?" Tamsin demanded, strutting into the kitchen and flicking on the kettle with an angry snap.

"There was this picture," I recounted, following her timidly. "An unframed canvas the gallery's owner would sit and admire with her morning coffee. It had been sold and was due to be sent out. I decided to make her a copy to keep."

Tamsin shook her head, her expression already betraying her anticipation of what was coming, as she filled her cup with boiling water for her herbal tea.

"What's wrong with that?" Rupert chimed in.

"I sent out the original and put mine up in its place on her wall," I admitted. "I mean she would have known, or someone would have if they'd studied it close enough. Anyway, she had her morning coffee, said goodbye to it, and that's when I said the original had gone out already and this was my version."

"So she sacked you," Tamsin finished.

"Why?!" cried my brother. "What an old battle-axe, you made her a present, and she gets rid of you?"

Tamsin made a dismissive flick of her wrist. "Of course she did, Rupert. What if our Minty decided to steal all the pictures in there and replace them for her own?"

"What? No!" Rupert spat. "That's ridiculous. She couldn't copy them all, could she!"

I didn't say anything.

"Rupert," Tamsin sighed, "I know your world revolves around you and your failed finances, but have you even bothered to go into your sister's room lately to see what she's painting?"

He looked angry, then defensive, shook his head as if to get back on track. "Minty… You couldn't though, could you, Minty?"

Now they were both looking at me. And maybe that was the moment I should have said no, but I was feeling a new emotion that was nice, and so I answered honestly. "Possibly."

Tamsin's anger dissolved, the lines on her face changed, and something new grew there instead, a strange expression.

"But," I conceded, "with the right equipment, you'd easily know they weren't the originals. It's much easier to copy someone's 'style' than replicate an exact picture."

"So… you could paint in someone's style, and they wouldn't know it was you? Even with the right equipment?" Tamsin pursued.

"Depending on the age of the painting I was trying to make," I said, "and if I had the similar paint, materials and aged canvas."

"Yeah, yeah," Rupert went. "If you had everything you needed and you did your best, would people be able to tell they were yours?"

I slowly shook my head. "Not always."

Tamsin did a single nod, and this same strange expression had now filled her whole face. It was something I had rarely seen but had often yearned for.

Respect.

Rupert clapped his hands together, making us jolt. "Alright, guys, I have a plan."

~NOW~

There were two distinct social circles in St Dunstan's Maida Vale Church: those who attended to get their kids into the school, and those who were going to get themselves into heaven. Maybe one or two that fitted in between.

Faith schools often had the best results in the area. If you couldn't afford a private school, they were often the next best thing.

The catch was, to get your child into one of these schools, and to keep them in, you had to attend a church, mosque, synagogue, temple or any place of worship 'religiously' (or simply for a school-place) and sign the register each time to prove you were there. Another holy war was taking place, but this time in West London, and instead of knights on horses, it was being fought by parents in SUVs.

As the church gradually filled, the air buzzed with muffled pleasantries. People shuffled along pews to make room or exchanged greetings with those they hadn't seen since the previous Sunday. The scent of polished wood mingled with the mustiness of old hymn books. The twins were seated on either side of Mum. Dad, next to me, was eager for some gossip. He always enjoyed the backstories about everyone, and if I didn't have the real tales, I'd invent them.

"Who's that chap there?" Dad asked.

"He runs the local butcher's," I said as people were taking their seats. "But the shop backs onto the morgue, and bodies have been disappearing…"

Dad chuckled. "He does have that look about him."

Today Dad was wearing a shirt and tie, with a thick woollen mustard-coloured jumper over the top, which I had chosen. Smart but cuddly, as dads should be, and I linked my arm through his. As more people entered and found a pew, his eyes were once again searching, squinting at people, something I had got used to over the years.

"And George over there," he said. "He looks like a good sort. Have you met him before?"

At the far end of the pew, there was a moustachioed man in his late 20s in a tweed jacket. He glanced over, and to my horror, Dad threw him an exaggerated wink and nod towards me, as if I were shy, but golly-gosh, did I like a moustache.

"Dad, you're killing me…" I gritted my teeth.

"Just helping things along," he murmured.

"Well, please stop," I murmured back.

"He lives with his mother, or it could be his wife," Dad recollected, "and I think she has a moustache too."

"Interesting."

Dad turned his head. "What about this old girl behind us, who do we think she is?"

The elderly lady in question was possibly younger than Dad.

I whispered, "She's a white witch and can heal anyone with a mixture of herbs and spices."

Dad whispered back, "I wonder if she can help your mother then?"

That was the first time he had ever hinted at Mum's condition. I studied Dad's stubbly face, waiting for him to say more. He didn't.

There were many things I needed to say.

"What about him?" Dad nodded.

And the moment was gone.

"You know exactly who he is, Dad, he's your ticket to heaven."

He belly-laughed, rolled his eyes as if there were doubts that he would pass the grading up there, and then the vicar began to speak.

The rest of my time in church was spent counting. Counting the minutes left, counting how many hymns on the board we still had to sing and counting how many parents' names were on the church school list, but who never showed up to sign themselves in.

Outside, as we left the church, a man in a mohair overcoat seemed to be watching us. When I turned back to look again, he crossed the road, as if spotted.

"We call them the untouchables," said Faith casually.

It was noon, we had dropped off the twins at home, and we were in Faith's Trinket Trove on Formosa Street. The shop was a sensory overload, with joss sticks burning, treasures twinkling, and every other spare inch covered in handmade crafts. Ducking between the wind chimes and hanging ornaments, I had spotted Faith, in a simple summer dress, perched on a stool by the till. And while my mother chose something, we had a chance to natter.

"Untouchables? Why?" I asked.

"Because," she explained, "those women on that list who

never turn up to church, their children also rarely get in trouble for anything, get picked first for everything good, and their parents don't have to follow the same rules as the rest of us."

"But that's unfair."

"Yeah, you wait until there's a play or concert, they always have their seats reserved at the front. Meredith, Karen and the other one."

My mother appeared. "Ah-hum," she cleared her throat politely, getting our attention, before putting her arm around my waist. "Did I introduce you to my youngest?" She proudly urged me forward like I was still her little girl.

Faith smiled. "You have, Margaret, and I used to see Minty when she came to visit you, and now our children go to the same school."

"Oh of course they do, righty-ho." Mum raised her eyes happily, while positioning an owl on the counter. "I'll have this, but I'll check for others I like." And she pottered off again.

The shop door pinged open, and a tall, thin, suited, bespectacled man came in, who looked out of place to be buying wind chimes.

"Minty…" Faith was saying behind me.

The man seemed to realise he was in the wrong shop, huffed and left.

"Why do you keep staring at my customers?" Faith mused.

"Because," I whispered, "I get the feeling I'm being watched." But outside I could only see Dad having a secret ciggie.

"Who would possibly be watching you?" Faith asked.

"No one, everyone, it's hard to say," I pondered.

"Darling,"' Faith said, letting off a throaty chuckle, "you may need help."

"Also," I added, "my neighbour's dead husband could be patrolling the back gardens at night," I gave a nonchalant gesture, "and in East Sussex, that type of thing never happened."

She looked like she had many questions but none of them were forthcoming.

By the side of the till there was a bowl of brooches, and one would have gone well on my pink cardigan. But I had no idea how much they cost; the labels were too small to read.

Labels should be larger or positioned further away, I reasoned, and my arms were clearly too short. I was putting off the inevitable – I needed a selfie-stick with a magnifying glass.

Or maybe just a pair of glasses.

Actually, the worst labels in the world were cooking instructions on the side of beef roasts, which for some stupid reason they printed on the reverse side, meaning they were always wet and torn. Another reason I was pleased not to ever be cooking one again.

"Oooh, let's have a lovely Sunday roast," Mum said, on leaving the shop, as if reading my mind, badly.

Dad shook his head.

Little over a year ago, at ten past one on a Sunday in July, the lunch I had been preparing was not going well. The Yorkshire puddings had come out looking decidedly squishy. Never a fan of my cooking, my then-husband Dustin, father of the twins, stormed out and his Triumph Herald roared angrily away. A moment later, Dustin parked outside our local mini-market and marched inside, muttering. Unknown to anyone, an old bucket-freezer there had faulty wiring and with the help of some ice, had become live. Supporting himself with one hand on his knee, Dustin reached into the bottom of the freezer, when his chest touched the edge, sending 220 volts through him. Not usually enough power to be a serious issue, however given his history of dark, silent moodiness and the close proximity to his heart, the resulting shock jolted him; he had lost balance and fallen in. Dustin had died buying a bag of Aunt Bessie's frozen Yorkshire puddings.

"We aren't having a roast, Mum," I growled.

"Why not?" she enquired.

"Because I don't own any glasses!!!"

That left Mum as confused as she often left me.

I put up Mum's new wooden owl into the last space on the wall, next to all the others. And I shared Cynthia's story with my parents.

"Espinacas!" Dad gawped, which meant 'spinach' in Spanish, a word Dad had picked up because he thought it sounded naughty, using it in place of 'Crikey!' although he liked that word too.

Mum gave him a jovial nudge before giving it all some serious thought. "Well, Barry, if you go first, I don't want you watching over me, covered in earth."

"I certainly will, Margie," he replied.

"Don't you dare!" She was serious. "It would scare the life out of me."

Dad smiled. "If the life was scared out of you, darling, I'd be winning you back."

Mum rolled her eyes, and he blew her a kiss.

I held up my hands. "That's all kind of creepy. What should I do?" I asked.

Mum knew. "You just keep yourself to yourself and ignore them."

"Who?"

"Any of them."

That wasn't helpful. "I wonder if we need a medium," I pondered.

"Or an exorcist," Dad suggested.

"While you're both busy doing that," Mum said, making clattering sounds from the kitchen, "I'll make us some lunch. Oh, look, what's this I found!" She had opened a cupboard and seen one of my make-a-do's, which were tiny standing paper animals, left in surprising places, with messages inside.

"I don't know," I helped her, "but it says, 'open me'." I unfolded it.

Mum picked it up and read the message out loud. "Today you have earned a rest. Let your daughter cook.'"

Dad winked, but I needed to buy something for us to eat, and so we all headed back out.

Inside Elgin Food & Wine, I was deliberating over the cold fridge selections and called Maxi again, and this time I got through. Maxi Kaur ran a small recruitment agency and was a tiny powerhouse in shiny heels; scary and utterly abrupt but got away with it, because she delivered her lines so beautifully.

"Yes?" she commanded.

"Can you speak?" I asked.

"Yes?" She was never one for dawdling.

I moved to an aisle on my own. “My can of worms is back,” I whispered.

“Oh god!” she said. “All the worms or just some of them?”

“All of them.”

“Shit!” she cursed. Although even her expletives sounded graceful.

“You’ll need to tell me everything. Let’s talk tomorrow in the gym.”

“The gym?” I asked.

“Yes, in the park.”

“The park gym?”

“Minty, your powers of deduction are astounding.”

“But I’ve never been to a gym before in my life.”

“Well then, it’s time you went.”

Nope. I did not like the sound of meeting in a gym.

“Hey, you know Paulie?” Maxi pronounced the ‘P’ as if it was a name she would need to change. “Well, last night he asked me to be his soulmate.”

“That’s so sweet!”

“Except by soul, he meant the soles of my feet. He really likes sucking my toes, but to each his own, I guess.”

I looked at the cheese in my hand, grimaced and put it back.

“What about you?” she asked. “Still watching *Mamma Mia* on repeat?”

“Mum likes it, and it’s always a new film for her.”

“Why aren’t you out dating, having some fun, aren’t you lonely?”

I stammered, “Are you kidding? The flat is full.”

“Oh, and I guess your parents won’t be around forever, will

they?"

"That's mean. But I guess not."

"And you're 35 now."

"So?"

"And that breed of dog usually lasts for around nine or ten years, and do you think the Harries will go to university?"

"I hope so, what are you getting at?"

"Well, we look forward to you dating when you hit fifty, because by then you could be all on your own in that flat. But you'll have plenty of space to swing-a-cat, if indeed you still have one."

I pictured all this.

"Harsh but true, the other line's going, see you in the gym!"

The line went dead, leaving me with the feeling that my stomach might not be the only part of me that was empty.

While this negative feeling washed through me, I was aware there was a man tutting somewhere, and that my right hand now had a pair of tongs in it, hovering over the fresh rolls. I apologised and let him go, then he let me go, and introduced himself as Phil, and said we should continue this over dinner, where there were plenty of bread rolls to row over.

We exchanged numbers on our phones and arranged to go out.

On leaving the shop, my parents greeted Phil, while Paddington and Muffin leapt up and put their dirty pawmarks on his shirt. I must say he did look slightly overwhelmed.

Later, alone in my bedroom, I noticed I'd already missed two calls from him. Clambering onto my bed, I flopped down on my back, closed my eyes, and pictured Phil winking again, repeating,

'Let's carry this on over dinner…'

I'm surprised at you, my little Mk 1.

I blocked out Dustin's distant, disapproving voice, and instead imagined my life with Phil, which would mean always wearing flat shoes, because at five-foot-five he was three inches shorter than me. Not a huge problem, I preferred trainers anyway. But he had also smelt damp and been quite huffy at the start.

Did I want to marry a small, damp, angry man?

I sat up, picked up my mobile and sent him my 'excuse-message' then deleted and blocked his number and sighed with relief.

The thought of going to a gym was bringing me out in a rash.

But how bad could it be?

I threw on some baggy grey sweatpants and a hoodie, the front adorned with a hand-dyed message I'd crafted myself. From the depths of the Harries' dress-up box, I unearthed an old pair of original brown boxing gloves. After tying these around my waist, I put my arms around Mum and Dad, and off we all went to the park.

Elgin Avenue had colourful flower baskets hanging from every other lamppost, and the trees that lined the street were a vibrant green. Inside the park café, my parents settled on one of the sunny terrace picnic tables, sipping coffee and chatting to people who recognised them. Dad lit a ciggie and I set up Mum's mini A4 whiteboard onto which I'd written where I was going and what time I'd be back.

A few minutes later, I entered the park gymnasium. The sounds of clanking and chinking of metal with sighs and panting gave me a rush of anticipation for what may be around the next corner.

With a quick rub of the St Christopher around my neck for luck, and with music playing in my earphones from Tamsin's old BlackBerry, I put my hoodie up, fixed on my boxing gloves, and bounded into the gym, looking for a punch bag.

There was none.

However, there were people happy to watch me search for one, as weights were pushed, pulled or dropped crashing down, along with the thud thud thud of trainers pounding along the conveyor belts in front of TV screens.

Women in full makeup found me most interesting. And they, rather like Prince Andrew, didn't seem to sweat. I, on the other hand, had always been somewhat lucky in that department.

In fact, my forehead was already damp.

A girl of around twenty prodded her friend to look over.

I couldn't exactly begin lifting weights with the gloves on though, and couldn't cycle; I mean, how would I hold the handlebars?

Over at one end, where the smell of rubber mats was more pronounced, there was a row of benches. Men were either straining with their exercises or encouraging each other; in front of them stood a wall of mirrors.

I began what I hoped looked like shadow boxing. After a few air punches, my arm caught the earphone lead, which yanked it out, and Rocky's 'Eye of the Tiger' blasted from its inbuilt speaker across the gym floor.

Tittering from various corners.

Retreating away to the safety of the water fountain, I pretended to be interested in posters about personal trainers while I fought to remove the gloves with my teeth.

A few minutes later, with gloves off and considerably fewer eyes on me, I sidled up to a vacant machine, which offered a bar dangling from a cable. Easy pie. Gripping it firmly above my head and walking away from the machine until my body could go no further, I let it yank me, spinning, back to the start. "Weeeeeeee!" I exclaimed happily. That was quite fun, so I did it again, this time leaving me with my hair over my face.

"Hi," a voice said. There was a man standing there. I brushed my hair back to see him more clearly. His confident bright green eyes stood out against his rich mocha complexion and shaved head. He was wearing one of those vests, presumably to showcase his muscled arms. His blue shorts and socks matched a stripe on his top. A thin gold chain adorned his neck, and he sported an expensive-looking watch. The whole designer look was thoroughly annoying and now he was frowning at me. He said, "I think you need help with this, don't you?" and flashed me a cheeky grin, revealing a pair of dimples.

"Very kind of you…?"

"Devon." He put his hand on his chest in case I didn't know who he was referring to. His voice was soft, deep, and from somewhere in North London.

"Devon," I repeated. "No, I really am fine."

"Are you sure?" he asked. That confident smile was back, lurking beneath high chiselled cheekbones.

"I'm sure." I offered a courteous smile. "But why do you

think I need help?"

"Err," he pretended to think. "Because you're doing it all wrong?"

"But how do you know what I was trying to do?"

"Were you trying to throttle yourself?"

"No." I put my nose in the air. "I was testing it."

"For what?"

"Elasticity."

He scrunched up his nose. "And did it pass?"

"Unfortunately, it failed."

At that moment, Maxi arrived, saving me further discussion. He moved to another machine.

"Pa!" I said loud enough for him to hear.

And he slowly turned, mouth agape.

Maxi, who had dressed like a smaller female version of Devon, all matching but with less aftershave, liked the running machines, but didn't like germs. "Don't touch a THING!" she barked. "Press the ON button with your shirt."

I put my hand under my top and did as commanded. "What about the rail?" I asked.

"Especially not the rail! With everyone's sweaty hands all over it. Even if you fall."

"Noted," I said, not meaning it.

Side-by-side we ran, while staring, without a hint of irony, at a video of a park.

"Who was that man chatting you up?" she asked.

"He was trying to be helpful," I admitted.

"Bastard," she commented, glancing at him. "And he's not your type. I doubt he'd call you a 'hooker' like Dustin used to."

"An escort," I retorted, "and a Ford Mk 1 Escort is a car!"

"How charming."

"It was just his way. And I liked it."

We ran in muted silence for a bit.

"Sorry, but you know we never got on," she admitted. "Anyway, that man, did you get his number? No, of course not, he's too perfect."

"I have the faintest feeling you're poking fun at me."

"Darling," she countered, "you're running in a top that says *Boris Pees in Pools* and you have a pair of mittens strapped around your waist."

"They're not mittens, they're boxing gloves."

"Really? How fascinating. So come on, give me the bad news."

"Okay." I took a breath. "Quinn's back."

Maxi stopped running in shock, and flew off the back of the machine, landing in a heap.

I helped her up.

"Jesus. He's not!" she gasped.

"Yes, he is."

"How do you know?!"

"Michael the Inspector told me."

"Oh my God, and does Quinn know where you're living?"

"No idea, and Tammy saw him in a crowd, just watching her."

"Fuck, fuck."

"Oh, and Oleg tried to sell the painting and discovered it's a fake."

"Fucking hell, Minty!"

"And of course, I haven't shared that nugget of news with Rupert or Tammy."

"You must, and you have to tell them everything."

"Really? Everything?"

"YES! They deserve to know what you got up to in that godforsaken mansion."

CHAPTER THREE

WHAT HAPPENED

~ THEN ~

Fear was threatening to consume me.

Rupert and I were in an antiques shop in Ealing. We had taken one of my paintings there in the hope of passing it off as an original.

"Why are you so agitated?" the antiques dealer asked my brother.

"I'm excited," Rupert replied. But I could see my brother's boat had been blown off course. "And it could be worth something," he added, rubbing his sweating palms on the knees of his jeans and hunkering forward.

The old man's eyes narrowed at him, evaluating, before his attention turned to me.

Run-chickety-chum-LOCKED!

I refocused on the man and provided him with an enormous confident grin, showing all my teeth. This jolted him. So, to even things up I became serious as if being told off, nodding to myself, and adding a fearful peek around the room while pretending to nibble at my nails.

"What is she doing?" the antiques dealer asked.

"My sister's special," Rupert answered.

The man grunted, and swivelled his squeaking chair back to my painting, which was behind him against the wall, pushing his face inches from the canvas. "Could be something," he muttered. "Hard to tell without sending it away, but that's the problem with these things." He straightened up and turned to study us again. "Unless you have some kind of provenance."

"Provenance? What's that?" Rupert asked.

"Something that proves you owned it or were given it, to help us age the thing."

Rupert slowly shook his head, obviously disappointed.

"Then I'm sorry—" the man began.

"But," Rupert leapt in as if remembering, "we do have an old photo if that helps?" And he began digging into his bag, to pull out the grainy black-and-white framed photo and pointed to a figure in it. "That's our great-grandfather standing so formally, and in the background, you can just about make out this painting on the wall."

The antique dealer's eyes lit up, and he smiled. "Oh yes, and I can see the family resemblance." He glanced up at Rupert.

"Really?" Rupert feigned surprise, then pride.

We were given a cheque.

Tamsin was waiting for us in the car outside – she never went in, she was more into organising everything.

Of course, there was a family resemblance. That wasn't our grandfather in that picture. It was Rupert.

~NOW~

At 3:40 p.m., the twins had arrived home, Harry had broken a glass, kicked a door, and begun a row with one of our dogs before disappearing into his bedroom.

Harriet shook her head at me. "Oh, for the love of Muffin!" She rolled her eyes. "Boys!"

I guess you could kind of understand it though.

My children's life in Sussex, of swimming in the sea and playing games with their friends in the sand dunes, had been exchanged for a new one, filled with colourful characters.

Harriet's first question as we first drove through London was, "Mummy, why is that man licking a lamppost?"

But what was I supposed to do? My parents needed someone living with them full-time, so once I managed to secure them a place in St Dunstan's, our new adventure began.

"It's not an adventure!" Harry shouted. "And stop saying it's character building! It's a horrible school with horrible children, with horrible teachers in a horrible town!" The door slammed again.

"Is it time for a gin and ha-ha yet?" Dad asked.

I checked my watch. "Not quite, Dad."

Harry hated everything, even his sister, and Harriet was struggling to make any friends. The twins weren't happy, so I took Paddington with me, to see if he could cheer them up.

"Whath wong, Harriet?" I asked in Paddington's husky lispy-voice. (All the animals had different voices. Easy when we only had two cats, but with the accumulated menagerie, it was getting harder.)

Harriet sat on the floor and gave him a hug. Harry, who was

playing on his games console, rolled his eyes with disdain.

"I can't do cartwheels," Harriet admitted.

"Cartwheels?" I repeated, positioning myself next to her and tugging one of her blond coils, which bounced next to her face.

She pushed my hand away. "Yes, Mummy, cartwheels."

"Honey, you've got lovely long legs like your Dad, they're not built for them."

"But every girl during every moment of free time does cartwheels. What am I supposed to do?"

"What do you do?" I was interested.

"I sit in the corner making my hands talk to each other."

"There must be someone else who can't do them?"

"Not in my class. Arabella can even do somersaults and backflips."

Arabella lived in one of the apartments behind the wall at the bottom of our garden.

"This is terrible!" I declared. "And a big problem later in life."

Her mouth dropped. "It is?"

"Yes, in hospitals doctors are always somersaulting their way into surgery, and you can't be a vet if you can't do the splits. How d'you milk a goat?" Harriet scowled while I pulled imaginary udders above my head. "Come on, you make me laugh, that's a better gift, and next year at senior school, no one will be doing cartwheels."

They'll have other things on their minds, like yucky boys.

"Well, it's important now," she said. "Now they are everything."

"Is that the only reason you're upset?"

"Also, they call me a baby for believing in fairies and mermaids, and they think I'm weird."

"They thought I was weird too." I cuddled her.

"They still do," muttered Harry from his game.

I fired him a look but carried on with Harriet.

"Why do you think they call you that?"

My daughter shrugged. "Because I sit in the corner talking to my hands."

"Maybe don't do that anymore. Stand up and take a big breath and join in."

I would regret this piece of advice.

I left them and headed into the garden to work on Maximus for a couple of hours.

One of the things I loved about metalwork was the mixture of textures: unloved rusty parts nestled alongside newer, shiny ones, and the way light bounced off chrome while being absorbed by lead. Once I had him assembled, looming high above us for added dramatic effect, Maximus was ready to face my harshest critic.

Ever since moving back in, making my father proud had turned into an obsession, a race against time I feared might soon run out. "It's coming along," Dad said as he made his way out into the garden, his arm outstretched along our wall for support.

Mum winked at me, but Dad's jaw was clenched, eyes pinched together as he studied it from different angles, licking his lips and about to deliver his appraisal, until he saw my face.

"It's fine," he concluded.

"No, go on, tell me," I groaned.

"I'm… you see, I'm still not convinced you've developed your own style, Minty," he replied.

Mum squeezed my hand to tell me not to worry.

Except for once, I was feeling defiant. "But what if this is my style?"

"I can tell you it's not," he said, his voice so utterly definitive, it prickled me further.

"I think it is."

"If this is your style," Dad's voice rattled, "we really do have problems, because there's nothing original or ground-breaking here. I've seen nearly the same piece by a young artist at the Tate last year." He perched on the wall opposite, hunkering forward, eyes evaluating my sculpture, then me with the same intensity. "Yes, the same one. And if you carry on down this road, you will never make a name for yourself."

I considered this. "You just don't like me welding."

"I think your paintings were better," he retorted, "but you could mould cow manure for all I care, as long as it's original, and people recognise your work, and say 'Look, that's a Minty.' And it would be nice for me and your mother before we're gone, to see the family name related to something positive instead of—"

"This is a Minty!" I interrupted.

His shoulders slumped. "It's not. You've given it a go, why not try something else?"

"Given what a go?"

He made a sweeping gesture towards my tools. "All this you're doing."

"You mean metal-art? Yes, Dad. I've given it a go for nine

years."

"And maybe that's where the problem lies?" He was staring into space, and then focused on me. "Go back to painting."

"You know I can't!"

"Well, this isn't healthy."

"I seriously have no idea what you mean by that."

"Margaret, the other day, I saw her picking rubbish up off the street! What she does with it I don't know."

"Well, I don't eat it, Dad, if that's what you think?"

If I find an exciting knick-knack and there's space to store it... what's the problem? Like once I saw the valves of an old trumpet and I used them as funnels of a sculpture of a steamship.

"Why can't you just give me some encouragement?" I pleaded.

"You don't think I do?"

"No," I answered.

"Well, then you're stupid." He was livid. "All those exhibitions I took you to, and the caravan painting holidays your mother organised."

"Yes, and thank you, Mum," I said. "But that's not what I meant. I just wish one day, some time in my life, you could tell me something I'd done, anything, which was good!"

"Well, I like it," Mum added quietly.

"You want me to lie?" Dad spat. "It's amazing, Minty, brilliant, and your choice of men has been outstanding, and we never worry about seeing you on the news again for fraud!"

"Barry!" Mum scolded.

I played "Summer Nights" from *Grease* in my head for a bit, and when I looked back Dad had his head in his hands and was crying. This was not why I was living with them. "Dad," I said calmly, "I'll paint something if that's what you want?"

Mum glanced from me to Dad and back again. "No, dear, that's not…." She shook her head.

Dad's eyes brightened instantly. "At last, Margaret, we can get rid of this mess in the garden. When?"

"Right now." I knew there was a large, stretched canvas under their bed which I'd been saving in the hope that one day my father would paint once more. I marched inside, grabbed the canvas, along with oil paints, turps, and my easel, and set it all up in my room without speaking. Mum helped Dad into a chair next to me and then hovered somewhere behind. And to really put the pressure on, Harry and Harriet came running in, throwing themselves onto my bed to watch. I squeezed out the primary colours onto my palette.

"What are you heading for?" Dad asked. "Landscape, still life, or, or something else?"

"I don't know, I'll just paint."

Harry tried to ask what was happening, his question stifled from Mum's finger-to-lips, and the large white space on the canvas stared back at me.

Two hours later, everyone had gone except Dad, still silently watching. The next moment, I felt his hand patting my shoulder. I waited for him to comment.

He didn't. He made his way down our corridor, returning a few moments later carrying an article from a magazine my sister had sent him about her latest zero-energy home design, which looked more like a spaceship than a house. The clipping, which he'd proudly backed onto hardboard, was headed 'Architectural prize for the most original design.' "I'll put it here," he said, and he propped it up next to my canvas. "To inspire you."

And he left.

The morning sunlight was making my curtains golden yellow.

Tamsin's magazine clipping was still there. My effort was finished. It was a landscape; it had a rumbling sky with the sun breaking through the clouds, which I'd taken from my memory of *Estes Park* by Albert Bierstadt; I had the horse and cart from *The Hay Wain* by Constable; I had a windmill taken from a painting by Jacob Isaacksz; and a few other bits added from various other famous paintings I knew. Everything was there, and I thought maybe I had managed to hoodwink Dad, but he knew.

And he was disappointed, again.

I scooped up the wet paint from my oil palette, all the different colours in one hand, and smudged them across the middle of the picture.

My phone buzzed. I had a text message.

Wiping my right hand on an old towel and awkwardly punching the code in with my left, I activated the screen. It was from an unknown number. And it said:

'Where is The Doctor?'

A sudden rush of adrenaline surged through me.

I had been waiting for contact. My heart immediately picked up the pace. And now, whoever had sent this would know I'd read the message. I took a long deep breath and held it.

Who was it?

Oleg? Or Quinn?

A cold, calculating Russian gangster, or a Glaswegian one with an unpredictable temper?

Hmmm, choices, choices.

And they had been straight to the point. Not… *Minty I hope you've been well, but I wondered if you would be so kind as to let us know what happened to that painting ….*

I let out my breath.

The thing is, if you were looking at earth from another planet in another solar system, this issue I was facing would be tiny, irrelevant.

But to a lot of people here, it was becoming big.

Should it be? Who decides how valuable something is? One person's cucumber is another's cauliflower cheese. We should change our thinking, and accept all art and fashion had the same value. Why should one brand be more expensive than the other? When this was believed, maybe the world would be a better place, people would be free, waste would be halved, our planet would love us again, and as my mind whirled with the possibilities, my phone buzzed, and the text read:

'WHERE'S THE FUCKING DOCTOR MINTY!!?'

Rude.

After staring at it for some time, I began texting back:

In his Tardis?? Fighting for peace, justice, and recycled vintage curtains?

However, I suspected my response may upset whoever they were, more than they were currently upset, if that were at all possible.

I deleted it and turned my phone off.

This was very bad.

Stirrings were coming from the twins' bedroom, which brought me out of my daze. I tiptoed out into the hall to slide quietly under the couch.

At last, Harry's legs came past, and I clawed at them, which once upon a time would have made him scream and giggle. Today he just said, "Not funny, Mum," and disappeared into the bathroom, leaving me there feeling dumb.

As I walked back from St Dunstan's School, people were rushing to get to work, parents returned from drop-off, kids, students and Ocado drivers everywhere.

But all of them were beginning to look suspicious.

It felt like *The Truman Show*, and I half-expected the entire scene to halt – all of them, even the man strapped to the tree on the opposite side of our street cutting branches, the postman, and the children – to turn and look at me in unison and shout, "We know what you did!"

That afternoon I received a call from the barmaid in our local pub, where we had lived in Sussex. She wanted the St Christopher I wore around my neck. She said it was hers. I told her she was mistaken – it was Dustin's, which he had worn all the time. She explained that she had given it to him due to his love for cars, and that St. Christopher is the patron saint of travel. She sent pictures of them together, kissing. Furthermore, she confessed that he had dubbed her with a classic car-inspired nickname.

I removed the pendant and mailed it to her.

When you've been called a "Mark 1 Escort" by your husband of nine years, and then discover he had a lover for seven of those years, whom he'd affectionately named his little "Triumph Spitfire," it was quite upsetting.

I shut my eyes and locked all that away in a spare room in my mind, deciding there was no need to revisit it.

It was 7 p.m. when we had the delivery. I took the parcel and sat down on the sofa and began unwrapping it. I was on my own at that point, but the hall door burst open, and the twins came bounding in.

"Did you buy us mobile phones?" Harry's face was all full of hope and wonder.

"No, I did not," I replied curtly.

Harry plonked himself down next to me, his hand delving into the box. "What is it then?"

"Not for you, hands off." I gave Harry's hand a playful tap.

Mum joined the fray. "Oh, that looks exciting," she beamed, "what is it?"

I moved away to finish unwrapping on the table. They all followed.

Dad in his usual chair.

Owls judging from their places on the wall.

Harriet read from the box, "CCTV night surveillance cameras?"

Harry huffed. "We didn't need them at home."

"This IS our home," I firmly reminded him.

Harry rattled on, "Then why do we need surveillance cameras?"

I shrugged. "Because I err…wanted to film…err…"

Harriet's little face lit up. "Pretty butterflies and night fairies?"

No, Glaswegian gangsters and walking corpses.

"Badgers," I managed.

And some Russian mafia too.

Harry's eyes never left my face. "Badgers?" he echoed, his tone cynical. "You don't think we're safe, do you?" He took a step back, as if needing room to battle.

"Oh for the love of Muffin!" Harriet exclaimed, rolling her eyes.

"Of course we're safe," I assured him. The battery-powered cameras were small enough to fit inside Maximus' ear. Harry was still scowling at me. "Look," I said, "why do you have to make such a big deal out of everything?"

His anger simmered. "Because we were happy in Sussex! We had everything. You tell me one thing we have here, that we didn't have there?"

Zombies clawing at the windows? Now, brush your teeth and off to bed and sweet dreams, everyone.

"We have…"

"Yes?!" he snarled.

"We have…"

"YES?"

I played my trump card. "Granny and Grandad, who love you very much."

Harry's shoulders slumped, he gave his granny a reluctant

hug and stomped off to his room.

Sleeping that night was a challenge; I jumped each time I heard a noise outside, so I located a pair of wax earplugs from my drawer and, inserting them into my ears, drifted off peacefully to sleep.

That meant I didn't hear my alarm the next day and awoke late.

Only fifteen minutes to get the twins to school. They were sitting in their pyjamas eating cereals at the kitchen table.

Dad was in his armchair, and he seemed relieved to see me. "Your mother is cooking us breakfast."

I found her defrosting a margarita pizza in a large saucepan on the stove. "Will you be eating with us, dear?" she asked, kissing my cheek.

"I'm not so hungry, Mum."

"It's just for you then, Barry!" Mum called.

"Oh, marvellous," Dad replied, "well, anything going, Margie, you know I'm happy."

Mum whispered to me, "I know two small people who may like to come out with us today." She winked and nodded towards the twins. Mum had always adored children and spent most of her life working with them.

"We would love to," said Harriet, "but we have school today, Granny."

"And in ten minutes' time!" I clapped my hands. "Now MOVE IT!"

Dad scratched at his stubble. "And I can't find your sister's article anywhere, it's still missing."

"I'm sure it will turn up," I assured him.

I went swiftly to my room, opened my cupboard and tentatively searched in darkness beneath my dresses, until I'd found Tamsin's magazine cutting I had hidden.

That was silly, Minty-Popps. You need to grow up.

There were no other things of interest there, just gubbins and a metal knob, which didn't look like it belonged to much. It looked sad and lost, but it would make a good eye or possibly part of a nostril, so I stored it in the jar with the others. There was my black fedora hat too, which I'd rescued from a hedge in Sussex. I liked that hat. It made me look fancy, but no gloves or shoes to go with it.

I straightened up, removed the paintbrush from my hair, and shook it free. I donned the hat and checked myself in the mirror. With my dark locks on either side at the front, it looked wrong, so I moved it to the side. The brim's shadow covered the faint lines on my forehead, which was helpful. Tugging it into various positions, I noticed the three cat-monsters gazing on nonchalantly from their positions on the bed.

By 8:45 a.m. we were back in the lounge, dressed and ready. Mum was chatting to the dogs and Dad was prodding some soggy-looking pizza with his fork at the table.

Before he could take a bite, I had removed it.

With the kids safely through the school gates, I was being pulled along Elgin Avenue by our dogs, while Mum and Dad followed behind. It was a glorious morning, the sun casting its warmth onto the pavement and lighting up the vibrant flower beds encircling each tree, lovingly tended by the local residents.

"Just look at that colour, Barry, just look at it!"

"Beautiful, Margie, like your hair."

"Oh, I think you need your eye drops," Mum responded with a rare joke. Dad chuckled and they kissed.

Into the park and I let the dogs off their leashes as we entered. The three of us made our way across the green and up a hill to a bench, where they could catch their breaths and admire the view.

A man walked past, and said, "Hey, it's the Dulux dogs!" He roared with laughter. "You know… from that advert?"

"Okay, George." Dad had no idea what he was on about.

"Has anyone said that before?" the man insisted.

I intervened politely, "I think we heard it once." (Everyone says it.) Then the man was off, guffawing and jabbering away about needing paint.

Muffin only liked exercise if it involved herding or a game of hide-and-seek with Paddington, chasing him between the bushes, but this day, there were no other dogs, and they wouldn't start their game. So, I ran around, hoping they'd chase me, but instead they just sat to watch. Trying a different tack, I hid behind a nearby bush and growled and barked at them. "Grrrrr… Ruff ruff ruff!" It was at that moment, through the undergrowth, I spotted a pair of shoes which had stopped on the path.

"Hello?" came a man's bemused voice.

Untangling myself from the branches, I stepped out to find Devon from the gym, in a light grey suit, different watch, shiny shoes, and just to really irritate me… almost perched on those cheekbones of his, were what looked like designer sunglasses.

"Goodness," he said, removing them, and his striking eyes

gave me an appraisal. "It's the boxer."

"Goodness, it's Devon from the gym."

He seemed elated. "Can anyone play, or is this something you do on your own?"

I took a leaf off my cardigan, and looked around for my dogs, but they'd gone. "Only me."

"Well, I'm sorry to interrupt, please carry on. But they look scared." He indicated my parents with his glasses. Dad's jaw hung open, as if I had become a werewolf and stolen his coat.

"And…" Devon leant forward to study my hair. "You have something…"

"A leaf?" I ventured.

"No, it seems to be just hanging there."

I ran my fingers through my hair and found a matted waxy lump. "That's an ear plug," I replied, not keen on detangling it in front of him.

"Oh." He seemed impressed. "Must be useful."

"Is that everything?" I asked, as Paddington came bounding back to me.

"For now." He smiled. Then, glasses back on, he was sauntering along the path, whistling to himself.

Our exchange was annoying, and yet there was something else.

What was it?

He had turned back, and caught me still confused, my head cocked, watching him. Beneath me, Paddington also watched, his head cocked sideways too.

"He seemed nice," Mum said, when I had joined them on the bench.

"And he has his own shoes," Dad put in, "which is always a good start."

I gave my father a playful prod. He was referring to Gabriel, a well-spoken young man we'd met in the park, who I quite liked. He had bare feet and had joined our table in the café to let us know the moon landings were fake, and then he'd lectured my parents on the evils of capitalism.

"He does slacklining," I had told them enthusiastically.

"That's a worthwhile trade," Dad had said. "They'll always need builders."

"No," Gabriel had answered, "you're thinking of dry-lining. What I do is tie a rope between two trees and walk slowly along it."

"Oh." Dad nodded. "Well, also… very… worthwhile."

Gabriel hadn't come to our table since.

It was evening, and I still hadn't found the time to set up the CCTV – a project I would soon regret delaying. While the twins did their homework, I settled into a lovely hot bubble bath, with my thoughts turning back to Devon.

Once, I'd been browsing in a shop with the twins, and a stylish elderly woman had commented on how beautiful Harriet's curly hair was. I offered her a compliment back, saying how glamorous she was. She had returned with, "Thank you, my dear, and you are so very…" The woman had fought for words whilst her eyes absorbed my appearance, in the end leaving me with, "different."

Different.

That day, I had worn my usual dungarees with rolled up legs, a dirty T-shirt, and bright odd-coloured socks and trainers. Some glitter on my cheeks and coloured ribbons and scrunches in my hair.

Today's look, in front of Devon, had been no different.

Hmmm.

And that feeling I'd had.

What was it?

I tried to remember the sun catching the trees, *the leaves, our voices, the smells and…*

And then I nearly drowned in the bath. But the good thing about choking on water was it tended to bring you out of your thoughts fast. This time it was my mother's voice that worked as she burst through the bathroom door to wave an envelope at me.

"We've been invited to something. How exciting!" She had found the plain white envelope with the words '*INVITE*' on our door mat. And before I could reply, she had wandered back out, leaving the bathroom door wide open and me with a cold draft, and lack of privacy. Mum's voice called from the living room, "It says they want to meet us next Sunday at a virtual bar, whatever that is."

"Who does, Mum?" I called back.

"Someone called Quinn," she proudly replied.

Then came Dad's thoughtful voice. "What kind of a name is that? You think we played bridge with him?"

"Oh of course we did," Mum answered, "with Marion Perkins from the tennis club."

"Get him on the blower then, Margie, and thank him, he's left his number on the card."

"No, Mum, don't!" I shouted, scrambling to get out of the bath, feet slipping on the wet tiles, grabbing a towel.

"I certainly will!" Mum shouted back. "It says RSVP and we don't know what to wear."

And she began calling the number.

I got to their phone and managed to stop the call, but not before it had already rung once.

He had our address, and now our home phone number.

I messaged Tamsin and Rupert and arranged a family get-together for Sunday. I'd tell them everything, face-to-face.

I needed a plan, but if there was one lurking somewhere in the recesses of my mind, it had so far enthusiastically evaded me. And I would fit larger locks on everyone's doors tomorrow.

Because he could be outside right now.

Tonight, the twins would sleep with me.

Sleepy-drain-hide-the-stain-SNAP!

~ THEN ~

"Who's paying for that?" Mum was gawping at the new car, which was sitting outside our flat.

"It's a company car," Tamsin replied, which I guess in some ways, was the truth.

"Well, you better look after it." Mum rolled her eyes at Dad, meaning 'goodness that is a lot of responsibility', and 'how proud we are' all jumbled together.

We gave them a tour of our flat, missing out mine and

Rupert's rooms of course, and steering them back downstairs.

We ate. Rupert made them laugh. Tamsin described her work at the architects and chances of promotion, and, once the plates were cleared away, I brought out the painting I had done for them and positioned it against the far wall. While Mum, Tamsin and Rupert waited awkwardly, Dad took his time, studying it. Sometimes up close, lifting his glasses to stare at the lines, then he'd nod them down again and take a few steps back. He checked our faces, then back at my work:

"Local scene, some interesting characters in the foreground, like the fruit-seller, and I think I recognise some of the shops, and yes, it's good, but it's not yours, is it?"

"Of course, it's mine."

"No," Dad argued, "it's a Cézanne. I mean he lived in Provence in the 1900s, but if he lived here now, and had wanted to paint the Kilburn High Street, that would undoubtedly be his."

Mum whispered in my ear, "It's very nice, dear."

It hurt. As it always had. But I cared less.

After they had gone, back in my room I surveyed the mess surrounding me. My make-shift bed took up a small corner on the floor, and covering every other conceivable space were paintings, all reproductions in the style of mildly famous artists.

And I could feel I was getting better. There were obvious signs like we were leaving places at a walking pace instead of a run. Which was always comforting. But there was something else. I was getting deeper with each artist, like I was stepping into their shoes, leaving mine far behind. And sometimes it felt as if their hands were gently guiding me. Not like ghosts, but I just began to understand them. I got them, and they got me.

Rupert acquired old, worthless paintings, so the canvases were aged, and I painted over them. In Rupert's bedroom, one complete corner was set up to look like a scene from the 1900s with one of our paintings hanging on the wall behind. We used a professional makeup artist to make Rupert look older and more distinguished, and the photos were developed in our bathroom/darkroom.

This was how we convinced people our painting had been in the family for years.

It sounded simple and it was.

Tamsin continued working at the architects, using her spare time to fabricate our items' provenances with a trail of forged ownership papers stretching back a hundred years or so. These were soaked in tea and lightly baked to achieve an aged look. Rupert made the calls, often sounding like a well-spoken old man. He would say, "My grandfather used to work for Lord Palmerston in 1856, no idea if it's worth anything, but I'm bedridden with a wound I received beating off one of the blighters in the Korean War, so I'm sending my niece, unusual sort, but a sweet girl nevertheless and hopefully won't forget your address, Richmond's Antiques…"

We started out targeting unscrupulous antique dealers, adhering to a simple rule: initially, we only dealt with those who attempted to deceive us. These were the dealers who undervalued my paintings, claiming they were works of lesser-known artists worth only a few hundred pounds, all the while secretly believing they had stumbled upon a lost masterpiece valued at over twenty thousand pounds. However, if a dealer recognised the painter and informed us of the artwork's potential value, we wouldn't sell to them.

In the beginning, it all seemed like innocent fun. I was 'knocking out' (as Rupert called it) around three forgeries a week, and my frustration with the overpriced art world was channelled into each piece. One, sold as a classic 19th-century painting of the Greek goddess of love, Aphrodite, was modelled on Pat from *EastEnders*. Another, purported to be Jupiter, God of Gods, was based on Timmy Mallet, the children's TV presenter.

Everything changed though when Rupert received Quinn's call. We had sold one of my forgeries to a friend of his, and he wasn't happy about it. His menacing, deep Glaswegian growl opened with, "Wha' you-s three dafty fuckin' eejits bin up ta egh?"

"Sorry?!" Rupert asked.

"Deh'n sorry me, laddie, I'll snip ye fuckin'posh baws-off, boil 'em up and dip me soldiers in them for brek-fist!"

Rupert was keen to keep his 'baws' away from Quinn's breakfast table, so we agreed to meet Quinn in a pub in Acton.

CHAPTER FOUR

DEVON

~NOW~

I welded one camera inside Maximus' ear and had him positioned at the bottom of the garden, facing us. From there, on my phone, I could log in and see our whole garden, and all the way over the fence line to Cynthia's patio doors. It also had an inbuilt microphone to capture anyone talking or zombie-gurning. Another camera was fitted in our front, facing the steps up to the pavement.

Michael the Inspector had left me three messages saying he wanted me to meet him at the Marylebone police station to go over a few things I did around the time of my arrest ten years ago.

I didn't call him back.

Instead, I took the Kray twins out for a walk along the canal path, off lead. It was raining lightly, but we didn't care. The summer rain brought out the earthy scent of wet grass and the subtle, comforting smell of the warm evening pavement cooling under the gentle shower.

And I began pondering, and my pondering went like this – I really should have considered the trouble my actions would cause. There could be now more than one criminal organisation I'd upset, and what with everything else going on, were my children in danger? And what if tonight, there was a strange noise coming from the garden, on the other side of my bedroom curtains, lurking in the darkness?

The possibilities were endless.

What if I got out of bed, went over to those curtains, and drew them back to reveal a man, swaying slightly in the moonlight behind the glass, pale grubby face, wet earth all over his boots and worms for eyes?

'Hey, kids, it's Kenny! He used to babysit me.'

'Goodness, Mummy, things were really tough in the olden days.'

While I was thinking, my doggies had a wonderful game chasing each other back and forth, leaping up on me at each turn, before we journeyed on to Paddington Central Rail Station to see the bronze Paddington Bear statue there. A train pulled in, and we were quickly surrounded by suited commuters. One particularly handsome man stopped to admire my dogs, which was nice until I had to bag a muffin-cake.

Why Muffin decided to do it there, I don't know.

Oh, and while I was scooping it up, Paddington disappeared into the crowd, and I was taught a valuable lesson. If you're teary-eyed, covered in mud, carrying a small bag of what looks like poop in your hands, bellowing, "Where are you, Paddington!" when you're clearly in Paddington Station, you'll be given a very wide berth.

Both dogs retrieved, we headed home.

Arriving back at our black metal gate leading down to the patio basement area, my parents' very serious neighbour Neil, who lived in the flat above, was waiting for me.

"Your dogs…" he began.

"Oh no, what did they do?"

"It's just all the teddies, and balls and ropes and things…"

I turned to survey the carnage that was our basement.

He carried on, "I've decided to rent my flat out and move to the country, so I'll be showing the place regularly. Do your dogs need all of them?"

"I'll confiscate a few of their teddies," I replied helpfully.

"Thank you, we have some people around later and I don't want to sound too grumpy," Neil added, sounding grumpy, "but during the viewing I was hoping your parents weren't sunbathing naked, your dogs weren't attacking each other, you weren't hammering and using your flame-thrower, and your children weren't being too crazy?" He forced a smile. "It's all about first impressions you see." And he disappeared inside.

My children too crazy?

Rude!

I opened my door to be greeted by Harriet waving my large pink dildo above her head.

"I found it in the drawer next to your bed, Mummy, look!"

"Harriet! Please stop waving it around."

"But what is it? It's so bendy."

"It's a candle," I said quickly. "I keep it by my bed, you know I'm into all that alternative medicine, it helps me sleep, it lights up at night."

"I can't make it light up, Mummy, but it does do this!" She turned it on, and it began buzzing, "Buzz buzz buzz," she shouted, racing around the lounge with it above her head. "Buzz

buzz buzz."

"Harriet, please stop, you'll wake up Granny and Grandpa!"

"They're in their room reading, can we show them?"

"NO!"

She carried on hopping and bopping around before I snatched it off her.

Marching into the bedroom, I slammed the door and buried my laughter in the duvet. Luckily my parents' door had stayed closed, and Harry was still doing homework. Small mercies.

SATURDAY

Devon's eyes were definitely part of the package. Yet it was his mouth that had ruffled me most. A perfectly smooth, smug mouth. That half-smile under his sunglasses as he walked away, so irritatingly assured. A mouth which thought it knew more about you than you did yourself. If he were a picture, he'd be painted by someone arrogant like Gustave Courbet, and no doubt it would be another of his controversial nudes.

I stopped, and realised I was applying lipstick to my shoe and my children were watching me curiously.

"How…" I muttered, "do you two move so quietly?"

"Socks," they answered together, pointing to their feet.

I wiped off the red and stood, checking my watch. "Well, why aren't your shoes on?"

"We can't find them." Harry glared, before shuffling away.

Harriet eyed me closely. She put a finger to her lips thoughtfully and asked, "And where do we think we're off to this bright sunny day, Mummy?"

I laughed. "To the gym."

"Why?"

"Fitness," I said as casually as possible.

She was grinning. "Do you think that man will be there?"

Dad had told them the story of the barking bush, which she loved.

"I have no idea, I hope not," I said, catching my reflection in the mirror. I pulled a T-shirt out of the cupboard. "How does this look?"

Harriet scrunched up her face. "You can't wear that, Mummy."

It was another T-shirt I'd dyed myself, with orange writing that read, *'Trump can't complete a sentence, unless it's in prison'*.

Harriet retrieved a plain top from my cupboard. "This looks nice on you," she said.

I agreed, although slightly miffed I had accepted fashion advice from my ten-year-old.

"And no hair-bobbles, paintbrush or ribbons today," I said, removing a yellow bobble she had just added.

"Can't I stay at home with the kittens?" Harriet whined.

"No, go and put your shoes on!" I answered, brushing my hair.

Harry appeared with one sad shoe, and I marched past him to their room. When the twins were younger, he was always the creative one, drawing, singing and dancing, and I thought he'd be in something like *Billy Elliot* or *The Sound of Music* in the West End, but now he just liked to slam things, moan a lot and amputate action figures.

"Where did Superman go?" I asked.

"You're looking at him."

I picked him up off the floor. "But his face is all pushed in."

"Yeah, he lost a fight."

"And one of his hands is missing," I noticed, turning the figure around.

"It's now an iPad."

"I see."

"It grows right out of his arm, cause his mum wouldn't buy him one."

I felt my lips tighten. "Really?"

"And he can use it anytime and she can't stop him."

"Well now, Harry," I said, feeling inspired, "how is he supposed to save people like that?"

"It's more likely he'll need a computer to save the world, than strong arms and a pretty face."

I sighed. He was probably right. "Have a look in Muffin's bed," I said. "I'm sure she ran off with something earlier."

He stomped off. I noticed myself in their mirror; my reflection here was more honest than in my room. Different lighting. I could see my skin had been gradually relaxing.

Don't give up on me yet.

A nasty smell interrupted my thoughts. "Granny's moved the tin of beans again!" I called. "Can someone put it back on the bin lid?"

In the park, with the twins safely in the play area, and my parents sitting nearby, chatting with some of their friends in the park café, I headed into the gym. Devon arrived not long after, wearing another sleeveless top, but this time he was with a woman. I stretched for a bit, did some running on a machine, and moved to one of the bikes before noticing the half hour was nearly up, and Mum would be fretting. A last sip at the water fountain, and that's when it all started. I was drinking with my head to one side, holding my hair away from my mouth, with the resounding clunking of weights and general gym-noises filling my ears, when Devon moved into my vision. Still no sleeves, but with some kind of designer-attempt to look like they'd been ripped from the shirt.

Come on, really?

He removed a polystyrene cup from the coffee machine dispenser nearby and stepped closer. His aftershave hit me, and it was the kind of scent some self-assured nitwit would wear. A bit mean but true. "It's a lot easier with one of these," he drawled.

I tried to respond, but no words came out. He waited for a moment, that smug expression creeping back onto his face as he moved past me.

"Devon!" I shouted, out of nowhere.

"Yes?!" He was startled and nearly dropped his water.

"Every year eight million tonnes of plastic are dumped into our oceans—"

He frowned. "Oh-kay?"

"Killing a hundred thousand marine animals, and all sea turtles have plastic in them, and that cup in your hand will be around for the next 400 years, whether it ends up in some animal's stomach or not, so yes, it may be easier for you, but not for me."

His eyes shifted to the foam vessel he held, unsure.

I opened my mouth to say more, but my feet had other ideas, turning me towards the door. Ignoring them, I spun full-circle back to Devon.

He was still there, looking confused.

But before either of us could speak, my feet had twisted me back, and this time my legs were taking me away through the gym, past reception and out into the fresh air.

A few metres up the grass-lined path, there was a *WHACK!* behind me as the glass gym doors burst open. "Hey!" called Devon's voice. "That's unfair!" He took a few steps towards me.

"What's unfair?" I replied.

"All of it is, because…" he said, searching, before his brow cleared, and he snapped his fingers in triumph. "You know my name, and if we're going to have any kind of relationship at all, I'm going to need to know yours."

"It's Minty," I responded politely.

He raised an eyebrow. "Fresh and sweet and tastes great after dinner." He cracked up, slapping his own knee to congratulate his genius.

"And what relationship would this be when you have a wife or girlfriend?" I pointed to the other side of the glass doors, where the woman was watching through the glass.

"That's my sister," he said.

"Oh." And I gestured to her, pointing to Devon with my thumb up.

His sister hovered her hand, as if he was just okay.

Devon shook his head. "I can't believe she did that."

Behind him she collapsed in laughter.

"What's more, you really embarrassed me," he said, "in front of everyone with this." He held up his foam cup.

"I didn't mean to, and you seem nice, but I'm not what

you'd want."

"Well, you can't blame a guy for trying." He turned to go. "But I'm adding this to my collection," he said over his shoulder.

"You collect cups?" I called.

He paused with one hand on the gym door, then turned his head slightly back, almost in a reflective gesture. "I know it sounds lame, but I think there's a story behind everything we do, and I translate the stories into memories, sometimes pictures. It's just a hobby."

And as much as he was not really my cup of tea, he was way more confident and attractive than anyone I'd ever been with, there was something intriguing about him and maybe beneath the exterior there was a man with a heart?

He grabbed a pen from the reception desk, and we quickly exchanged numbers, deciding to meet on Tuesday for coffee at the park café. He mentioned he'd bring along one of his creations to show me, piquing my curiosity about this unusual hobby of his.

~ THEN ~

THE QUEEN'S HEAD IN ACTON

Tamsin parked the car and turned to us. "Rupert, you take the lead. He's familiar with you, so use that to build some trust. We'll follow your cue," she instructed, then glanced at Minty. "And Minty, try to keep it quiet unless absolutely necessary."

That was perfectly okay with me.

There was a large blacked-out saloon car, parked directly outside the Queen's Head, and its driver was leaning against the wall, smoking. His eyes never left us as we passed him by.

The air inside felt heavy, carrying a stale odour of spilled beer and old cigarette smoke from the days when you could smoke inside still oozing from the worn-out furnishings.

And here was Quinn, sitting behind a wooden table.

He was hard to miss.

He was a giant.

Giant shoulders; giant arms; giant head; and he huffed and puffed, swore and coughed between sentences. While he talked to us, his large hands adorned with heavy gold rings squashed a burger into his mouth, with ketchup and mayonnaise seeping from his massive chops. A couple of his large friends on either side glared at us with threatening contempt.

I kept wondering what it would be like to be his petite girlfriend, who had popped over to land a kiss on his cheek before retreating to drink Bloody Marys at the bar. How would she ever sleep? I bet he snored like a hippo, and every time he turned, she'd be catapulted into the air. If his bladder was anything like mine, he was up every few hours, with the floorboards complaining as he stepped over them, creak-creak huff-puff, fookin' cough cough…

"Minty!!!" Rupert was glaring at me.

"What?" I answered.

Rupert and Tamsin exchanged glances, Rupert taking a relieved breath. "We have been asking… what you thought about Quinn's kind offer?"

"Sounds intriguing," I answered, which did nothing to satisfy the looks I had already accumulated from everyone in the pub. "Do you think I could get another glass of water?" I asked politely.

Rupert ran through the details again.

Quinn's offer involved not providing us with early graves, if we worked with him. He would supply us with X-ray, spectrometry, radiography, microscopy, and infrared images of the valuable paintings hanging on walls of stately homes. How he'd get them, we never asked.

These detailed images were a gold mine for anyone looking to master the art of replication. They revealed the initial steps an artist took, possibly starting with pencil sketches beneath the final layers of paint. You could decipher the buildup of the composition, whether a palette knife or brush was favoured, the intensity of each stroke, the specific pigments employed, and even the lead content in the paint. Important too was whether the artist reused canvases or preferred fresh ones. Although you'd only learn about this piece, artists often used the same method, meaning you were unlocking the secrets to their entire body of work. It was like unearthing their soul.

And if I was able to do it well, then when the investigators used the same machinery and imagery to see beneath my work, they should be convinced they were originals.

Choosing the right subjects to paint was crucial. It involved deep research into an artist's history to find hints of a piece that might have been lost over time, or at least the chance that a work had gone missing. You couldn't just paint anything. It was about finding evidence of something the artist might have seen or an idea or composition they would have been drawn to for a painting.

This was always Tamsin's area.

With Quinn's connections, he could also have highly professional documents forged, which would back up the provenance, or backstory, behind each painting. We would get a percentage of each sale and I'd need to drop off my paintings with the landlord of the Queen's Head, who was our go-between.

I listened to everything they discussed, while one of his friends glared at us. In contrast the other was more interested in his phone.

Towards the end, Quinn demanded in his casually unpleasant voice, "Gimme forgeries." A forgery was a new idea, or painting, in the style of an artist, not an exact reproduction. A replica could never be sold while the certified original was in play. "Forgeries…" Quinn repeated, pointed a giant stubby finger towards me, and in a quiet, wonderfully dark rasping tone, threatened, "Nae be makin' me fookin fakes…" And when I didn't respond at all, he clapped his massive hands in front of my face. "WAKEY-WAKEY!!!!"

The phone-staring friend next to him had been about to sip a full pint, but with Quinn's resounding CLAP, his hand clutching the glass nervously jerked, sending an arc of beer across the table and onto Quinn's lap. Quinn studied his wet sweatpants, and without warning or looking up, swept the back of his hand, hard, into phone-man's face, sending him tumbling backwards through the air into a heap against the wall, glass everywhere.

The pub went silent.

I did not like that. This was a cruel, vindictive man. Quinn returned to me, and said, "You get it?"

When I didn't reply, he glanced at his remaining friend next to him, cocking a giant thumb towards me, and huffed, "Dat dere's a dafty numpty if ever dere was one."

Rude.

Quinn had the fake ownership papers and documents professionally produced, arranged for the paintings to be transported to the discovery site, and organised everyone involved in their reappearance.

Over the next year, I did a number of paintings, from different artists. Some from the 1900s and some from this century. Each one fetched between £50,000 and £300,000, and we received 10 percent commission. With the money we opened a small high-class gallery in Hampstead. Rupert was out the front, handling our rich clients, while Tamsin silently worked behind the scenes. We were slipping Quinn's commission through the books as art sales. Inflating the value of our sold items. (The gallery was also making a small honest income.) We had a family business.

We would celebrate each successful sale and sometimes joke that it was probably like in the movies, where you're one step ahead of an investigation. But we never truly believed there was one going on.

We were very wrong.

One day, my brother came back with news.

"Quinn wants the next one sold at Sotheby's or Bonhams. That's where the big money is, but he wants to go bigger."

"A bigger canvas?"

He shook his head, looking at the floor.

"Come on, spit it out," Tamsin said impatiently.

"He wants Minty to do one from a well-known artist."

"How well-known?"

He shrugged. "Super famous, a household name."

"But one of those would be…"

"Worth millions, yeah."

"This is getting out of control," Tamsin said. "And anyway, it's impossible, Minty won't be able to get away with it, and they'll know it's a forgery."

"Not if I have the original next to me when I paint the new one," I said. "Then I could live and breathe the artist's mind."

Rupert balked. "They won't exactly let us take a painting out of one of those houses, Minty."

They didn't let us take the painting out.

Quinn organised for me to go in.

CHAPTER FIVE

TIME TO TELL

~NOW~

SUNDAY

Not far from the splendid black metal horse statues at Minster Court sat the Walkie Talkie Building, with the Sky Garden Restaurant at the very top. It would be a year on Monday since Dustin had met his fate in the mini-market, and the twins wanted to do something special to commemorate him.

Tamsin and her husband, Thomas Francis Junior, had invited us out for a special family lunch. Afterwards, we all planned to walk up Parliament Hill on Hampstead Heath where we had scattered Dustin's ashes. Harry suggested we have a minute's silence, and as Dustin had been a man of such few words, it seemed fitting.

The lunch would also be my opportunity to quietly come clean with Rupert and Tamsin about what I'd done in Oleg's mansion. My sister wouldn't be able to be too cross with me. After all, neither her husband Thomas nor my parents knew she had ever been involved in our escapades. Still, I didn't expect the meal to end with an ambulance.

We all met up at the bottom of the Sky Garden lift.

Tamsin was wearing another summer green suit, with her hair in an immaculately coiffured French hair-knot. She apologised, "Crispin and Clementine wanted to stay at home with the au pair. I know the Harries will be ever so disappointed."

The last time the cousins met, Crispin had been thoroughly unimpressed with any of Harry's toys, and Clementine had spent all her time talking about boys (or 'yucky boys' in Harriet's words). If the twins were disappointed, they handled the news well.

The doors opened on the 43rd floor, and we stepped out into the stunning, chic, modern restaurant, surrounded by lush greenery. A few metres away, behind a wall of glass, the breathtaking view of London stretched out beneath us.

Mum shooed us all forward. "You go on, I'll wait for you downstairs," she said, working her way to the corner of the lift, frantically searching for the down button.

After some gentle coaxing, we had her out, and once we had moved to a table hidden from the view, Mum was happy. I sat next to Tamsin, so I'd be able to share my news with her.

"Hey, gang, wallets away," Thomas announced in his friendly-but-firm voice, taking off his corduroy suit jacket and folding it carefully. "We're paying, but you never know if clients or the press are close by; so best impressions all around, please."

Rupert did his 'best impression' of a duck, which made the twins giggle.

Mum spotted one of her favourites on the menu. "Your father and I would like the risotto, please."

"What about a steak?" Tamsin offered. "They have filet

mignon here."

"It's their teeth," I explained. "They'll need something softer."

"We like wine though," Dad confessed, searching for the waiter.

"Don't worry, Dad," Tamsin assured him, "Thomas is choosing a bottle."

While Thomas Francis Junior pored over the choices on the menu, Dad made a serious face, as if he appreciated the solemnity of the wine choosing, which I doubt he meant. "Your business must be doing well?" my father said, sitting back to survey his surroundings.

Tamsin replied, "We had three more orders for zero-energy homes this month."

"Good heavens!" Dad exclaimed, his face full of pride.

I took my chance to prepare the ground for later. "By the way, Tammy – I have something serious I need to discuss."

Rupert was intrigued. "Is it a business idea? Because I've one of my own…"

"No, Rupes." Tamsin shot him down. "We are not investing in your hare-brained schemes. Dad, what about a starter?"

"They won't eat it," I answered.

Thomas spoke without taking his eyes off the wine list. "I'm sure your parents can speak for themselves, and your mum loves prawns if I remember rightly."

"Sounds lovely," Mum said diplomatically.

We all ordered, and Tom chose a £100 bottle of wine, the vintage of which he endeavoured to discuss with my father, who had topped his own glass to the brim to show his appreciation.

Two large plates of prawns arrived for my parents, who passed them down the table to Rupert, because they thought they were ordering prawn cocktails, while I busied myself attempting to slip water into Dad's wine.

"Minty," Thomas said, catching me. "Let your parents live a little, surely they've deserved that?" He often liked to remind me of the trouble I'd caused them.

Harry made a toast to Dustin.

Drinks were drunk, more wine appeared, starters were finished, and we began our mains. "Tamsin, when's that exhibition again?" Dad asked, moving his food around on his plate with his fork, as if reorganising was all that was required.

"Next week," she replied, refilling his glass.

Dad grinned. "Good-oh."

I wanted Mum to sit between them, so she felt more included in the conversation, and while we were swapping chairs, I overheard Thomas: "Your family always loves a drama." His statement was the catalyst for a hushed row.

Tamsin hit back, "I don't know why you keep saying that!"

He replied, "Swapping chairs, we couldn't sit near the window, and what about the starters?"

I interrupted. "Guys, I need to speak to Tamsin about a serious matter."

"Go on then," Thomas snapped.

"Privately…"

Thomas smirked. "See, more dramas—"

"I don't feel good," Rupert said.

Mum, at this point, took off her shoes and tucked them into her handbag.

"Your shoes don't go in your bag, Mum," Tamsin pointed out, gently wrestling with her.

Thomas raised his eyebrows, as if his point was being proved. I hated those eyebrows of his.

Dad, now sloshed, began talking to the next table about art.

Trying to defuse things, I said, "Let Mum keep them in her bag if she wants, and I need to talk to you urgently."

Tamsin snarled at me over her shoulder, while trying to get a shoe out of Mum's firm grip. "Is it an important matter, Minty?"

"I'm guessing," Thomas chuckled, "it will be a life-or-death one."

"Actually, Thomas, it is," I admitted.

"Oh, for fuck's sake," Thomas sneered. "And can everyone just remember, we are on show here!"

At that moment, Tamsin yanked at the shoe, Mum let go unexpectedly, sending it flying across the table. It struck a glass of Bordeaux, which toppled over, soaking Harriet in red, and she screamed.

Tamsin wasn't pleased. "We DO NOT LIKE DRAMAS!" she bellowed at the restaurant's startled guests.

Rupert let out a gurgle and keeled forward in toxic prawn-shock, clutching his neck, while Harry began crying, because that was what Harry did on Sundays.

I called the manager. "Can you order an ambulance for my brother, taxis for us, and a first aid kit for my father," who had slid under the table, with blood pouring from his knee. I wasn't sure how that had even happened.

Thomas was rather disappointed with our public performance and took Tamsin straight back to Tunbridge Wells.

After my parents had slept off the booze, it was 7 p.m. We saddled up the dogs and headed up to Parliament Hill on Hampstead Heath, where Dustin's ashes had been scattered the year before.

From the viewing point, you could see across London all the way to Canary Wharf, and with dotted clouds amongst the blue, it was a truly magnificent view. And I may have been imagining things, but I was sure a couple of men sitting on a bench near us were observing us all.

"Well, I think this idea is very mature of you, Harry," said Dad, breaking my thoughts.

We were going to hold hands for a minute's silence, while we sent Dustin all our love and thoughts. My own love and thoughts for Dustin had somewhat diminished since my chat with his 'Spitfire' girlfriend. But there we all were, holding hands, looking down, eyes shut.

After a moment I heard Mum ask, "What are we doing?"

We opened our eyes again and I re-explained, "A minute's silence for Dustin."

"Right." She smiled. And she put her arm around the twins. "Don't you two want to play with those children over there?"

"Not yet, Granny," said Harriet kindly. "We want to send Dad our thoughts first."

"Barry – they're sending you thoughts."

"No, Mum," I pointed out, "Dustin was the twins' father, who died."

"I know he did!"

"Well, we're sending him our thoughts."

"Go on then!" Mum snapped impatiently.

We shut our eyes but were interrupted again. "Minty!" a voice called.

"Damn it!" swore Harry, to my father's disapproval.

Striding up towards us was Phil, my damp corner-shop admirer. "I never thought I'd see you again!"

"Who's he?!" demanded Harry bitterly.

Phil arrived next to us on the hill, slightly out of breath. "Did you block my number?"

"No," I lied.

"Really?" He scratched his head. "That's strange, I couldn't get through. Anyway, glad you're feeling better, with the sickness and all."

"Much better, thank you, Phil," I said. "But I'm here with my parents and children and—"

"No need to apologise," he interrupted, his palms up, "you didn't mention you have kids, but I'm fine with it. Actually, I'm heading to the pub for a roast dinner, would you all like to tag along?"

"Oh, that does sound nice!" Mum said, picking up her bag and heading down the hill.

"NO!" bellowed Harry. "We do not… like… roasts!"

"Oh, come on, little fella," Phil said, nudging him. "Who doesn't like a roast? And that pub does one of the best."

I shook my head. "They really don't."

But Phil was determined. "Beef, chicken or pork, pigs in blankets, lashings of gravy over some nice Yorkshires, why on earth not?"

Harry screamed, "Because my dad died buying a bag of Yorkshire puddings!" And he slumped down, weeping openly with Harriet consoling him.

"He did," I admitted. "That's how he died." No one spoke for a bit.

Phil's eyes flittered about awkwardly before he shrugged. "I hear they do a good burger too?"

"Let's catch up another day," I replied.

He nodded eagerly. "Yes, let's."

He walked off, and that's when I locked eyes with one of the men on the bench. There was no doubt they had followed me. He muttered something to the other man, and they both got up and left.

Instant messaging calls, with their encryption, were the safest way to buy or sell drugs, guns, or carry out a range of other spurious activities, I had been assured after reading various articles on the web. What I had to tell my siblings fell into another bracket, of which there were fewer articles. Rupert and Tamsin entered the conference call, and before I could speak, Rupert began, "Does Mum still think she worked at Selfridges?"

"To be fair," Tamsin said, "we don't know, she may have done."

Rupert wasn't convinced. "In the '30s? With Mr Selfridge?"

"She's getting confused," I admitted, "but that's not what I wanted to discuss."

Tamsin sounded surprised. "It's not about our parents then?"

"No." I took a deep breath. "And what I'm about to tell you may come as a shock."

My brother interrupted. "What I'm going to say will also be a shock – we're going to be rich!" he boomed in our ears.

"Are we?" Tamsin's enthusiasm a mere pinch of his.

"Yes," he assured us, "but first you need to trust me."

"But we don't trust you," Tamsin replied.

"At all, Rupert," I added.

"Well, that's something you have to get over," he said, "because I need you to lend me £10,000."

"I don't have any money," I said.

"And I'm not lending you any," Tamsin put in.

He sounded hurt. "You would if you knew what it was for."

Tamsin controlled her voice. "What's it for, Rupert?"

"Okay, you're going to love this one." His tone rose with excitement. "Minty, think of something you like but hasn't always been that good for you."

"Cheese?" I suggested.

"No, men!"

"Ignore him, Minty," Tamsin said. "I can't believe you just said that!"

"And," I added, "there are loads of dating apps already."

Rupert enthused, "Hey, and it's good to know, sis, you've been trying them all out."

"I haven't!"

"Anyway," my brother pushed on, "it isn't an app. It's a cushion with an arm attached. So, when you're on the couch watching a sad film on your own, you can wrap the arm around you, kind of like a hug from a boyfriend, but with less commitment. He comes with three changeable one-armed shirts: lumberjack, football jock and—"

"Quinn has been in touch," I blurted out.

"And office jerk," Rupert petered out.

It was Tamsin who spoke first. "Why?"

"He wants to meet me."

Tamsin panicked. "What on earth for? You're clearly not in the copying business any longer!"

I took a breath. "It's about that painting, *The Doctor.*"

"The one in Chelsea, on that oligarch's wall?" Tamsin asked.

"Yes," I croaked. "And well, *The Doctor* has been examined—"

"How ironic," Rupert observed.

"And they've discovered it's not an original," I said.

"Really?" Tamsin said. "Are you sure?"

"Oh, yes," I confirmed, "100 percent sure."

"But it has to be," Rupert argued.

Tamsin agreed. "We know he had the original, you saw it, and it was certified by many experts even—"

"Ahh, indeed," I interrupted, "it was an original back then. They're not doubting that. But it's not anymore."

"God. That's weird," Rupert observed.

"Well, yes," I went on, "and you remember Quinn told me never to do a fake."

"No," said Tamsin, "don't say this. Please don't."

I shut my eyes. "Well, Quinn did say a famous fake would never fool the experts, and I guess he was right."

"What happened?" Tamsin snapped.

"Shit-the-bed no!" came Rupert's fearful voice.

"TELL US, MINTY!" Tamsin shouted. "WHAT DID YOU DO?!"

~ THEN ~

The Doctor was hanging on the wall of a stately home owned by Oleg, a 'businessman' who had risen to power after the breakup of the Soviet Union, as so many of the oligarchs had. Around 2012, Oleg was already under the spotlight for corrupt activities, and the UK government had frozen some of his assets. Facing cash flow problems, and unable to sell any of his art, Oleg was offered a chance by Quinn to make £10 million, without any risk, which was too good an opportunity to miss. On the wall of his Holland Park mansion was his greatest treasure: a famous painting from the 1961 series by celebrated French artist Antoine Rousseau. There had always been some wonder as to whether Rousseau had painted more. *The Doctor*, *The Farmer*, *The Cobbler*, *The Baker* and *The Chimney Sweep* were all dark, brooding unframed oils on canvas, one metre square. And as some of his last paintings were lost in a fire he started, which had ultimately killed him, we decided *The Teacher* was one piece that could have been his final work, never to have been seen. And maybe it could be the most valuable of all. If we managed to pass it off as an original, in return for allowing me into his home and letting me analyse Rousseau's masterpiece, Oleg would receive a percentage of the sale value. The exposure and renewed interest in the artist would likely push the value of his painting skyward too.

However, I was having second thoughts about the whole thing.

By chance, Maxi had popped by when Quinn had been occupying three seats on our sofa. And later, Maxi had been furious with me. She explained I had often been her moral compass and was so disappointed in my behaviour.

This struck a chord with me, and so I tried to back out of it all.

"I wish you had said this before," came Tamsin's reply. "The train has now left the station and yes, after this, we will stop, I promise."

Rupert and I arrived at a high wall with gold-plated, ostentatious gates leading to Oleg's home. The intercom clicked, followed by the low hum of a motor, as the gates began to move back smoothly, allowing us entry. White paving stones and pillars lined the courtyard, interspersed with the sweet smell of lavender and peonies. We passed a cabin where some estate security personnel waved us through. Then, another officer, accompanied by two black German shepherds, checked our bags.

At the large white front door, another two officers waited, with cameras monitoring every angle.

"Follow me," one of the security personnel said.

And we did, with the other falling in behind us. I knew this because I kept turning around and there he was, right behind me.

Once we were safely inside and standing in a vast hall, one of them grunted, "The Principal is away today." His voice echoed testily off the high ceilings and marble floors. "But he gave me strict instructions about your visit," as the subtle scent of polished wood and a faint trace of citrus from freshly cleaned surfaces hung in the air.

Rupert grinned. "We're just here to do our job."

"Actually," the guard added, "only one of you is."

Which prompted an argument between the two of them, but my attention had been taken by some artwork in the distance near a staircase.

Watercolour paintings, as you know, involve some degree of chance, especially if you were painting on an easel, which was why Dad loved them so much. With enough water on your brush, the paint would drip or bulge, smudging, merging sky and land, like viewing the countryside through a rainy car windscreen, *the smell of damp cagoules all around whilst rain thumped on the metal roof, sipping hot chocolate from a thermos, Mother's sandwiches.*

"Stop, no, stop, I'm talking to you, don't touch it, put it back, I told you to put it back, don't move!" (I guess he'd been saying all those things separately, but to me when I clicked back in, the words piled through at once.) I froze as instructed, and now he was behind me. "What were you doing?" his voice sounded, breathlessly.

"I was having a gander," I replied to my invisible questioner.

"No. You do no gandering," he barked. "You will ONLY be allowed in ONE room during your time here."

"If I need the toilet?" I enquired.

"You will be escorted."

"If I'm hungry?"

"You bring a packed lunch."

"Okay, what shall I do with this?" I lifted the picture above my head.

There was a gap when I guessed they were exchanging glances behind me, before I was allowed to un-freeze and replace it on the wall.

"You will be escorted for every minute of every second of

your time here. Is that understood?!"

"Yes sir!" I answered briskly. "Kind of like buddying up in camp?" I suggested.

No reply was given, but my brother smiled at me with a mixture of love and distant concern.

Unlike its usual placement behind a special non-reflective glass screen surrounded by extensive security measures, *The Doctor* was now presented differently for my task. It was temporarily relocated to a large, bare, white-walled room, where it was securely clamped to a beautiful bronze stand. The room, devoid of the usual elaborate security features and surveillance cameras, contained only the painting, myself, and a laptop displaying X-rays, infrareds, and other essential images needed for my detailed study of *The Doctor.* And a security officer, sitting in the corner, unable to see what I was painting, but able to stop me touching the original. No surveillance cameras in that room. Oleg did not want the security team knowing what we were doing. If we were successful and *The Teacher* was hailed as an original – it would be in all the papers, and people could talk.

As I stood before the blank canvas, my brushes were arrayed before me, ready for the task. The scent of linseed oil and turpentine filled the air, a familiar aroma that always stirred my creative spirit. I dipped my brush into the palette. Each stroke I made on the canvas was deliberate, as I sought to emulate Rousseau's unique style.

Frequently, I paused to study the X-ray and infrared images displayed on my laptop. These technological insights revealed the hidden layers and techniques of Antoine Rousseau's masterpiece, guiding my hand as I replicated brushstrokes and blended colours. The room was silent except for the soft swish of my brush and the occasional creak of the easel. In this solitary space, with only the silent guard in the corner, I felt a deep connection to the art, as if each brushstroke was a conversation across time with Rousseau himself.

I painted two canvases simultaneously side-by-side, on two easels. This was how I liked to work. When one was drying, I continued on the other, which doubled my chances of getting one perfect. By the halfway mark, I usually left the worst one and continued with my favourite. On the first day, Oleg popped in a few times to watch me, telling his employee to leave, before asking me questions about my painting process and informing me about his knowledge and appreciation of fine art. And when I offered little in response to this revelation, he became stroppy, like a child not receiving recognition.

I saw him less after that. It was just me and the guard, who as it happens, was barely interested in what I was doing; always with headphones on listening to music or talking very loudly on his mobile. The room was locked each night after I left and was opened for me every morning.

At the start of the second week, Oleg arrived again, visibly irritated. He waited for the guard to leave before he let loose. After a cursory glance at both canvases of *Teacher* I had been working on, he shrugged dismissively. "Terrible composition. Any child could tell they're not by the great Antoine Rousseau," he sneered. "They are bad, not good at all, and a complete waste of my time."

"Shall I go then?" I stuttered, feeling my face flush.

"No, no," he retorted, already striding towards the door.

"You may as well finish the week. Fuck Quinn and fuck your paintings. I'll see you Friday."

After he left, I found myself sitting in a daze.

He had been rude and hurt my feelings. And for reasons I couldn't quite articulate, it mattered to me. More than I wanted to admit.

His behaviour had taken me by surprise and given me no time to mentally prepare and it had stung, leaving me embarrassed for blushing so visibly. Worse still, he had noticed my discomfort, making my cheeks flame even hotter in self-consciousness.

Taking a few deep breaths, I forced myself to calm down. My heart was racing, too agitated for the steady hand painting required.

Then, an idea struck.

On a spare canvas, I began to paint a replica of *The Doctor.* It was astonishing how Oleg's actions had fuelled my creativity that day. Both the imitation of *The Doctor* and my new creation *The Teacher* turned out to be the finest works I'd ever produced. I crafted the replica with a singular purpose: to challenge him, to see if he could discern it from the original. I wanted to witness the surprise on his face, to prove a point. Nothing more.

And on Wednesday, I had finished my copy of *The Doctor.* It would take two days to dry properly and give me time to complete *The Teacher* by Friday.

Friday arrived and I couldn't help smiling. Because I was sure Oleg would be shocked. However, he never returned. A message was sent, via the guard, that Oleg had more important things to deal with than my 'amateur painting'.

I had put so much love into creating this beautiful copy of which I was proud. I glanced back at the guard who had delivered the message, however he was already back plugged into another song on his phone. There he was jigging about in the corner of the room, peering from the window (as usual, at the women in the mansion opposite).

But this time, I wasn't embarrassed. I was angry.

I calmly got up, unclipped the original from the stand, put my copy in its place, and opened my folder to pack the original of *The Doctor* away, along with my new creation *The Teacher*.

I don't know why, I just did.

As I began zipping it up, the guard whirled around unexpectedly.

And that's when my strength melted with the realisation of what I had done. My heart began thumping in my chest, my face felt hot, and I lost my breath.

"What," his voice dropped, "what are you up to?" Something was fishy. He could tell and here he came, marching over, a deep scowl etched across his face.

"Nothing," I tried, innocently looking up, "but do you really think that Oleg… does not like me?"

"Oh." He nodded and heard my timid tone. "Probably not."

His shoulders relaxed, as if here was a silly woman still getting over being humiliated by his mean boss.

I shrugged. "I did my best for him."

Now he'd never seen anything I'd painted, having been told to keep on the other side of my easel. He had no idea what I could produce, solely that Oleg thought it was 'amateur'.

He glanced at what he thought was their original, still in its place. "If I was you," he said, "I'd pack your things away and get out."

Later, I was escorted from the building as usual.

Yes. It was that easy.

I walked out of that mansion with all its high-security, surveillance cameras, patrols, guards, dogs, and alarms, with a global household name masterpiece under my arm. Afterwards, I sat in the back of a black cab, being driven across town with two paintings next to me: my new painting in Rousseau's style *The Teacher* and also Rousseau's original, *The Doctor.* His was considerably more valuable than mine, by somewhere near £50 million.

My cab stopped next to the Queen's Head in Acton, and I skipped inside, handed *The Teacher* over the bar to the landlord, (who worked for Quinn). Then on to our flat in Willesden Green.

~*NOW*~

WHATSAPP CALL CONTINUED…

I had finished explaining everything to Rupert and Tamsin over the phone, and now there was just silence on the line, the kind that begged for a response.

Finally, Tamsin's voice came through, tinged with patient hope. "After Acton, what did you do with it next?"

"With what?" I replied.

Rupert screamed, "With the goddamn original Rousseau!!!"

"Oh! Okay, so I dropped off my forgery and carried on to our flat with it."

"But why," asked Tamsin sounding exasperated, "did you take it in the first place, Minty?"

"Oleg was rude," I explained, "and so was Quinn."

"People ARE rude!" Tamsin's voice rose sharply. "You have to get over this thing!"

"Shit!" cried Rupert. "Just tell us where you went next!"

"I headed to the flat," I said, "but I guessed you'd both be mad at me."

"We would have been," Tamsin's tone softened, "although by then, we had been arrested."

"And," Rupert chimed in, "thank God you did not go into the flat with it under your arm."

I firmly grasped this positive point with all my might. "Yes! Now that WOULD have been bad. What with all those police waiting for me in the dark in our flat, it WOULD have been the end of it all, because it's not like stealing a lipstick from Boots, and I must say… still to this day, when I turn the lights on in any room, I fully expect to find it full of police staring back at me again. Anyway, now I guess Quinn thinks we diddled him and sold it, because I've had quite a few angry texts, although some could be from Oleg or the Russian mafia, because they can't be happy either and of course the police will be keen to recover it."

Tamsin broke in. "Stop stalling! Where… Is… The… Rousseau?"

"I stopped off on the way," I answered.

"Yes…?"

"And I got rid of it," I added.

"What do you mean?" she pursued.

"Well, I binned it," I replied.

"When you say binned," Rupert said, through what sounded like gritted teeth, "do you mean you stored this priceless artwork somewhere safe?"

"No," I answered, "I mean I dumped it in a wheelie-bin and hopped back into the cab."

After a pause, Tamsin spoke.

"Holy mother of Mary."

CHAPTER SIX

THE INVITATION

~NOW~

Were teenage girls the meanest creatures on earth?

From my memories of school, they were certainly right up there with honey badgers. And honey badgers didn't hunt in packs or follow you home from school. I didn't want Harriet going through all that, but surely at this age there was nothing to worry about. Although, watching the twins trundle off through the school gates, bags hanging limply from their slumped shoulders, I wondered what I could be sending them into.

While all this was leaping about in my head, the school bell sounded, causing panicking parents to mutter and hastily push their children inside. I found myself standing next to a glamorous-looking woman wearing a cream cashmere jacket and large sunglasses.

"I'm not trying to be cool," she said to me. "I have a terrible hangover."

"Oh, I get them too." My voice sounded like a teenager at a disco.

"You know, I don't drink in front of my children," she added. "Which is a crying shame, because it means I don't see them much either." She lifted her glasses and winked. "Joke. Hi, I'm Meredith."

I smiled. "Minty… I have the twins."

"Oh, the new cool kids, with all their pets. Arabella is rather jealous."

"Cartwheels!" I blurted out.

She frowned.

I clarified, "Your daughter is very good at them."

"She should be," she said, "she's had gymnastic lessons since she was five."

And then she began talking, and somewhere behind her I noticed an SUV without a mummy or daddy inside, and instead sitting in the back, as the car drove slowly by, was a large, angry Quinn.

The PAST is coming.

I was aware Meredith was waiting for me to speak. "Sorry?" I asked.

"I said P.A.S.T. is coming up this Thursday," she repeated. "It stands for Parents And Schools Together. You must come along, 4:30 – 6:30 p.m., anyone who's anyone will be there, and this month we're holding it at my place."

I said I would try to make it.

Faith had a bit of a thing for Meredith. She admitted this later when she stopped in for a quick cup of tea after the school run. "But I'd never tell her," she said. "I wouldn't want that power in her hands…" Faith explained that P.A.S.T. were a tight-knit group of high-powered parents, mostly bankers and lawyers, some with children at St Dunstan's and the rest from private schools, and it was all very selective and secretive. "You

HAVE to go because if the twins make friends with Arabella, then the whole class will want to be their friend. And you'll all be invited to the parties, and you'll be set for life, or at least until the end of the school year, when I guess you'll be cast off like a wet sock."

I did not like the sound of this. I often had wet socks after dog walking and didn't like them one bit. But I agreed we'd go.

"And," she bubbled, "you better start planning what you'll wear. It will have to be something good!"

Hmmm.

I woke up thinking about Devon. I had received a text from him. It said, 'See you later for Round 2. Ding-ding.'

If he were a sandwich, he'd be a tuna, lettuce, mayo, salt and crisp sandwich. And there was much you could enjoy munching about him. Parts of him were good for you, but shiver-me-timbers, there were bad bits too. And his mouth, with that double dimple…

This was not good.

Why wasn't he married? He had to be in his forties. Where had he been hiding? But that was the trick, wasn't it? Selling you the impression that they were a toy only you had discovered, still sealed in its original packaging, unused, on its own at the back of a dusty attic, hoping to be found.

And if he liked women that much, enough to chase one out of a gym, a woman he had nothing in common with, then how much chasing had he been up to? But it's not like he knew me, it must be something physical?

Standing in front of my reflection in the wall mirror, there I was in my homemade tie-dyed top, my long dark wavy hair embellished with random plaits, ribbons, and other bits just doing their thing. My button nose, thin lips, and the twinkly crinkles around my eyes when I smiled all came together in the person looking back at me.

He had no real interest in me. Why would he have?

I bounced over to the door and quietly locked it.

Ran back and whipped my shirt over my head, poking my head through to evaluate what I could see, prodding my naked side, releasing it, and watching as the blood filled in around the white finger mark. I wasn't tanned, but working outside and dog walks gave my face and arms some colour.

He couldn't like breasts. Mine had never been big.

My body was always on the overly thin side, but hours of hammering, squatting and shaping metal had altered it.

I now had a bum-bum. And my forearms had veins.

Maybe he liked bum-bums and veins?

Most women would surely find him attractive, but maybe deep down, he was sweet, and kind, and all this time, he'd been searching for something more, a connection…a creative connection…

'Fresh and sweet, and tastes great after dinner.'

Yeah right! Stop this utter-fluttery ballyhoo nonsense, Minty!

I sulkily pulled my head back through my top, sent the polite 'excuse-message' cancelling, then promptly blocked and deleted his number. Immediately I could feel myself relaxing, a wave of relief washing over me. I was glad that this silliness would finally be over.

Trilby and Fiddlesticks, my ten-year-old cats (brother and sister), were rescues, from when I lived in Scotland. Trilby disappeared from our home in Sussex during the Scottish referendum and may have run back there, to lead them to freedom. However, Scotland stayed in the UK and Trilby returned six months later, irritable, meowing and swiping at the dogs as they passed.

Fiddlesticks went missing during the Brexit vote and was discovered after a few days wandering around Hastings, looking utterly bewildered, eyes vacant, mouth hanging open.

Rather like I was at the time.

Two weeks ago, Princess Jasmine, an incredibly fat cat, was left on our doorstep in a box along with a 'Curly Wurly', which I ate, but Jasmine had shown no interest in politics so far. However, she was not fat, she was pregnant, which accounted for the sick I trod in. And she produced seven new furry members of our family.

I checked my CCTV phone app each day. Cynthia's garden was visible. I flicked through the footage; sometimes she sat outside but no zombies or gangsters were hiding in bushes yet. The camera was motion sensitive though, so it had picked up a few foxes. Muffin didn't like foxes. Once, during a thick morning mist in the park, she landed in some of their poop, and we were followed home by a screeching, horny fox hidden deep in the fog behind us. The whole experience left poor Muffin visibly traumatised.

AROUND 12 NOON

My theory about mess went like this.

You tidy a table. And a minute later your child leaves something there. Then the next child sees it and thinks it's allowed. The mess begins multiplying. And soon the table's purpose is transformed into a dumping ground. And everyone likes a dumping ground, even me. It stops you having to think.

Problems, like mess, were multiplying. In three days, I would have to tell Quinn that *The Doctor* was landfill, and my inner voice incessantly urged me to plan and panic.

Planic. Was that a word?

It was now.

Anyway, first it was time to clean the flat.

The washing machine was always full of everyone else's clothing and sheets, with my few casual clothes at the bottom of the washing bin under stinky towels. There was a choice; to clean I could wear an evening dress or a fairy costume.

I opted to be a fairy.

It even had wings which, curiously, made the whole process of dusting, sweeping, and mopping much more enjoyable. As I swept around our snug Victorian basement flat, the soft rustle of my costume's nylon and netting mingled with the soft murmur of my parents chatting and reading their books in the living room.

"For every job that must be done," I sang, "there is an element of fun—"

The knocker on our front door boomed. Resting my broom to one side, I passed my parents and opened the door to find Devon standing there, in a brown leather jacket and jeans.

"What…" he said but trailed off. "Do you have guests?"

"No, I was cleaning," I replied honestly, flattening down my wings.

"Right," he nodded, "silly me."

"How did you find our flat?"

"Your dogs. They're kind of famous around here," he said, nodding towards our 'Beware of the Dogs' sign. "I think you're overreaching with that one," he added, as Paddington leapt up with a teddy in his mouth and Muffin licked his leg.

"Traitors," I scolded them. "So, how can we help you?" My tone was polite and matter-of-fact, as if we had just met.

"We were meant to be meeting and then I received your text… which makes no sense, by the way."

"It makes perfect sense," I replied defensively.

"There is no such thing as 'date-anxiety loose-bowel-syndrome.' And who even writes such a kind of thing?"

"Me, I'm not well."

"That much I guessed," he replied.

I removed my crown.

"I only came by," he said, "because you told me you like collages, and I had made this for you." He stood to one side to reveal behind him, propped up against our back wall, a large board with random bits of painted cloth and the foam cup glued to it.

"It's lovely," I said.

"Yeah," he sighed, "but I can see you're just as shallow as all the rest."

And before I could reply, he was gone, and I was alone again. The gate had shut, and the dogs were glaring at me.

That's unfair.

Mum was waiting inside the flat as I came dashing past.

"Darling, your father says you have a disease?"

Dad was looking aghast once more.

"Stop earwigging, Dad," I called back.

In my bedroom, from the wastepaper bin I recovered the small piece of paper which had Devon's number scrawled on it, and ran back through the flat, past my startled parents, grabbed my phone, before I froze.

Why was I doing this?

Because maybe…

Did I like him?

Yes, he was a bag of smooth, dimpled trouble, and my world certainly did not need more of that, but wasn't life about taking chances?

What about the twins? Was it fair on them? No!

And I wasn't ready for this.

But we had coped before, and thinking about him was making me smile, and a happy mummy meant happy Harries.

Imagine.

No!

Oh please…

"Shut up!"

Before I could change my mind again, I had ripped up the number, lifted the tin of baked beans off the kitchen bin and sprinkled the pieces into it.

"Shallow? Ha!" I slammed the can back down on the lid, breathing heavily.

"Shall I make us all a nice cup of tea?" I heard Mum suggest.

However, through the open door, I could see the board, with its patches of coloured cloth and that cup stuck to it.

"Aggggh! Show me the money!" I cried.

After 20 minutes on my mobile phone's settings trying to get Devon's number back, I donned some rubber gloves, opened the bin and began searching.

Mum came out of the kitchen to watch me. Bending down so her face was upside down next to mine she asked gingerly, "Would you like a digestive?"

"I'm not scavenging for food, Mum, I'm trying to find something!"

Dad joined in. "No doubt she's working on her next masterpiece, Margie, adding more rubbish to our flat."

I ignored his sarky remark.

But I could only retrieve half the bits – the others had slipped down amongst the food waste. Yanking my front door open, and oblivious to the young couple waiting on the steps above. I barged out still dressed as a fairy, muttering, carrying the black refuse sack, and proceeded to empty the rubbish all over the basement floor. Flopping down in front of it all, I began riffling through, holding bits up to study. That was when I noticed them. "Good morning!" I bellowed cheerfully. "Are you… waiting for Neil?"

"Yes."

"Oh good, it's a lovely place to live and," I said, holding another piece of rubbish up to the light and peeling some food from it, "you'll feel very safe here." I stopped, looked up and grinned. With the last piece of the number in my hand, I cleared up, went inside, and carefully taped the pieces together, to call the number.

Devon picked up after one ring. "Hi." It sounded like a

smirk.

"I'm not shallow, and usually not rude!"

"You're forgiven."

"And if you knew me better, you'd know—"

"Sounds like you're asking me on a date?"

I fought for a reply. Nothing came to me. In the end, my shoulders slumped, head down, hair over my face, I gave in. He'd won. "I'd maybe, like that," I admitted from beneath my hair.

"Good," I heard him say. "I can make dinner Thursday, 7 p.m.?"

"Okay. But I'm bringing my parents."

He laughed. "Fine!"

And the line went dead.

I wanted to lose myself in his charm and his looks, his body and his smile. I had never been with anyone like that in my life. Dustin had never made any effort for me. Not in what he wore, said, did or even how he smelt.

Devon had made me a collage.

At least I thought he had.

I turned my head sideways to study it a little longer. And just admitting that I really did like him, to myself, was making me flush.

After taking a shower and borrowing some rather fetching flowery clothes from my mother's drawers, I heard my name being called from outside. I finished dressing and ventured out. It was Neil, my very serious upstairs neighbour on the steps above, and he didn't look happy.

"Minty," he said.

"Yes?"

"Earlier were you searching through rubbish, dressed as a fairy?"

"Yes," I admitted. "But I tidied up the teddies." And I flashed him a big, helpful smile.

"Thanks."

"Did the couple take the flat?"

"No, no they didn't." He indicated with his finger as if new thoughts were still forming. "And the huge metal horse staring at me through my bedroom window?"

"It's going, very soon. Anything else?"

"No." His eyes seemed to drift. "That would be it for now."

"Righty-ho," I replied.

Time to saddle up the dogs for a walk.

On the corner of Elgin Avenue, there used to be a shop called P & J Butchers, and as kids they let us nip through, dodging hanging animals and leaping over bloody puddles (which was probably what had put me off meat), out to the back, through a door in the fence and over two walls to our garden.

I had noticed the butchers had gone, replaced by Jenny's Crafty Kids, the kind of place you could leave your children doing arty things.

There was a sign on the window: *'LUNCH COVER NEEDED, APPLY WITHIN.'*

Inside, the musty smell of poster-paint filled the air, mingling with the happy screams of 20 children, who were generally causing havoc. A woman, whom I presumed was Jenny, shouted over the top of the din. "You can't bring dogs in here!"

"You need lunch-cover," I said hopefully.

Batting a child away from her, she asked, "Have you worked with children before?"

"No, but I have two of my own." I grinned hopefully and blinked.

She looked unimpressed and handed me a form to fill out. "What about art?" she said. "Had any experience with paint?"

~ THEN ~

I opened the door to our flat and switching on the light, I was greeted by a Met Police 'surprise party' in our living room, and then handcuffed and taken in for questioning.

The sterile police interview room was illuminated by harsh fluorescent lighting and exuded a sense of impending solemnity. A small, square table stood in the centre, surrounded by three chairs. Across from me sat a police officer, and next to him, Detective Michael T. James (not yet an inspector) in a white office shirt, top button undone.

"We know all about your operation," the Detective said, "that you and your brother have been up to; mixing forgeries within your gallery, peddling them out, and we have all the evidence we need on you."

"Right, so why am I here then?" I asked curiously.

The Detective fixed me with a cold glare, which simmered with anger. "We traced some of the pictures you painted, which you managed to sell to various antique shops."

They had found all the paintings in my room, and those in Rupert's bedroom, searched our gallery and found two displayed there, and two waiting to be posted out. As Rupert later admitted, we had been 'caught with our pants down.'

He carried on, "You and your brother have been identified by some key witnesses."

The weight off my shoulders felt good, to have everything finally over. I felt cleaner. I admitted everything I'd done. Except for the two Rousseaus I'd created: *The Teacher* and *The Doctor*, because I was still too curious to find out if these ones which I was most proud of would be discovered, or would they slip through the system cleanly?

"What about your sister?" he asked. "What part did she play?"

"None," I answered.

He looked up. "She didn't know about any of this?" I shook my head, and they exchanged a look.

"And Quinn?" he said. "We know he was helping you."

I shrugged. "Who?"

Questions about Quinn would inevitably lead them to Oleg's mansion, and the revelation of my art theft certainly wouldn't bode well for my trial. As it turned out, they later dropped the case against Quinn. He proved too wily, and they doubted their ability to secure a conviction if they expanded the case to include him.

"Your forgeries managed to fool a few antiques dealers," Detective James continued. "But they were not of the level needed to deceive the true experts."

The other officer added, "The auction house told us, and I'm quoting them here, 'this was a very poor imitation, which would never have passed through our books.'"

"Thanks," I replied, slightly offended.

"We have listed the forgeries you were trying to sell," said the officer, handing me a sheet of paper with ten or more items. "And a list of the ones we think you have sold." Another sheet of paper was handed over.

"Now," the Detective resumed, resting his elbows on the desk, folding his hands and letting his chin rest on them. "Tell us. Are there any other of your forgeries not listed there?"

I studied both sheets. "Yes," I answered honestly.

"How many are missing from our notes?"

I studied it for a bit. "Around, maybe, I'd say a hundred or more."

"One hundred!" he spluttered. "And where are they stored?"

"I don't have them anymore."

"Well, where are they?"

I thought about it. "In galleries, some auction houses, stately homes, smaller museums."

He swore. A few times.

CHAPTER SEVEN

THE PARTY

~NOW~

"Why don't you call this chap back, then?" my mother enquired.

The evening began with a feeling of being stalked and harangued by the Inspector, marked by another stern message on our home answering machine, requesting my attendance at the police station.

"I will at some point, Mum."

"Darling," my mother said, "this isn't like a call from an old friend—"

"Well, it kind of is," I murmured.

"You should phone him back. It sounds important and—" She gasped. "It could even be about the lights on Widley Road!"

No. It was not.

And there were more important things afoot.

I had 4:30 p.m. P.A.S.T. with the twins, then 7 p.m. was dinner with Devon (and my parents). For my date with Devon, my parents were washed and changed and in clothes I'd chosen to make them feel rather special. Dad wore a reclaimed 1920s pinstriped gangster suit and Mum a lovely blue dress with a pink sash. My cousin Nathaniel had arrived, to show me his latest homemade clothing range.

Nathaniel and his wife lived in a barn they'd converted themselves, in Oxford, only eating home-grown produce (or roadkill) and he often came down to London to sell his creations in the markets and now, happily, to see us. He was supremely creative, from making furniture to designing clothes, and the twins adored him. He wore clothes he'd made from recycled materials and had glasses so thick you couldn't see his eyes. Which was such a shame, because behind those glasses were thoughtful, considerate, kind eyes. Nathaniel rarely spoke, but when he did, it was very quietly, and very slowly. "My wife…" he began.

"Yes, Nathaniel?" my mother answered loudly, reminding us all to be quiet, which we duly did.

Nathaniel found her help bemusing, and his face lit up. "My wife wears the same colour each day of the week."

"No, she doesn't," Mum argued quickly. "I've seen in her in lots of different colours."

Nathaniel frowned. "Aaah, yes, but on Mondays, it's always maroon, Tuesdays are turquoise, Wednesdays are white, Thursdays thistle and so on, and on Sundays, she doesn't wear any clothes at all."

We all considered this.

Dad spoke first. "Surely she must wear clothes to church?"

"No," Nathaniel replied.

"Espinacas!" Dad liked this. "No, she doesn't wear clothes, or doesn't go to church?"

"Can we cover this another time?" I interrupted, fretting

somewhat. "I've no idea what to wear, time is running out and I have two very different social situations to survive."

The first was P.A.S.T. at Meredith's, which from what Faith had said, would be populated by women whose lives were intertwined with wealth and privilege, and they would be adorned with designer dresses, expensive jewellery, exuding elegance and refinement.

My mother had an idea. "Let's put you in this nice grey cardi." And she stood back to admire her work.

"Thank you, Mum, but I can't wear a cardigan, and it's on back-to-front."

"It doesn't matter," she persisted, "if you want to wear it like that, you can."

"But I don't want to, Mum," I fretted, taking off the woollen straitjacket. "And I need to decide how to look later, for this date,"

"Well, you should do something," Mum said, the crotchety part of Alzheimer's kicking in, "because your trousers are horrid, that top needs a wash, and your hair is an ugly mess!"

"Thanks, Mum."

She shrugged. "You look like a man."

After a quick stocktake in the cluttered, messy bathroom, I noticed gunk stains and something missing.

I found Harry in his room and asked him, "Did you use all the shampoo to make gunk?"

He didn't look up. "It's called slime, Mum," he replied nonchalantly, "and yes I did, all of it, today."

"Thanks!" I snapped sarcastically. He had wanted me to buy some slime. I'd refused, but with the help of the internet (often my biggest adversary) he'd made it himself. I was about to go when a thought dropped in. "Hold on," I said, "to make it, you need something else."

"That's right." He nodded with fake sincerity. "I used all the shaving foam too."

"Harry!"

Greasy hair and unshaven legs. Not the best look, but it wasn't over yet.

"Remember, Mum," he smacked his lips, with a sly grin, "it's not just shampoo and shaving foam… it also takes…"

I screamed, "TOOTHPASTE!"

Ten minutes later, I had dry-shampoo-sprayed my hair and freshened my teeth by dipping my toothbrush in a glass of Dad's crème-de-menthe. Laid out on my bed for my later date with Devon, I chose something safe: close-fitting jeans and a nice top. P.A.S.T. needed something different. I had plumped for a long burgundy sustainable tube skirt made by Nathaniel, which hid the furry legs. I accompanied it with an oversized black suit jacket, with my flowery hat, fun clumpy wooden clogs, Mum's cream silk scarf, and my auntie's homemade pink dangly feather earrings.

It had all looked quite fun and definitely a statement. But at 5 p.m., as we stepped up to Meredith's front door, something in my children's demeanour worried me.

"Why couldn't you just try and look like them?" Harry nagged.

"Because I would have failed, and it's better to do something big and bold, than try to fit in badly." My finger hovered over the Bains' buzzer as muffled party sounds came from the other side. But a wave of social anxiety was gradually engulfing me.

"Oh, come on!" Harry snapped, pressing it himself.

Chimes went off, and after a moment Meredith came to the door in a light blouse, gold belt around a tiny waist, with a fuchsia calf length suede skirt. The mixture of shiny and matte was something I could appreciate.

"You've made it!" she said. "How wonderful! Come and meet everyone."

We passed through a hall, with various framed photos of Meredith on one side, some with her standing on a stage, and on the other wall lots of a man with a gleaming grin. The Harries were removed and taken away to join the children's screams, which threatened to drown out the faint sound of opera music. I was led through to a large cream French-style kitchen full of women chatting around a marble-topped island in the centre.

"This is Minty, a newbie at our school."

Heads turned, a few gawps, then polite smiles and conversations resumed.

"Can I help with anything?" I asked Meredith, who was directing a girl nervously filling champagne flutes.

"You are sweet," she replied, handing me one, wrists jangling with gold. "If I can think of anything for you to do, I'll let you know, but my troupe are handling it famously." Her heels clicked away, leaving me with a waft of perfume.

By troupe she meant her staff, who were carrying canapés on trays, or topping up glasses.

"It's just nice to be out of the flat," I said, catching up with her as she joined a circle of others. "We live behind the trees." I took off my hat and flattened my hair. "Our garden is on the other side."

"Oh, we're neighbours," she remarked. "How charming, do you get much sun over there?"

"My parents sit out on their deck chairs most days."

She stopped. "Hold on, it's not the one with all the sparks, is it?" I nodded.

"What on earth are you having built?" she laughed.

"Nothing, it's me."

"You're… a metal worker?"

"Scrap metal actually."

The circle of mothers took a step back.

"I make things out of welding and shaping forgotten steel. It's art." I held up my phone's screensaver to show them and they gingerly returned.

"Oh, look at that delightful horse!" Meredith exclaimed, and shoulders relaxed.

"How do you see the sparks?" I asked.

She waved her glass. "From the top floor."

"The roof?" I frowned.

"No, our bedroom."

I felt my jaw drop. "These aren't flats…?" The whole kitchen went quiet.

"No, dear, it's all ours." She offered a micro-smile. "Oh, here he is, and hopefully one day our prime minister, God-willing."

The women made a collective sigh of approval.

A man joined her side, late fifties maybe, poky face, and grey swept back hair. He grinned broadly. "You never know." Then he winked. "But it's certainly in the ten-year plan, ladies. Hey!"

He pretended to whip out a gun from a holster and pointed at me. "We've met, haven't we?" The room turned.

I copied the same gun-holster thing back. "Don't think so!"

He guffawed loudly, hand on hip, leant over to peck Meredith on the cheek, then sauntered out, tossing crisps into his mouth as he went.

Meredith returned to her group. "Any thoughts on senior faith schools? We can't go private," she said. "Politically unwise, I'm told."

"Which church do you go to?" I interrupted.

"She doesn't have to," one of the mothers said with a sly wink, "because Meredith has an admirer..."

Meredith choked on her champagne theatrically. "And that's my cue to get us another bottle of Dom, back in a mo."

And I was left alone with the group, who formed a tight circle with me on the outside, whilst they played a game. "Okay, let's do Charlotte's next," one was saying, "I think her shoes are Jimmy Choo, and her top is a Calvin Klein." I edged toward them.

"No, darling," another said, "she wouldn't do Klein, it has to be Gucci."

"Okay, what about Trudi?"

"Shoes are Valentino, because she has the matching bag."

They stopped to turn and glare at me.

I shrugged. "Anyone want to do me?"

They shook their heads.

"My earrings are fly-fishing hooks made by my auntie," I revealed proudly. "My hat is from a bush in Sussex, and my skirt's made from potatoes, and I think it's even edible." I grinned.

A woman blurted out, "I've eaten!" Then covered her mouth.

I left the smell of canapés and their chatter, and weaved my way out into the corridor, past a row of Andy Warhol prints of tins of soup, which Dad would say had their own style. (I stuck my tongue out at them as I passed.) At the end there was an open door leading to a plush bathroom, adorned with marble and smooth gold fittings. Once safely inside, I flopped onto the toilet seat. There were two black-and-white framed photos on the walls. One was of Meredith on a stage, and the other, of her husband, and this time he was more serious, and now he did look familiar.

He wasn't smiling, and those eyes – they were almost scary. Hmm, where had I heard that name, *Mr Bain*?

Mr Bain will be, will be… And wallop, it hit me.

~ THEN ~

THE CENTRAL CRIMINAL COURT OF ENGLAND & WALES

It had been six months since Rupert and I had been charged with fraud and deception and it was the day of the court hearing. We were in a conference room within the court and were discovering our chances of being kept out of prison had greatly diminished, since our legal representation was off sick.

"Now," said our new barrister, adjusting his curled, traditional tie-wig, as he spoke to me and Rupert, his voice low, "can one of you summarise the case," he double-tapped the two-foot-high pile of paperwork in front of him, "because I know nothing about it but you're pleading guilty so, if you'll forgive the pun, I'll just paint the best picture I can."

"Are you serious?" Rupert collapsed into one of the leather and oak chairs, his face ashen with fear.

"Oh, we have to be serious today," our barrister answered, picking up a file off the top and studying it vaguely. "Because Alistair Bain can be truly evil."

"Who is he?" asked Rupert. "Your wigmaker?"

He discarded the file into the pile, and wiped his hand on his side as if its very content could taint his reputation. "It's unfortunate for you, he is not."

"Who is he?" I asked, taking a chair next to my brother.

"His Honour, Judge Bain will be…" He ran his tongue over his lips, pausing briefly. "Sadly, presiding over your trial."

"Bollocks," declared Rupert.

"Maybe he will like us?" I suggested hopefully.

"I doubt it," our barrister sighed. "He's an utter bastard!"

And I must say, Alistair Bain did not seem to like us at all.

~NOW~

Determined to leave sharpish, before Alistair would recall where he'd seen me, I ventured out just as Meredith emerged from a side door.

"Where are you off to?" she demanded, and before I could answer, she had one end of my loose scarf. "Come along." She spun on her heels, holding one end of the material in her hand and launching back along the corridor, suede hips swinging, making me trot along behind her like her pony.

"Look what I have found, all lost," Meredith announced, leading me through like a prize.

Alistair, who was back in the kitchen, spun around, his eyes lit up. "Ah, here's our lady of mystery, and I'll get it any moment," he jested, and he drew his gun-finger again. "Chelsea Flower Show '98!"

I shot my gun back. "Definitely not!"

"Then Ascot 2002?!"

"Oh do stop it, Alistair!" Meredith chided. "He really is a terrible tease."

As their guests tittered, I realised that although Alistair knew he had seen me somewhere, it was clearly not at these events he kept suggesting for everyone's entertainment. This was just a sly dig at me, and I began to presume I'd been invited rather like a jester or clown would be at the Queen's party. I decided it best to leave before retreating inside and embarrassing my children. "I really have to go," I tried.

"Oh, nonsense. Here," Meredith picked up a jam-jar from a row neatly labelled, "you must have one of these."

I turned it over in my hand. "What is it?"

"Homemade plum jam," she explained. "Too many trees, and the plums get caught in the mower thingy."

"I thought that was a communal garden," I admitted.

"All ours, for our sins," Meredith revealed. "More champagne?"

Who has a garden in central London that size*?* I considered, as the lovely smell of horse chestnuts drifted in from somewhere. When I tuned back in, Meredith was speaking:

"I couldn't believe it," she was saying, "but… as you all know, my DS is so much fun." More guffawing.

"Harry has a Nintendo DS too!" I exclaimed brightly.

The laughing dried up, heads turned. I fought on, "He likes Mario Kart and Pokémon."

"DS," someone translated, "stands for 'darling son'. DD is for 'darling daughter'."

During the resulting silence, it occurred to me as smoke wafted through, that the aroma wasn't horse chestnuts at all. It turned out my DS had thrown someone's doll onto the fire and someone's DD was crying. As the place filled with fumes, and the mayhem ensued, I downed another glass of champagne and gathered my own 'troupe.' And while Meredith and I searched for Harriet's shoes, I overheard the other mothers talking.

"What an angry little boy."

"Maybe it was his mother's hat. I mean it upset me!" More guffawing.

"And with the scrap metal and deckchairs," someone added. "Jules here thought the Pikeys had moved in."

Rude.

I put my hat firmly on my head.

Like a disgraced team being sent home from a tournament, my two made their way, heads down, towards the entrance hall. And while they crouched down to tie on their trainers, our hostess patiently waited for us to leave so she could return to her non-fire-starting guests. It was me who spoke first, the effects of the champagne beginning to hit. "What is it you do, if you don't mind me asking?"

"I am an opera singer," Meredith replied. "I sang at the

Royal Albert Hall last week."

"Goodness," I exclaimed, wondering if my two could speed up the shoe process. The hall door with an ornate stained-glass window had been closed (to stop us returning?). "You have the most beautiful home," I said. "I'll have to learn to sing."

"Oh no, it's not the singing that made the money." Her voice lowered. "It's divorce."

Such a strange personal revelation. "So what…" I said. "You like, just keep changing wealthy husbands?"

She glared. "No! Alistair used to be a divorce lawyer, then a judge, and one day a prime minister!"

"Oh." I nodded. "That makes more sense."

At that precise moment, Alistair flung the hall door open. "Henley Regatta 2005!!!" he screamed, while the sounds of sirens built from outside.

Meredith stepped past me and pulled open their front door as four police cars complete with blue flashing lights pulsed into their drive, and my friend the Inspector got out.

I span back to Mr Bain, whipping out my gun. "No, Crown Court, 2013!" I shrugged. "You sent me down."

"Minty Hutton," announced the Inspector, "we'd like to ask you some questions at the station."

It was then that I guessed my days with P.A.S.T. were numbered. Time to join the PTA instead.

~ THEN ~

I was given two years in prison, which I deserved. But when you're given a two-year prison sentence, you don't serve the full two years. You do one. Why they don't just say you have one year in prison is very strange. Rupert received a suspended sentence.

In court, Judge Bain read out a letter submitted on behalf of a group of auction houses and museums, detailing their deep concerns about me. Judge Bain concluded, "Due to the peculiar nature of your talent for forgery, these people are very concerned about you ever picking up a brush again. I can't ban you from painting unfortunately, but I can use a prohibition order which forbids you to sell or attempt to sell one of your paintings for ten years." And that was it.

The most harrowing part was seeing my parents' faces in the gallery and the pain and stress I had caused them, as I descended the steps to the cells below.

CHAPTER EIGHT

THE METROPOLITAN POLICE ART AND ANTIQUES UNIT

~NOW~

The police carried out a thorough search of my parents' flat, while they and the twins and I were also taken in for questioning. It was quite a family affair. My children were thrilled to see the inside of a police station, my mother loved the attention, my father less so. And a multitude of possible scenarios played out in my head, including my children screaming as I was led away to the cells. These images were not welcome.

And I must say, police stations were just as bleak and morbid as they had been last time I was questioned. In our interview room, there was a mirror along one wall, with the others bare. Across the table from me sat an attractive young woman in a navy-blue shirt who identified herself as PC Pepper, and next to her, Inspector Michael T James; untidy as usual, white shirt, unshaven and gruffer than before.

"Hi," I greeted them. "May I call you Michael?" I asked hopefully.

"Let's stick to Inspector," he replied without any hint of a smile. "As you know, we've obtained a search warrant for your parents' flat, and they are currently being questioned."

"And did they tell you where I was?"

PC Pepper answered. "You'd written it on a board in large red writing."

"Ah-ha."

He proceeded. "Minty, we'd like to ask you about some paintings."

"I'm glad you mentioned that," I enthused. "I didn't want to be rude, but these walls could definitely do with a splash of colour, maybe a Kandinsky or Pollock, not originals, because they're rather pricy I'm told." I laughed loudly, and for too long, but the relief to be momentarily rid of fear was overwhelming, so I let myself disappear inside to sort things out for a bit, while murmuring a nonsensical rhyme. When I arrived back, I could hear the young PC was upset.

"– And that," she whispered, "was a spell, for Christ's sakes!" My eyes returned.

The Inspector looked unruffled; his assistant looked disturbed.

"Hi." I greeted her again gaily.

Michael coughed, took a breath and said, "We'd like you to look at this valuable—"

"Very valuable," chimed the young PC.

"Painting." And Michael turned a screen-tablet around with an image on it, pushing it across the desk toward me. "I'm sure you recognise *The Doctor*, or *Le Docteur*, as it's called in France, by Antoine Rousseau?"

"Yes," I leant forward to study the image, "you already

mentioned this before, it's lovely."

He continued, "It was bought in 2005 by a rich Russian businessman and it's been hanging on the wall of his Holland Park property ever since, and at some point, it was replaced."

"With one of yours," added his colleague.

"Oh, how sweet, and flattering," I exclaimed proudly.

"No," Michael growled. "He didn't buy one of your paintings to replace his Rousseau. Why would he do that?"

"Because he appreciated my art?"

"No, his original was at some point swapped, for a replica."

"Oh dear," I said. "How unfortunate, when?"

"At some point in the last fifteen or so years," PC Pepper helped.

Michael resumed, "Now tell me HOW you did it. And was Rupert there too? And what about Tamsin?" he suggested, from beneath his furrowed brow. "Getting her fingers dirty for once."

"Inspector, you know my sister was never involved."

He made a grunt.

"According to what you say," I offered thoughtfully, "this Russian gentleman may have had the wrong painting on his wall for over a decade and never noticed."

"Correct."

"If he's been that happy with the one he's got, I don't see the problem."

PC Pepper threw me a bitter smile. "You don't see the problem?"

"No," I answered honestly. "Is there one?"

"Oh, there's a problem…" she affirmed. "It's illegal, and we call it… theft."

I was beginning to feel she didn't like me.

"If it is a fake," I said, trying to sound helpful, "you know there must be countless artists who could have done it."

"Maybe—" PC Pepper began.

"But not like this," the Inspector cut in, his eyes never leaving mine. "Only a dozen, at most."

"I would love to help, really, but I don't know anything about it." I sat back and folded my arms, hoping that would end their questions.

There was a silence as they just observed me, and I probably should have kept quiet but felt I needed to prattle on a bit. "Who did you say owned it?"

PC Pepper piped up. "His name is Oleg, and he's wanted for crimes here and in the US. He's fled back to Russia, his assets have been frozen."

"Nope, never heard of him." My voice was even unconvincing to me.

My older friend took a sip of his water, and cleared his throat while getting himself comfortable, as he prepared himself for the big finale. "Minty, in August this year, it was reported in the art news…"

"Art news?" I repeated, as if the words were foreign. "Is that a thing?"

"To artists, yes," PC Pepper helped.

The Inspector continued, "It was reported that *The Doctor* had been stolen, and barely two weeks later, you arrive back in Maida Vale."

"So?" I hit back.

"Well, the thinking is," and he leant forward, "you have the original and you've returned for one reason only…"

"To look after my parents?"

"No," he replied. "You're going to move it."

"I really haven't. I've come back because my mother keeps pouring soup in the toaster."

"Unfortunately," Michael grunted, "that's not what everyone thinks."

"Who's everyone?"

"Us, and the CIA," PC Pepper jumped in.

Jeepers Creepers.

I looked up. "Why would the CIA be involved?"

Michael took up the baton. "Oleg is wanted in the US for money laundering, and financing activities which threaten US security."

"Oh," I said.

"And he didn't pay his taxes," PC Pepper added eagerly.

Michael's mouth twitched, betraying slight irritation. "Anyway, the US think the painting is rightfully theirs. And there is of course the Glaswegian underworld as well. And they all believe you have it."

"I really don't."

No one said anything. We all looked at each other.

"Sorry." I bit my lip to show how much I'd like to help them if I could.

At that moment, the phone went, and Michael snatched it up. He looked disappointed.

"The team at your flat has found nothing so far."

"Oh good, then may I leave, please, Mr Inspector?" I asked. "As I have a date."

His eyes narrowed at me, but then a begrudging sigh. Warmth returned to his eyes.

The twins hadn't eaten, and Mum was still looking forward to the restaurant meal she'd been promised. We were all hungry after our grilling. Besides, if Devon wanted to get to know me, he'd need to meet my children sooner or later, so it might as well be today. Thus, we all went on the date.

And because we were late, the police kindly gave us a lift there.

The Paradise was a quirky, beautiful restaurant in Kensal Green which I'd heard about but never been to. I had texted Devon to let him know my children would also be attending the date. As he stood on the steps in a velvet black suit jacket over a roll neck sweater, diamond stud earrings, checking his glistening watch, presumably about to leave as we pulled up, it would have dawned on him that I wasn't joking.

My mother was first to get out of the police car, in her middle-class leather biker-gloves and a cardigan she'd insisted on wearing back-to-front, then my father, in his gangster suit with the twins, and lastly me, in my edible skirt. An eclectic collection of characters we were to be sure, as we made our way toward him.

His mouth had shaped into an O as if it were the start of a word, but that word never came out.

Introductions and cheek kisses. He smelled of spice, and we followed him inside.

The restaurant walls were adorned with a mix of artwork, ranging from psychedelic murals to abstract sculptures, with candles and soft lighting casting a warm glow over the entire space, while mismatched vintage furniture and velvet curtains added to the charming atmosphere. With the adults on one table, Harry and Harriet on another nearby, we settled into our seats. And yet our arrival, so far, hadn't been addressed.

"What…" Devon asked, shooting a glance toward the door.

I leant forward. "Yes?"

"Back there… that was…?" He left the sentence hanging.

And because I had done quite enough lying for one day, which had left my head feeling rather woozy, I stuck to the truth. "They were the police, and gave us a lift in their car, didn't they, Mum?"

"Yes, they did," my mother replied. "Have you been in a police car?"

"No, Margaret, I haven't," Devon conceded.

"You should," she answered, "they're very nice and my daughter can probably get you a ride in one if you wanted. We've been in a few, haven't we, Barry?"

Devon was attempting that O again. I smiled. Dad rolled his eyes before picking up his empty glass, looking for the waiter. At last, Devon's mouth formed words. "Well, you're here now, aren't you. White wine? Margaret? Barry?"

"That's kind of you, George," my father replied.

"Devon," I corrected him.

Dad shrugged. "As long as the bottle's full, I don't care where it's from."

We ordered wine, and water for me and Devon, who said, "If you don't mind me asking; the children's father, is he still in the picture?"

"He's dead, isn't he?" Mum said.

"Yes, Margie." Dad downed his wine.

Mum looked pleased with her memory. "Well, I thought he was."

"Please, guys!" I cast a look over at the twins, who were more interested in the dessert trolley.

Devon whispered, "I'm so sorry, did that happen recently?"

"Last year," I replied. "My husband fell—"

"Into a fridge," Mum added quickly.

"So, you be careful," Dad advised him.

"Why should he be careful, Dad?" I rasped. "It's not likely to happen twice, I didn't push him."

My father raised his eyebrows.

"And why are you doing that?" I panicked. "Now Devon thinks I have."

"I don't." Devon took a quick glance over his shoulder before lowering his voice. "But seriously, why the police, and how did you get him into a fridge?"

"I didn't 'get him' in there, he fell."

"Right," Devon nodded, "but the police think otherwise?"

"Oh no." I waved my hand in the air vaguely. "They wanted to talk about a completely different thing."

Devon slowly shook his head. "Which… was?"

I sipped my drink. "More like a burglary."

"Oh god, you were burgled?"

"No," I replied, "someone else was."

"Locally?"

"A big place in Holland Park."

He blew out a breath. "Oh dear, and you're a witness?"

I shook my head. "Not quite."

Devon nodded. "Actually, I will have some wine."

"Me too," I exhaled.

"Hurray!" Dad was always happy when joined in his drinking or smoking.

"Ah-hum." Mum leant forward. "Are you dating my daughter?"

"Margaret," Devon answered, "I came tonight to meet your daughter with an open mind, but come on…" And he swept his hand in our general direction. "How could any man resist all this?"

There was silence. Then my father and Devon were howling in laughter.

"What I liked most," Devon managed, "was your entrance. I can't wait to see how you leave."

Dad mused, "My guess is, in an ambulance like last time."

And off they went, guffawing again. After he had regained his composure, Devon leant back in his chair, and eyed me with a cheeky grin. "I am pleased to see you're over your recent illness."

"Were you ill, Minty-Pops?" Mum asked.

"No, Mum, Devon's little joke." I threw him a playfully scathing look.

Dad asked his usual question. "What is it you do, for a job?"

"I work for a charity," Devon replied.

Dad liked that. "He has his own shoes though AND a job." He added a cluck and wink. "What more do we need?"

"WE," I glared at my father, "don't need anything." Devon was smirking at me.

I drank a mouthful of wine.

The meal began to go well. We talked about many things. He worked for an animal charity and nearly married a woman. "But she was too wild, always doing crazy things like jumping off bridges into rivers, so we broke up."

"Why?" I asked.

"Always worrying about her was too much. Maybe I'm too boring, but it's a lot to take."

"Well, I promise not to bring any drama to your life," I said.

"Yeah, right," he laughed. "Hey Margaret, how did you and Barry meet?"

Mum shuffled in her seat. "Oh, Barry, you tell them."

Dad winked. "Okay. During the Blitz I was moved to a school in Oxford. One day, I was caught fighting and caned so hard by the headmaster I needed stitches and was sent to the school chaplain to confess my sins."

"The good old days," Devon joked.

Dad took a sip of his wine. "When I arrived, the chaplain asked what my interests were, I told him I liked painting, and he got me to start an art club."

Mum jumped in. "My father was the chaplain!"

"Wow!" Devon exclaimed.

Dad squinted into the distance remembering. "And because of him, I found my first true love."

"Painting?" Mum suggested, searching for a compliment.

"Give over, Margaret! It was you!" Dad laughed, reaching for her hand across the table. "And she's put up with me ever since."

Something exchanged between them, leaving Devon and I

very much on the outside watching in. A look flickered over Devon's face that I hadn't seen before, and then it was gone.

"Why are you still single?" I asked him.

"Maybe," Devon replied, "I haven't been attracting the right women."

"Or," I suggested, "you waste all your best lines down the gym?"

"Talking of which," he countered, "how's the equipment testing?"

"Good, and did you find the sleeves for that shirt yet?" I coughed and said the word 'Vein' at the same time.

Devon raised his glass for a toast. "Here's to you, Minty-Pops."

"Well, I must say," said Dad, who had been avidly watching our exchange. "This is exciting stuff."

That feeling hit again. The one I'd had the day Devon walked away in the park.

We ate our desserts, and Mum began humming to the restaurant's background music. "Oh, I know this one." Her eyes twinkled, her body beginning to rock to the song. "It makes you want to dance, doesn't it?"

"Then you should, Margaret," Devon encouraged.

Mum replied, "I would if we weren't in a restaurant."

"Restaurants are the best place," Devon persisted. "More attention, less competition." And then he was up, jacket coming off to reveal a tight long-sleeved black roll neck top and with those big shoulders moving beneath. He looked like one of Harry's superheroes. "Do you mind, Barry?"

"Not all," Dad replied. "I'd join you both, but I'm better

drinking."

And then, Devon danced with my mother, to Cyndi Lauper.

~ THEN ~

From: Minty at HM Prison Holloway

To: Mum & Dad
144 Elgin Avenue
Maida Vale
W9 2NT

Dear Mum and Dad,

You may think there is little to laugh about in prison, but you'd be wrong. Inmates who have been here a while always find ways to entertain themselves. Like when I arrived last night, and Wendy in the store handed me oversized jeans, because she had wanted everyone in HMP Holloway to know I was a newbie, which does kind of break the ice a bit. This morning, I was fine on the way down the metal staircases, holding my jeans up with one hand. But collecting my breakfast tray at the bottom, and carrying it back meant two hands; and while climbing up, my jeans fell to my ankles and the elated women on the landings above began rattling their cups against the railings, yelping and screaming; "New girl, New girl!"

They all seem so friendly, and I've been invited to meet a few of them properly tomorrow – eeks!

All my love, Minty xxx

CHAPTER NINE

THINGS HEAT UP

~NOW~

The next morning at 8 a.m. I sent Devon a text, thanking him for an amazing night.

He read my WhatsApp message because the two little grey ticks had gone blue. Read it, and not responded, going offline shortly afterwards. If you were talking to someone, and they listened before turning their back, it would be classed as rude.

Wouldn't it?

And why had I texted him first anyway?

There had been no kiss at the door.

None.

I searched for him on Facebook. Found him. There were a few photos, not many, but enough to annoy me.

Luckily for me, men weren't the only thing I had to think about, there were other worries; word had spread amongst the mothers from St Dunstan's that we'd left Meredith's in a police car. Living with my parents was meant to make their lives easier and less stressful, and to make Dad proud of me. If I wasn't mistaken though, I seemed to be achieving quite the opposite effect.

I tidied the messy-police-searched flat, while everyone slept. And I noticed the BT van was still parked opposite our flat. And that man was still doing things up a pole opposite.

Afterwards I found a new article on the web detailing the missing Rousseau painting, and it featured eight possible suspects. All had been fraudulent artists with a bio under each one. Including me at number eight (but under my maiden name). No picture. The piece made quite a story and was thoroughly intriguing, although less so for me, I guess, because I remembered doing it.

And in two days' time, on Sunday, I had to meet Quinn, and I hadn't a clue what I was going to tell him yet. And he wouldn't be happy. No siree Bob.

But by the afternoon, I could confess it wasn't any of this that was causing a major disruption to my digestive system. It was Devon.

He was troublesome.

And deep inside me, he was arrogantly running amok.

To stop me checking my mobile every few minutes, I turned it off. Then rationing myself to once an hour, clicking it back on, waiting for the screen to load, so I could find the messages app, to discover… nothing. Welding gave you the opportunity to hammer your thumb, burn your hand, blind yourself, inhale dangerous fumes, or with arc welding, possible death by electrocution.

This could be worse.

Talking of welding, you could kind of understand why Dad thought it was a bad idea. He didn't like it, so maybe clay should be the way forward. I made a clay figurine of Devon, and then smashed it flat with a rolling pin.

After school pick-up, my parents were peacefully afternoon napping and Harry was in the kitchen making a mess. To calm myself I began drawing pictures at the dining room table with Harriet, occasionally swapping coloured pencils.

She kept singing, "Mummy's got a boyfriend…"

In the end, I snapped. "Who exactly is this boyfriend?" I demanded.

"You know who." She raised her eyebrows as if I was hiding something.

"You mean the man from last night?"

"His name is Devon," she said, tilting her head from side to side while she drew, humming to herself. "And yes, you luuuuve him."

"I do not! And he's not texted, and I know nothing about him."

"I love Ellie and know nothing about her." (Ellie was her stuffed toy.)

I sighed. "You know everything about that pesky elephant. She's been with you since birth. You have complete and utter trust in her, and she in you. Your love is without fear, or jealousy, you never argue, and she will never let you down. I've met an arse from the gym with muscles, who's more in love with a mirror than anything else, and I'm certainly not in love with—"

My phone beeped and I snatched it up. "Devon!" I breathed.

Harriet giggled.

One message. From him.

"Who…" I said, changing my tone, "I may or may not forgive later."

And I liked saying his name out loud... Strange.

I didn't read the text yet though. Better to hold on for a few minutes at least, otherwise it would give him my read-receipt and he'd know I'd been waiting.

This was so awfully complicated.

Harriet was thinking again. "Daddy was a bit like Ellie, wasn't he."

"How's that?"

"He didn't say much."

We drew for a bit.

"How's school?" I asked her.

"It's okay, except playtime."

"Why don't you like playtime?"

Harry passed. "At least you get playtime!"

I called after him, "Maybe if you behaved, they'd let you out more, and you'd be happier!"

"I'd be happier," he retaliated, "if you didn't hide things in our packed lunch!"

We waited for the inevitable slam of their bedroom door. There it was. I whispered to Harriet. "He didn't like the glitter then?"

"No, it fell out all over the floor when he opened his lunchbox," she giggled, stealing the pencil I was holding. "I liked mine, although I didn't like the bar of soap you put in there last week."

"That was Granny."

"And the pinecones?"

"They were mine."

She let out a slow raspberry while she thought. "Sometimes I want to be naughty at school too, so I don't have to stay in the playground."

"Oh honey!"

"I'm always on my own, trying to look like I'm happy being alone, and today…" She crunched up her eyes tightly.

"It was sooooo embarrassing, but I tried to join in like you told me."

"What happened?"

"Arabella promised they wouldn't tease me if I tried a cartwheel, so I did this." She got off her chair, planted two hands on the floor and jumped about a foot to her right. "How did it look?"

"Not like a cartwheel I've seen before."

"Yeah, they laughed."

"Okay, but did you laugh with them?"

"It wasn't that type of laughing, Mum."

I gave her a nudge. "I thought it would be better since we went to Meredith's?"

She slowly shook her head. "It's worse."

"Do you tell Harry when you're upset?"

"Not anymore."

"Why?" I asked.

"Last time I told him, he threw one of their toys on the fire."

"Oh, I didn't know that. Maybe I should talk to Arabella's mummy."

"No, no, please don't!" she cried.

I gave her a cuddle. "Anyway, maybe today will turn out to be… *Freaky Friday.*" *Freaky Friday* was a film where the mother's and daughter's bodies were switched, so the mother went to school in her place, and I thought it would cheer the twins up. But after we put it on, Harriet was clearly unimpressed with the kissing.

"Ugh!" She turned her head indignantly. "They obviously didn't learn the rule you're taught in reception, to keep your hands to yourselves!"

"Baby!" teased Harry.

They argued for a bit, and Mum kept asking why the mother was acting so childishly, and Dad kept asking for wine, so we opened a bottle and watched *Mamma Mia* instead, again.

And then I opened Devon's text. It was a picture of himself (of course) blowing me a kiss. With the line, 'When can I meet the convict again?'

So, he'd found me on the web.

After that I drank a whole bottle of wine on my own.

THE SCHOOL FÊTE

You would want to know if your child had been a bully, wouldn't you?

Having avoided any other parents since the whole wooden-horse-fire-admitting-prison-police-car-bit, and now blessed with an award-winning hangover, I found the thought of confronting Meredith unattractive to say to least.

We arrived late, and the playground was already bustling with children and parents everywhere, chatting, laughing and moving between stalls.

Over to one corner, Mum put her arms around the two Harries. "This is exciting, isn't it?" she said, ushering us into a huddle, making that secret-squirrels granny-face, meaning *I'm about to spoil my grandchildren.*

"What are you up to, Mum?" I called above the din.

"I think," she replied, "these two need a little something to spend on the tombola." And delving into her handbag, she continued. "Close your eyes and hold out your hands," which they did, and for once, Harry seemed excited. My mother then pushed a tissue in each of their hands. "And don't spend it all at once!" she finished with a flourish.

They examined the paper in bewilderment.

"Come on, you two," said Dad, oblivious to what she'd handed them, "what do you say…?"

"Thank you, Granny," they replied in unison.

Mum ruffled Harry's hair and pushed him away. "Now run along."

I took my parents' arms, one on each side. "Let's see what mischief we can get up to, guys."

The school fête was a noisy, colourful place. Children were milling about, laughing and shouting. Near the food stalls, the smell of sausages cooking made my stomach rumble while people tried paying with credit cards, to be told once again it was cash only. Balloons were everywhere, bobbing in the wind with all sorts of bright colours.

Over by some stalls, Meredith stood, in another wrap-around suede skirt, this one purple, along with a cream blouse and a lot of gold. She was surrounded by several dads blatantly fawning over her, until she spotted us and strutted over. "Minty darling, can you take over children's nails?"

"Gladly," I replied.

My own nails were often covered in dirt from metalwork,

but when they weren't, they had random multi-coloured splodges of colour, perfect for children, I thought. "And I just wanted to apologise," I began to Meredith, "for the fire, and for, you know, the police, and things."

She put her hand up. "No need in dredging up the past, Alistair and I are firm believers in rehabilitation, everyone deserves a second chance, even those young children on the corner of our road."

"Which ones?"

"The dirty little hoodie fuckers that scratched our Bentley."

"Oh, right."

Meredith's eyes scanned the people around me as if searching for all the other people she had tasks for, and I could see our conversation could be over any moment, so I took the plunge.

"Also, I heard something about Arabella recently…"

"Well, don't tell everyone." She put one red nail to her lips. "It's meant to be a secret, but yes, she's headlining at the Maida Vale Centenary Show!"

"Ah, right, that wasn't—" I mumbled but didn't get any further when she slapped a note into my palm.

"Now be a poppet and get us some drinks," she said with a wink.

I was left with her ten-pound note in my very confused hand while she grabbed Faith, who had been heading towards me, and my mother, and led them away. After queuing at the refreshments, I returned with water to where Meredith was organising Mum behind a stall. "Sorry," I said, "but Mum won't be able to do that."

"Don't be silly," Meredith chided me. "Margaret is our newest and best member of the PTA, and your father will enjoy the freedom to browse the stalls." She then spoke to him in a louder, more deliberate tone. "But it's all for charity, Barry, and the prices are on the boards."

Faith blurted quietly into my ear, "She asked me what the police wanted with you, I said your dad mistakenly left a shop without paying."

Meredith took Faith at that moment, leaving us with a new problem: my mother would be painting faces.

"Mum, I think this is a bad idea."

"I certainly know how to paint children's faces," Mum tutted at me. "I've done this many a time, don't you know."

And there it was. I would be doing nails, and to my mother's absolute delight, she would be painting children's faces next to me, and although this terrified me, I was kind of interested to see what would happen.

Mum and I sat back-to-back, with eager children on either side, lining up and nattering about what colour nails they were thinking of, or which cute animal picture they were going to ask for, and of course expecting their faces to look exactly like the ones on the board.

My first customer, a rather confident girl of about eight, put her pound in the jar and said, "French polish, please."

"But surely you'd like something fun?" I offered.

"No," she answered curtly, "I always have French polish."

Behind me, as I dealt with nail polish, my mother expertly glided her sponge perfectly over a child's eager face.

I turned back to my job in hand. My hands, clammy from

the heat and hangover, struggled to get the top off the bottle of cream. Her first nail looked okay, but they got steadily worse as the fingers went on.

"You're not very good at this," the girl noted haughtily. "And your hands are shaking."

"Or…my hands are still and the whole world is shaking," I suggested hopefully.

"No," she retorted, "it's definitely your hands, and you look sick." She hopped down and skipped off to her friends.

A new customer climbed up into the chair. Pigtails and seemed a total cutie pie. I grabbed the bottle of red, the top of which broke, leaking crimson all over my fingers. "Show me the money!" I swore, edging towards her with my blood-coloured fingers.

She dropped her pound in my jar quickly.

The first nail I kept inside the cuticle, but the second was a mess, then I hit a knuckle, and as I tried to get it off, I drew a thick line across her wrist. "Almost done," I teased.

Afterwards, the girl examined her hands in wonder, eyes like saucers.

"You're welcome," I said cheerily. "Next!"

Beside me, my mother was surrounded by a swarm of happy children, checking themselves in the mirror. They looked amazing.

As I watched the scene, I remembered.

Minty-Pops, do you want to be a fairy or a beautiful butterfly fluttering about in the garden, or shall we make you into a tiger, like Tammy?

A shadow moved across me, and I came back.

There was a large man in a woollen beanie, towering over

me.

"This a new hobby you're doing?"

I imagined he was someone's disgruntled father. "First time actually and finding it harder than I thought."

"Well," he replied, with a strong Scottish accent, "maybe you're used to bigger canvases?"

My stomach lurched, as our eyes met, his gaze filled with unmistakable malice. Then just as quickly as he had appeared, he vanished into the crowd.

SUNDAY

Following Quinn's instructions, I connected via a VPN and slid into a virtual world, in a virtual pub, which served virtual drinks, for our chat.

Then about an hour later, I met Rupert and Tamsin in a real pub for a real drink and got really sloshed.

"Before I tell you about my meeting with Quinn," I said, "you guys should probably know this…" My brother's attention was only partially with me, the women around the bar seemed to be of greater interest until I added, "The police took me, Mum and Dad and the twins in for questioning."

"Shit!" cried Rupert, straight back with us.

"Language, Rupert!" scolded Tamsin. "What do the police want?"

"They want the original Rousseau," I replied, "because they don't seem too happy with the fake one."

"AAGH!" Tamsin exclaimed, squeezing her eyes shut. "But they don't know it was you who did the copy, do they?"

"Not yet."

Rupert began taking off his coat and trying to sip his beer at the same time. Neck twitching.

"And," I said, "they told me the original no longer belongs to Oleg anyway."

"Oh!" Rupert sighed. "That's a relief." They both relaxed and sipped their drinks.

I clarified. "It now belongs to the States, and the CIA want it back."

Tamsin spat her drink out all over her brother.

"Christ!" cursed Rupert.

"Fuck-a-rooney!" cursed Tamsin, now happy to join the swearing.

Rupert held his hands over his eyes and twisted in his stool, as if trying to escape the problem.

"And as you know," I added, "I threw it away."

"Yes, you did," Tamsin replied carefully.

"Popped it into a bin on the Edgware Road," I admitted, "along with my packed lunch."

Rupert growled. "Just tell us what Quinn said!"

"He said we were all being watched by the police, which is why he met me online."

"No!" my upset siblings said together, glancing around at other customers in the pub.

Tamsin lowered her voice to the barest of whispers, making us all huddle forward as she asked, "And what about you destroying the Rousseau?"

"He was very disappointed."

"And?" she pushed.

I lied, "That was pretty much… it."

"Really?"

"Yup."

They buried their heads in their drinks, deep in thought.

I didn't tell them what I had seen online.

I didn't tell them that Quinn's avatar was twice my one's height, and he wore a butcher's apron, and when I arrived in the virtual bar, he was sawing some other avatar's body in half, and blood was squirting all over everyone sitting around the bar watching.

I also didn't tell them the bubble from Quinn's mouth was full of the foulest threats and most disgusting language I'd ever read. And that two of the other avatars were holding someone else on a chair who was begging for their life.

When you played Sims, that never happened.

What I had witnessed with Quinn was horrible.

He knew Rupert, Tamsin and I were not rich, so we obviously hadn't sold the original, but he'd also made up his mind that we'd tried to sell it and lost it somewhere in the proceedings.

But he didn't care now.

Now he only wanted a new, big, famous forgery.

I informed him it was unlikely my hands still held the necessary dexterity to paint that level of forgery, if the children's nail-bar was anything to go by. And if anyone I knew was ever hurt, my hands would cramp up for good.

Quinn got this. And he kindly gave me an ultimatum – I had until Friday to paint another one, or it would be me sitting in that chair begging for my life. And my limbs would be removed one by one.

I had only five days in which to planic.

~ THEN ~

To: Minty Hutton

HM Prison Holloway
Parkhurst Road
London
N7 0NU

Dear Minty,

How are you coping? We're so glad you're making friends in there. But we do worry about you, so we have been doing some research, and started watching a series called Bad Girls to learn more about daily prison life. This is what we discovered so far, hope it's of some use:

- *Grass has many meanings.*
- *Inmates love smoking it, but despise people that are one.*

That's all we have. Hoping we get more of the lingo soon, and although we may never understand why you did all this, Minty-Pops, we love you very much and miss you.

All our love and kisses,
Mum and Dad.
xxxxx

Chapter Ten

EVERYONE KNOWS

~NOW~

"Why don't you want to go to school this morning?" I asked, sitting down next to Harriet, who was still in bed. I tried to find a space for my feet on the floor, which was covered in papers and books and toys and bits of toys.

"I'm sick," Harriet moaned, unconvincingly.

She was about as bad at lying as I was.

"Now," I said, "why don't you tell me the truth."

She turned on her side to face the wall. "Arabella kissed a boy, and I said that was 'gusting."

She meant disgusting, but I never corrected her, because I liked the way it sounded. The same as when she asked if I thought she may be a 'lez-be-numb' because she didn't like boys.

"And now," she added, "they all think I'm immature."

"No, they don't," I assured her. "Do they, Harry?"

"I do," he replied.

"Shut up, Harry!" I snapped. "Did you finish your homework?"

"Sure," he said, his eyes glued to his Game Boy. "And if you don't believe me, you can call the police."

"Why would I do that?"

"Because they have our laptop; it was confiscated, remember?" He gleefully chuckled. "My homework's on there."

I mouthed various things, but nothing came out.

Harriet resumed, "And now I've stopped putting up my hand in class."

"Why?"

"Because I know if I get it wrong Arabella and her gang will laugh, so I stutter," she said.

"Right." I headed into the lounge and began talking to my parents. "That child has been mean to Harriet again. I'm going to call her mother."

"Good! You do that!" Mum said, while Dad nodded his enthusiasm.

I snatched the home phone, put it on speaker, and punched in Meredith's name, and her number began ringing.

"Meredith Bain," she answered.

"Hi, this is Minty."

"Minty, my dear, how are you?"

"Fine, but we need to talk, and this is a little awkward actually."

"Oh, do you need to return something?"

"Return something?"

"Yes, Karen and I noticed your father was way too near the raffle for safety's sake, simply a disaster waiting to happen, what with his light-fingered reputation."

I took her off speaker, while Dad mouthed 'light-fingered' to himself, staring quizzically at the ceiling again.

"No, it's about Harriet. She's always been very insecure, and now she's pretending to be sick because she doesn't like school."

"Oh, the poor thing. New schools can be a daunting maze of fearful challenges, I don't envy them at all."

"Indeed, and I feel… there is a possibility, however bad this may sound, and I hope it doesn't… and if it does it certainly wasn't meant to, or sound accusing in any way…"

"Spit it out, Minty," she sighed.

"Okay, I will. Do you feel sometimes your daughter could be a bit of a bully?" There, I said it.

"Arabella? A bully?"

"Maybe? Do you think?"

"Are you asking me if I think my daughter is a bully?"

"Between those show-stopping cartwheels, yes, do you think?" No reply.

I blabbered on. "And I didn't want to say anything but I'm sure you'd understand if it was happening to a—"

"To a what?" she demanded.

"To a, to a DD of yours?" I finished hopefully.

Silence. Then came her curt reply. "Can you hold for a moment?"

I checked my parents. Dad gave me the thumbs-up, Mum had her hand over her mouth.

After a moment Meredith returned. "I have just spoken to her," she said.

"Oh good!"

"I have just spoken to her…" Meredith said louder, indicating she hadn't finished the sentence, "and Arabella insists she's done nothing wrong."

"Oh, but Harriet says—"

"One girl's word against another," she interrupted. "Do you think maybe Harriet invented all this?"

Blood cooking... Stay in the room Minty-pops.

"No, of course not!" The phone began to shake in my hand.

"Not to put too fine a point on it," Meredith continued, "but you said yourself Harriet is insecure, maybe she just needs to toughen a little?"

"Why should she? Why can't your daughter just be nice to her?"

"Darling," Meredith said in a tone dripping with condescension, "it's all normal school behaviour. I really don't know what you want me to do."

"But you're her mother!" came my exasperated voice.

"And you're THEIR mother and maybe that's where you should be concentrating, I mean Harriet sounds like a tell-tale and I doubt Harry even knows what break-time is."

"Why are you being so rotten?" was all I could mumble.

"But from what we know about you all, and from the papers I read this morning, it's not really a surprise."

"The papers?"

"Yes, like father, like daughter, who knew the PTA would attract the Pink Panther family."

"What… papers?"

"I'd start with *The Daily Mail*, then *The Times*, oh and *The Telegraph* has a good article too." And the phone went dead.

THE TIMES

A Maida Vale mum has been named as the prime suspect in what surely may be the most spectacular art theft of this decade. Minty Hutton, 35, who was described today as a 'friendly loner' by another mother we spoke to, has been out of the spotlight since her arrest and conviction ten years ago for multiple counts of art fraud. Although not yet charged the police are.... ...and it went on.

Having bought the papers from the corner shop, I decided it would be best if the twins were off school today anyway.

Oh deary me, the net did feel like it was closing in.

Feeling a tad trapped. Or would be soon.

Breathe.

I studied the paper again.

Described today as a *friendly loner.*

???

I felt I should be more annoyed by that description, but it did sound like me.

How though, did I move from 'suspect' to 'prime suspect'?

As if to answer my question, I had a call from Michael, the Inspector. "We have located one of the guards who was working around the time the painting may have been swapped. We'd like you to come to the station and take part in an identity parade to see if he recognises you."

I told my family.

"Oh how exciting!" Harriet said, clapping her hands together after my call. "Is it like the Notting Hill Carnival Parade, Mummy?"

"Not quite."

"Can we come?" she bubbled.

"No."

"Will we see it on the tele?"

"I hope not."

"Can I tell everyone in my class?"

"I'd rather you didn't."

"There's a girl in my year," she said, eyes sparkling, "whose parents met at the Lord Mayors parade, you should take Devon to this parade with you, on a date!"

"I think he was looking forward to Eminem, sweetie."

"Oh dear, that's a shame."

Dad shook his head. "I just wonder what we did wrong, as parents." I grabbed Harriet and we went into the garden to search for fairies. But Dad followed us out, so while he perched himself on the wall, I told Harriet to go check on Granny.

I began unpacking some clay. "You don't mind if I create while we chat."

"You go ahead," he motioned, taking out his pack of ciggies.

I began pounding it on the bench, warming it up so it would be easier to use.

Dad's face had gone red, which meant something was coming. At last, drawing on the cigarette, he said, "You haven't been at it again, have you?"

"At what?" I answered innocently.

"Doing illegal stuff," he grunted.

"No. Of course not."

"And that painting that's gone missing?"

"*The Doctor*? Beautiful, isn't it? I always loved that one, he has his own style, doesn't he, Dad?"

"Yes, great artist, great style. Where is it?"

"You're... asking me..." I began, pretending to be

thoroughly absorbed in clay-modelling. I looked up. "Sorry, what was it again, Dad?" But I could see from the deep angry breath he took that his patience was running out. "Oh, I remember," I said quickly. "You wish to know if I took the painting and sold it in Camden Market. No, I did not."

"And Rupert?"

"He's your son, Dad."

He didn't smile but stuffed his now-lit cigarette between his teeth.

"Please don't worry about what the papers say." I grinned. "I'm not."

"But…" he huffed, "that means nothing, does it? You aren't norm…" He shook his head.

"Not normal. Thank you, Dad."

The trees in the distance took his attention for a bit, while he took another drag. Then his cigarette was tapped on the garden wall next to him, knocking off the cherry, and he tucked the remaining half back in the packet. When he looked up again, his eyes were wet.

"Oh, come on," I said.

"Just you promise me," his voice choked, "you won't let that boy lead you astray again."

"Who, Rupert? I'm a grown woman, Dad, but I promise." And I went over and gave him a hug.

Over my shoulder, he asked, "So… what's that?"

I stepped to the side to let him view what I'd been doing. "I'm going to call it…" I answered with a touch of pomposity, "'Cat.'"

Dad got up, and with his stick made his way over to my

bench.

"Or," he offered, "you could call it 'Feline Treasure', because it looks remarkably like page three of the artists yearbook in the lounge."

"It could be," I conceded.

"But why?"

"I liked it."

"But why don't you ever do your own work?"

"I don't want to."

"When was the last time you did?" he asked, squinting into the distance, as he tried to retrieve memories. "Were you ten? Twelve? No, it was younger than that…"

"Dad!" I said, bringing him back. "The reason I don't, is because…"

"Yes?"

"There are so many beautiful artworks out there already."

"No, that's not the reason, is it? We both know why you won't." He shook his head and left me standing there.

What? Why? What did he think? I liked copying. And that was it.

I felt for the comfort of my phone in my dungaree pocket.

There it was.

Reassuring.

I would text Devon. He needed a text, I wanted to tell him something nice.

I miss you.

There, sent.

Dad could 'stuff it.' (One of his phrases, not mine.)

I checked the CCTV app and found the camera had caught

our night zombie at last.

At 1 a.m., a young man climbed out of a window, shimmied down the steel drainpipe, landed in Cynthia's flowerbed with both feet, then stepped onto her paving. Lit up what looked like a joint and leaned back against the wall taking deep drags. A few minutes later he chalked something on her blackboard, then climbed back up a different drainpipe above the paving (hence no other prints in the earth).

No dead Kenny.

How disappointing.

But the police were getting closer to knowing I was at Oleg's mansion, and once they proved that, it would be hard denying it was my fake.

Hmmm.

Next, they'd be getting me back in court.

And once I was in the dock, they'd accuse me of lying to the police, stealing and then hiding the original, storing it somewhere safe, and then waiting all these years to move it.

And you know.

They'd be right.

Because of course I had hidden the original.

And it was nearly time to get it.

Tum-te-tum-te-tum.

~ THEN ~

To: Minty Hutton

HM Prison Holloway
Parkhurst Road

London
N7 0NU

Dear Minty

I hope you're well.

You have written to Mum & Dad but haven't replied back to Rupert or me yet.

When you have time, please do write to us.

Also, although I imagine Mum and Dad will tell you, I have exciting news. I met someone incredible called Thomas, we moved in together and are thinking of getting married.

Hope you're getting along okay there, keep your chin up.

Write to us when you can.

Love,
Tammy
xxxx

CHAPTER ELEVEN

DATING DEVON

~NOW~

I had received some encrypted files from Quinn. They contained all the X-rays, radiography, microscopy, etc., images of a painting he wanted me to forge, within two days.

Thinking of Devon instead though brought comfort and warmth, which spread throughout my body. And now we were going on our second date, which meant I'd need someone looking after my parents and the twins.

Tamsin was busy, and I wasn't asking Rupert. My brother had babysat once, but never again. At the time, the twins were toddlers and he had put on a film, which Harriet kept pointing at saying, "Tooth-fairy." My brother had assured her confidently this wasn't the tooth-fairy, but a flesh-devouring cockroach monster. Later I explained to him she hadn't been saying "Tooth-fairy," but what she was trying to say was, "Too scary!"

He didn't babysit again.

However, my cousin Nathaniel was great with the twins, and came over to sit with my parents while Devon and I joined Maxi and her boyfriend Paulie to travel to the O2 for Eminem's concert. Nathaniel also needed to pick up the bag of Muffin's dog-hair I'd kept for him, because he had a spinning wheel, and liked unusual material for making clothes.

I was trying to find this box of hair, leaving Maxi, a time-panicked, every-second-counts businesswoman, typing away on her laptop alone with Nathaniel, in his homemade jumper, super-thick glasses, and who took longer to say a sentence than she took to fill three temp vacancies.

"There is a sign," began Nathaniel, in a deep, slow, deliberate, monotone voice. "On that wall."

Maxi's fingers stopped. "Sorry?"

"It says beware of the dogs," he added.

Maxi looked from Nathaniel to the front door, then back again. "Outside! Yes! It's for Paddington and Muffin."

"We have the same sign, except," he pondered, "where it says dogs, our one says chickens."

Maxi's fingers paused. And you could see her face trying to work out why she had been given this information, and what she needed to do with it. "Chickens?" she repeated.

"We have guard chickens," Nathaniel explained. "The chickens peck your ankles until they're called off."

Maxi seemed to like this. "Huh! Maybe I should get some for my flat. That would get Paulie up in the mornings." One of Maxi's mobiles buzzed, she texted on it, while answering another. "Book me in with the client at eleven, no make it at two, because I have a spinning class first."

Nathaniel's brow cleared. "I like spinning too, it's one of my hobbies."

Maxi replied, "It's fine, just a bit smelly and sweaty."

Nathaniel gave her an odd look. "Maybe you should wash it

first then, if it still smells."

Maxi's brow furrowed.

He continued, "It's only sweaty because it's been trapped without air for so long, I dunk mine in a bucket of soapy water, to get rid of the stink."

Maxi's jaw dropped, her one-woman factory halted, fingers hovered in the air.

Nathaniel's eyes lifted. "Before you start, always give it a jolly good scrub."

As much as this was entertaining, I thought I'd help them out. "Nathaniel is referring to a spinning wheel – he makes clothing out of hair and recycled food."

"Oh, thank God." Maxi threw her head back, in little miniature hysterics. "I am so sorry, Nathaniel," she dabbed at her eyes with a tissue, "I was talking about cycling classes."

"If you want," he replied, rarely able to see the connection to humour, "I can make you a Christmas… dog-hair pullover?"

"Amazing, please do," said Maxi.

"You want to know what I like doing most?" said Nathaniel.

Maxi closed her computer, now enthralled by my cousin.

"Nathaniel, yes, I do want to know whatever it is, I'm interested."

"I play in a musical band."

"Is… there somewhere we can see you perform?"

"We have a gig in the Pig and Parrot in Kent, if you want to come."

"We'd love to, what is it you play?"

"The acoustic toaster."

"Incredible, the toaster, I'll be there. By the way, Minty, have a look in the bag on the table."

I opened the bag. There was a box in there from a posh shop.

Inside was a pair of black, high-heeled, over-the-knee leather boots.

"How lovely," I said, without conviction.

"They're a present for you," Maxi said. "But I know you don't like them."

"Sorry, but they're not really my thing."

"That's the whole point. Your thing would be found in a skip, and Devon can't be a chest man, can he?"

"Probably not."

"You have good legs, make the most of them. And wear something tight that you didn't make, find or borrow – no offence, Nathaniel."

I didn't wear them.

And I knew I should have been doing Quinn's painting, or at least figuring out what to do. We'd had three reporters ring our doorbell asking for my story, and now there were two suspicious vans parked outside, plus a news van. All too much to cope with, so I went to the concert at Twickenham Stadium, which was amazing. Devon was super fun, and we sang and we danced and he lifted me up onto his shoulders.

We loved it.

Maxi not so much.

"Eminem turns up late," she observed, "then stomps around the stage in a track suit."

"Yeah but…" Paulie began.

"Paulie!" she snapped. "It seems you paid for a very angry

young man to shout at me for two hours, I'm not impressed."

"That wasn't shouting, Maxi, that was rapping," Paulie tried.

"And it was amazing!" I helped.

"And don't get me started about the toilet facilities," she continued. "Did they seriously expect me to use a hell-hole porta-loo wearing Ralph Lauren?"

Devon and I shared a cab on the way home, giggling, the other two heading in a different direction. Devon kept repeating, "A hell-hole porta-loo wearing Ralph Lauren?" We still hadn't kissed, but I tucked myself around his arm and nestled in against his shoulder.

Arriving at our road, we found Nathaniel and Dad standing outside, in the street. They were distraught.

Mum was missing.

My parents had gone to bed, but Mum had woken up confused and left the flat while my cousin was napping in an armchair. She'd been found wandering around near Marble Arch, asking people for Dad. Very confused, she was taken to a homeless shelter on the Edgware Road.

When we got there, the police wanted to ask me a lot of questions about Mum and where she was living, and the twins, and the dogs, and cats, and they said we may possibly get a call from Social Services. Devon stayed with me throughout, even holding Mum's hand as we drove home. It was 1 a.m. before we closed my parents' door, their snoring sounding peacefully.

I took Devon's hand and silently led him to my room. We lay down on my bed facing each other. His face had been so full of concern. For once, no teasing or jokes from his side, just compassion and an understanding that transcended words. I traced a line with my finger along his jaw line and over that perfect mouth of his, he lightly kissed my finger. Our eyes locked. My usual doubt and shame in these situations dissolved into trust.

We kissed.

He pulled me in close. I breathed in deeply. That intoxicating spice scent. Rolling up on top, my legs around his waist, removing my T-shirt over my head.

Kissing him deeper.

There is more, but I want to keep it to myself. I hope you don't mind.

Afterwards we lay there, and for the first time things for me had happened, and I wasn't laying alone.

We were woken the next day by Paddington pawing at my bedroom door. Devon pretended to be Paddington talking. "Who's in your room, Mummy?"

"He doesn't talk like that," I pointed out haughtily, walking over to let my doggie in, shutting the door behind him. "He's got a lisp because his tongue hangs out all the time."

Devon changed to a throaty voice, "Whooth thith stwange man in your bed, Mummy?"

"Ohhh yes, much better." I skipped back to bed and threw the duvet over us. Underneath our mouths were opposite each other, an inch apart, and the warmth from his lips reached mine. Hidden in our den, from the outside world, giving us an intimate cocoon. We kissed and I whispered in his ear, "He'th got a thscary thsnake under there!"

Devon began tickling me, making me giggle. "Stop, stop,

we'll wake everyone up!"

We peeked from under the duvet. Paddington's panting head was very close, making us laugh more.

I left Devon to go back to sleep and took the dogs around our block. When I had arrived back, Tamsin was in our lounge, drinking coffee with Mum and Dad, who were still in their pyjamas. She had received my frantic messages about Mum from the night before. My mother, though, couldn't remember a thing about it, so we didn't press the subject, and Dad was simply relieved she was home.

Tamsin and I began flicking through Devon's social profile on my phone.

Dad called from his chair, "She met him in a bush." Then gave us a cluck-and-wink.

"No," I corrected him, "at the gym actually."

"You in a gym?" Tamsin's voice, high with incredulity.

"Sometimes," I confessed awkwardly.

Her eyes returned to his social media account. "And what's he like?" she asked.

"Nice," I said. "He works for an animal charity."

"And these photos," she studied my phone even closer, "they're current? I mean he still looks like this?"

"Yes. Mum and Dad met him," I answered defensively. "Mum?"

"Yes, he's very nice." Mum nodded, and Dad gave a thumbs up.

"And he's your boyfriend?" Tamsin couldn't sound more sceptical. "Sorry, Minty, it's just he's not your usual type… he looks clean for a start, but I guess everyone chooses their best photos for Facebook," Tamsin finished, shrugging.

At that precise moment, Devon appeared in the lounge door with just a towel around his waist, his chest all smooth, toned, face slightly stubbly, that smile, dimples showing. He was like an image from a catalogue, but real and mine.

"Jeees…" Tamsin's jaw dropped.

Devon looked sheepish. "I didn't know anyone was up."

"It's fine." I waved him in.

"Morning, Margaret, and Barry," said Devon, "I love your watercolours on the walls."

Dad winked. "Thanks, George."

We nuzzled noses and he gave me a peck on the mouth.

"Hey," Tamsin interrupted, "if you two want a day out by yourselves, I'll stay with Mum and Dad?"

"This is my sister Tammy," I said quickly.

"Hi," Devon greeted her. "Why not? We could all go away for a few days."

"All who?" I stammered. "Away where?"

Devon laughed. "Us. You, me, and the twins?"

"The Kray twins?" I enquired.

"Not your dogs. The Harries," he said. "We could head up to the Lake District. It would give you a break, away from the news."

"Nice," I said, "but they have school, and Mum and Dad need me."

Mum disagreed. "We are quite capable of looking after ourselves, aren't we, Barry?"

"Trumpers-pumpers, Margie," Dad agreed, but looked concerned.

Tamsin leapt in. "Keep the twins off school. They need to stay away from this circus for a bit, and I'll look after Mum and Dad."

Devon put his arms back around me. "And your parents said how much you loved the lakes."

A romantic trip it was then.

I waited until Devon had gone before running back down our stone steps and grabbing hold of Tamsin's shoulders, who had followed me outside. "YAY!!!" I whooped, bouncing up and down.

"Just do me one favour," she said, trying to calm me down, "don't tell him a thing about the 'old firm'…"

~ THEN ~

From: Minty at HM Prison Holloway

To: Mum & Dad
144 Elgin Avenue
Maida Vale
W9 2NT

Dear Mum and Dad

How are you both? Wish I was there to give you some hugs.

But how are things here (I imagine) you ask? Well, let me fill you in on my main news.

Everyone on our wing thought I was behaving strangely and decided I was trying to cover something up. They came to the conclusion I was a corrupt policewoman who had been put inside.

I'm pretty sure I'm now the most unpopular woman in our block and maybe the whole of Holloway Prison.

Wish me luck!

:)
Love Minty

~NOW~

We had finished packing and were ready to leave. Devon had arrived in his black sports car, which he double-parked outside the flat. He swiftly loaded our suitcase into the boot, then settled into the driver's seat, waiting for us as we wrapped up our goodbyes.

Harriet was excited and wouldn't be a problem. Harry was a different story. Would he even make an effort? On that subject, he put my mind at rest…

"No," Harry hissed as we approached Devon's car, "I will not! And why are we going in HIS car?"

"You know I can't drive," I answered.

"Dad used to build cars from scratch. Why can't you even drive one." He sulked.

This was going to be a fun trip.

Devon's immaculate car smelt new and was not covered in kids' mess like ours, or empty crisp packets like the Inspector's. This one was spotless. Along with the new-car smell was a heavy mix of Devon's aftershave next to me and a hint of leather from his green and white varsity bomber jacket. Another gleaming watch adorned his wrist, making him look more like a US football star than any charity worker I'd met.

As we journeyed on, Harriet had been happily chatting before she fell asleep, while Harry had remained silent. That is, until we hit the M6 toll, when he suddenly felt compelled to share. "I really need to go," Harry announced from the back seat.

I flipped the sun visor so I could see him in the mirror. "We can't stop here, sweetie. We can in another 10 miles?"

"Mum, I won't last." He shook his head definitively. "I'm desperate, and it's coming now."

I sighed. "You'll have to just hold on."

"I can't."

"What's the problem?" Devon enquired.

Strange question, but I guess he'd never had children.

"He needs a wee," I clarified. "Children have smaller bladders."

"Oh." Devon sounded genuinely interested to learn this exciting snippet of information.

"Can I just pee in a bottle," Harry asked, "like I usually do?"

Silence from Devon. He was probably absorbing new details about the family travelling with him.

I took a breath. "Devon, can he pee in a bottle?"

Devon's voice returned, all squeaky. "Is that really necessary?"

"Well, it could be worse if he can't hold on…"

"Fine." Devon was now clearly revolted. "But please be careful, Harry."

My son made a face at him from behind. Pretending I hadn't noticed, I said, "You have that empty juicy bottle in the back there, Harry, don't you?"

"Yes, Mum," Harry responded.

"Then do it carefully." Everything under control.

Devon's mouth was back in that O again, and his eyes were crinkling like he had driven down a dead-end and couldn't figure out how to turn around.

I tried to help him. "You must have peed in a bottle when you were young?"

Devon threw me a look. "No, that must be a Maida Vale thing, we don't pee on our car seats where I'm from."

"He won't get it on the seat." I called back, "You won't get it on the seat will you, Harry?!"

"No, Mum."

"See."

Harriet was still asleep in her corner. Behind us there was the sound of the bottle being opened, and then a trickle, while Devon's breathing turned into short puffs like he was in a Lamaze class. From behind us the trickle became a torrent, and the tone went higher as the bottle began filling up.

"He's very accurate," I said, "aren't you, Harry?"

"Very accurate, Mum, but I think there's a problem."

"What kind of problem?" I asked.

Harry's voice had a depth of concern. "I can't see if it's full because of the label."

"Well," I remarked, "when it feels heavy, stop."

"And I think I'm running out of bottle…"

"You've filled it already?"

"He's filled it," Devon panicked, "Harry, stop, please can you stop now?"

"Okay, okay," Harry said, "no need to wet the bed."

"Harry!" I scolded, stifling a smile.

"Mum… it's right at the top and now, oh no, I can't seem to…" We were approaching some booths on the motorway.

"Do you have a card?" Devon asked me. "For the toll."

"Yes," I answered. "Harry, my handbag's in the back."

"Hands are kind of full, Mum, and I can't get the bottle off."

"Stop mucking around," I said, "just take it off carefully."

The car in front of us went through the barrier, and we were moving slowly towards a man in uniform working in the booth.

"I can't, Mum, I've got it trapped, it's made a vacuum, when the air came out."

"What?" I looked behind; his winkle was now stuck in the bottle. "Okay, stop yanking at it!"

"Jesus Christ, what's happening?" Devon shouted.

We were drawing alongside the tollbooth man.

At that point Harriet woke up. "Mummy! Harry's doing something really horrible to a bottle!"

"He's winkle is caught, honey. Harry, stop pulling or it will go everywhere!"

"Stop pulling, Harry!" cried Devon. "Stop pulling."

"Hello there," tollbooth man said politely next to me.

"Hello," I replied.

"Fuck," said Devon.

"Will he have to have it chopped off?" asked Harriet.

"I hope not, darling, everyone keep smiling."

Romantic weekends? Eat your heart out, I could run a travel site.

A few miles ahead we saw a sign for a service station. "Oh, good," I said, "we need to empty the bottle."

Devon sounded in pain. "Because it's plastic… You want to reuse it?!"

"No, I mean we'll throw it away, that's…" my voice trailed off as I saw his face, "– what I meant. Do you want to be by yourself for a few minutes?"

Devon nodded. The poor man was utterly shell-shocked.

I spoke to the twins without taking my eyes from him. "Kids, Devon's gonna need to take a moment on his own, let's go find the loos." Sadly, I guessed that a man in his forties who had never had children was likely to be one who'd never wanted them. This holiday may prove to be a very steep learning curve for my Devon, especially the way we were. And later, driving through the Lake District, things hadn't improved. "Honestly," I said, "I just think you're a little uptight, you need to relax more."

"You're wrong about me," he answered, tight-lipped.

"Really…?"

The atmosphere between us was frosty, to say the least.

We stopped for lunch.

Getting out of the car, we began towards the gastro-pub.

"Kids, go with Devon," I said, "I'll follow on in two minutes."

No, this was NOT going to be my romantic trip. I opened my suitcase in the car boot and, finding Maxi's present, sat on the edge of his car to tuck my jeans into the high-heeled boots, zipping them up. Then, I stood rather precariously; the four-inch heels were an inch higher than I'd ever worn before.

I felt like a tart.

Inside the pub, I found my children and Devon had settled themselves at a table by the window and were looking through their menus. Standing un-noticed by the door, I took a deep breath and hobbled to the drinks bar. My grumpy ankles did their best to steady me, whilst I leant forward, poked my rear out as far as it would go, and ordered a shot. When I turned around, Devon was watching, jaw open.

Well stone the crows, Maxi was right.

"Are all men really that basic?" I whispered in his ear, as I arranged myself next to him.

He took a deep breath. "Pretty much. What about you? Anything like that work for women?"

"Nice-smelling charity workers," I revealed, honestly, "does it for me."

He laughed. "Yeah, it can be rewarding, especially when you get a call about a poor horse that needs saving, or a beached whale, that one was incredible." He took a sip of his drink with a satisfied smile on his lips.

"Tell me more...." I breathed.

And he did, and by the time we arrived at a country lodge, we were well and truly back on course. While the twins were unpacking in our room, I went to Devon's room. He opened the door, I jumped on him, and he stepped back carrying me, until we landed, kissing on the bed, me on top. Him lying beneath. My hands all over his chest, his jacket was still zipped at the bottom, the cool of the satin lining over the backs of my hands as I explored.

There was a knock on our door. We froze. Harry's voice. "When are we eating, Mum?"

"Get showered first, sweetie!" I called back.

We looked at each other, suppressed giggles and then,

slowly, quietly, we carried on.

This was like nothing I'd ever felt before, each new sensation and experience bringing renewed joy. Watching him interact with the twins, caring for their safety when we took a dinghy across the lake, our secret exchanges, winks, in-jokes, and the opportunity to grab each other when we were alone for a passionate kiss, before holding hands, me skipping next to him.

Harriet was thrilled (Harry less so).

I messaged Quinn. I told him I needed more time. He didn't reply.

Once the twins had gone to bed, we spent that evening chatting about life and sharing stories, and we made love many times.

We decided to take the scenic route back down and make a stopover in Manchester for the night. Daytime, in the city centre, and as we walked past an Ann Summers store, Devon whispered a playful comment about how I would look good in that type of lingerie. That made me pause. Taking a deep breath, and leaving Devon and the twins by the door, I ventured inside. The store was surprisingly quiet, with customers silently perusing the aisles, giving it an almost library-like atmosphere. I navigated through, on a mission to find something a little less frumpy for our next evening together, when I heard my daughter's screams.

"Mummy, Mummy, look!" Harriet cried, in delight. "They have your special pink candles there that help you to sleep, but your candle is much much bigger!"

They weren't candles.

My jaw dropped.

So did Devon's.

Discreet laughter broke out across the aisles.

We left in a hurry.

Once on the motorway again, and much to my protests about cows and their gas-trumping killing the planet, Devon bought us lunch at a well-known burger chain. It was the first time the twins had been to one, and annoyingly, they loved it.

And later they had ice cream from another awful chain – lots of firsts. During lunch, Devon encouraged me to write a rather curt email to the school, complaining about Arabella.

This was what everyone had talked about. I had always wondered if I would ever get to feel like this. I was thirty-five, for goodness' sakes.

Now I did. Golly gosh.

Dustin had kind of accepted me with something close to reluctance. Like he knew he could do no better, and I'd felt lucky he had decided to stay with me.

But with Devon, I felt equal. That was a new feeling.

Crikey, as my father would say.

In fact, with all these new feelings and questions rushing through me on the way back from Manchester, when we took a route through London's Holland Park, I was lost in love and thrown off-guard when we took a turn into the very same street where I had painted *The Doctor*, slowing down at the Russian's property. I even gasped, "But this is…" before my mouth clammed shut. Devon saw, and a new look fell over his face.

Was it my imagination?

And then the twins were chatting, and things moved on.

But what had just happened?

~ THEN ~

From: Minty at HM Prison Holloway

To: Mum & Dad

144 Elgin Avenue
Maida Vale
W9 2NT

Dear Mum & Dad,

I so miss you both so much. Here has been very much like being back at school.

Only this time I don't have Tamsin here to look after me.

Things change.

So does life.

After my cellmate spread that rumour about me being a corrupt policewoman, who had been put inside. Things became tougher.

Love you both.
Minty. xx

CHAPTER TWELVE

INTO THE DARKNESS

~NOW~

Back home from our weekend away, Devon had left, and Tamsin was her usual stressed-out self, pulling me outside. "I can't do it," she admitted, her voice quivering with frustration. She lit her cigarette and took a long drag, then rattled off the next words while holding in the smoke as if it were a joint. "I thought I could, and I tried, I really did, but I can't." She let it out, shoulders deflated.

"Can't do what?"

"The country would have been perfect, I thought – Dad could paint, Mum could enjoy the flowers, and even bring some of those horrible owls with her. I mean maybe she likes their eyes, because her own eyes are deceiving her since the Alzheimer's?"

We considered this.

"No," I answered, "I think Mum just likes owls."

"And I thought they'd be better off, and happy in RTW, but no, Minty, no. Not after these last few days here. Mum doesn't ever just sit, ever!"

"Well, she can if you do a puzzle with her."

"But that's it! She requires constant attention."

"Like she gave us," I pointed out.

"Yeah, but I can't, I mean I don't even do it for my own children, that's why we have a nanny for Christ's sake, but…" She prodded her cigarette toward me. "You… you can and they're happier here." She took a breath. "How were the lakes? And what's-his-name, are you guys still…?"

"Yes," I answered. "Very much still… although…" The image of Oleg's black gates as we drove slowly past his house came to mind.

"What?" she asked.

"On the way back…"

"Oh God, you didn't make him pull over so you could go scavenging in some motorway rubbish-tip for art?"

"No."

"OH, you didn't tell him you still listen to The Cure or never shave your armpits?"

"I shave my armpits."

"Good girl, some things do change." She watched me, scrutinising. "Oh shit, you told him you love him? Oh God, you do love him, don't you, look at that face!"

"I don't know but Tamsin, seriously, but on the way home something happened. We took a strange route back."

"Strange how?" She shrugged.

"Maybe it was a coincidence, but he used the M4 and cut through Holland Park, driving down the exact street…past that house."

Tamsin's face grew ashen, and somewhere in the background I was aware of a dog barking.

"You know..." laughed a man above, who had stopped to lean over our gate, "Sir Barks-a-lot never seems to like your dogs." His yapping miniature labradoodle attempted to get under the gate to bite Paddington's and Muffin's legs. We smiled politely. But he wasn't finished. "We call him Sir Barks-a-lot, because he does like to talk."

We waited until he had left and were about to resume our discussion when Thomas appeared by the door.

"Interrupting anything?" he asked.

"No," Tamsin sighed, "not at all."

Thomas kissed her and fixed me with a disapproving eye. "I picked up a letter for you off the kitchen floor. Looks like it's from the council."

And it was.

Social Services were doing a spot-check this week. A health professional would be knocking on our door, unannounced, to evaluate the safety and wellbeing of my mother and children.

Hmmm.

"Oh," added Thomas, "and I can't believe your parents haven't yet been bought a smartphone, so I got them one." He handed it to me.

"Oh you," cooed Tamsin, "you're such a doll!" A smartphone?

Seriously?

A year ago, Mum would have been able to teach me how to use it. Not anymore. Things for her had changed so quickly.

"How thoughtful," I said carefully.

Harry will love it though.

Later I went to Kilburn and purchased a disposable

unregistered 'burner' mobile. It was surely time to get the picture back, so I called the number. But there was no answer.

That evening Harry was staring forlornly at his maths homework, and I seized the opportunity to help him.

"There is a pond," Harry read out, "with 18 blowfish in it, and some eels with the ratio 12:2. How many eels are there?" He waited, hopefully.

"I think they're trying to catch us out," I speculated. "Let's make this simpler and break it down into pictures." I drew some eels and blowfish, while Harry waited patiently. "No," I said, "that's not helping. Let's get some trees in there and a proper pond." I drew a bit more, and added a storm breaking in the distance, geese, an old man with a hernia, an Asian water buffalo and a pair of friendly fluffy ducks. Around that point Harry lost patience and went off to ask my father instead.

My own homework – the X-rays and other files Quinn had sent me – was still waiting. I flicked through them all, let out a long raspberry, took a deep breath and deleted the files.

Bet Harry wished he could do that.

Then disaster struck around 10 p.m. Harriet, who should have been asleep, came running into my bedroom. "Mummy, Mummy! Jasmine's crying and her kittens have escaped!"

Harriet's face was a mixture of love, worry and determination.

Our white wooden doors off my bedroom to the garden had a square hole at the bottom. The swinging cat-flap had been too close to my bed and kept me awake, so I had removed it, and the brood had jumped through to freedom. With my dressing gown and slippers on, I unlocked the door and grille the other side, clicked on my phone's torch, and grabbing a plastic washing basket in the other hand, I ventured out into the darkness, locking the grille behind me.

The kittens were not there in our triangular garden; however, there was a brick missing from the wall. I came back and tried telling Harriet we could search in the morning.

"Help them," she pleaded, "they'll be lost, alone and scared!" Her big eyes blinked at me from the other side of our grille.

I went back and ventured to the darker bottom of our garden past Maximus. Climbed over the wall, my feet landed on the other side amongst bushes and twigs. Beneath me, my dressing gown was getting caught on brambles and legs scratched as I tripped and scrambled through the prickly, thorny maze. Then something close by crunched.

I stopped. In the stillness, only my breath sounded.

But beneath it – was that more breathing?

Who is out here with me?

And how long would it take me to get back over the wall and back to safety?

The sound of kittens mewing broke me out of my trance. Poking my head through some thick undergrowth, there, under the moonlight, playing together on the grass, were Jasmine's kittens. I climbed out onto the green and bending down, scooped them up one-by-one and dropped them into my plastic washing basket. "Come to mummy," I sang softly. Tiptoeing further from the bushes, I scooped up another furry mischief-maker into my temporary carrycot when I must have tripped a motion-sensor, as daylight flooded the lawn, and that's when I noticed the building ahead with a curtain which had been drawn back revealing the Bain family: Meredith, hubby and kids, all standing frozen, slack-jawed watching me. Meredith with one hand mid-gesture. Her husband, equally stunned, clutched a half-eaten sandwich, its contents threatening to tumble out. Their children, wide-eyed and unblinking.

I lifted a kitten up by the scruff of the neck. "Cats!" I bellowed to them.

They didn't look any less scared, so I dropped the kitten into the washing-basket and went back to my work, chasing the last few around their lawn, muttering to myself about Meredith's accusation of my mental health with my dressing gown billowing in the breeze as I ladled more kittens into the basket. With the Bain family still in their annoyingly immobile state, I recovered my last furry escapee, along with one slipper which had fallen off. I gave my rigid audience a thumbs up and, still crouched over, tip-toed my way back into their bushes.

To Harriet, I was the best thing in the world, and for a few days, I began to imagine I had got away with it, but their CCTV had other ideas.

Miss Belvedere, the twins' form teacher, was quite large and imposing, and reminded me of the horse-loving country women who took their 'dawgs' on a five-mile walk before breakfast, then mucked out the stable, shot a pheasant, skinned it, plucked it, cooked it, put it in a pie and had it on the table by lunchtime.

"Thank you for inviting me in," I said, arranging myself on the chair in front of her desk.

"Now, you are Minty Hutton, so that means the two Harries are yours, correct?"

"Yes."

She jabbed a finger towards me. "You found one name you liked, why mess around with two?"

"Well, they are different, Harry and Harriet."

"Wrong." She swiped her finger away. "Harriet is the female version of Henry, and Harry is the 'spoken' form of Henry. Populandos in Latin, did you know that?"

"I didn't."

"Which means Home Ruler." She took a sweet and started sucking it, still looking at me. "Do they rule your home?"

"No."

"Just as well. They're too young."

"Indeed, they are."

"They've had another late mark, days off school, and you've only been here a couple of weeks."

"That's my fault."

Miss Belvedere emitted a huff, to show her contempt for lateness. The sweet moved around inside her mouth, and there were a few more sucking sounds before she asked, "So what's he done this time?"

"This isn't about Harry. It's about Harriet, I emailed you."

"Agh, yes, she doesn't put her hand up anymore, I noticed that."

"Because, well, in a way, she's being bullied."

"Bullied, in a way?"

"Yes."

"In which way?"

"In the way a child sometimes is bullied."

"And you think it's Arabella?"

I nodded, weakly.

"Our school captain?"

I shrugged.

"Gymnastics genius?" she said, rising from her chair and leaning forward. "Captain of hockey, netball, football and chess? Digital leader, learning mentor, music ambassador, even though I'm not sure she even sings or plays an instrument?"

I sighed.

She continued, "What you are saying here is that one of the most productive and accomplished children we've ever had in the school, is in fact a bully?"

"Sometimes it's not just about the achievement though, is it? But how they achieved it."

"Exactly, look at Stalin." And she sat down and carried on observing me. "Maida Vale's 200-year birthday is nearly upon us. A celebration for the best talent its residents can offer. There is a two-minute spot left. Maybe your two could shine and win class approval."

"That's a great idea."

"Good. Now I believe you have already spoken to Meredith?"

"I tried…"

"Even though taking matters into your own hands broke our school rules."

"But—"

"No buts. You can't call up another mother and yell at them."

"I didn't?"

"One mother's word against another, and we take that type

of thing seriously, but what with everything you're going through with the police, we will make allowances this time if you agree to forget your complaint."

"What about Harriet? They laugh at her in the playground?"

"What would I say? No laughing? Remember to let the children's laughter remind us how we used—" she let out a low burp "—to be." And she was standing. "Wise words, I'll keep an eye on the situation." I was being ushered to the door.

"Maybe the twins," I suggested, turning back to her, "could read out that poem they wrote together?"

"Lovely."

"Is Arabella doing anything?"

"Backflips over miniature burning buildings, while her mother sings a requiem. Have you heard her mother sing? I hear she's rather good."

MORNING

Dad had a speeding fine for doing 34 mph in a 30 mph area and I had a fine from our local authority for being late to school three times. One fine for being too fast and one for being too slow. Our family needed to find a middle ground somewhere. The school lateness and my mother's trip to the police station wouldn't be doing us any favours with Social Services.

Quinn sent me a vile and threatening encrypted message. I told him it was all looking hunky-dory, but I needed more time. He gave me until Saturday.

I tried THAT number again on my new 'burner' mobile, but still no answer.

In the evening, Devon came over. We shut ourselves in the

bedroom and had lots of sex and wine. But I couldn't shake the feeling that our conversation was often being steered toward the investigation, and who may possibly have taken the painting. And never far from my mind was our journey back past Oleg's mansion.

"Aren't you worried?" Devon asked at one point.

"About what?"

"The investigation!" He sounded almost angry, exasperated. "And everything, everything else."

"Is there any point?" I snuggled up to the smooth warmth of his muscled chest. "Have you never dated a blacksmith before? We're all quite chilled, you know."

He moved my hair away from my face. "You're certainly no drama queen."

The next morning, however, hungover and paranoid, I took my phone into the bathroom, ran the shower and as quietly as I could called Tamsin on messenger and told her. She had already spoken to Rupert about the drive back, and when I mentioned Devon had yet to invite me into his home and was really laying into the questions…she decided it was time the three of us confront him.

Harry's muffled cry, "AAGH! For the love of Muffin!" came from the hall. Wrapping a towel around my waist and wetting my hair to add to the shower effect, I went out. Harry was waiting outside the door. "First everyone thinks you're a thief, and now this!"

Harriet wasn't having that. "You know Mummy isn't a thief! What a horrible thing to say!"

I had to agree. "You are being quite mean, sweetie."

He marched off, and I followed him through to the lounge. My parents were eating breakfast there, and the aroma of coffee and toast wafted from the kitchen, where Devon was.

"Hey," Devon whispered, "what's with the tin of baked beans?"

"Keeps the bin lid shut," I confessed.

"Of course," he nodded. "Remarkable ingenuity."

Harry reappeared. "I downloaded TikTok on Granny's phone, and it's trending!"

"What is?" I sighed.

"You and your box of cats!" He handed me the mobile.

Devon grimaced. "You have a box of cats?"

"A basket of kittens actually," I reasoned.

Harry bellowed, "Does it matter?!"

Granny was curious. "What is a Tick-a-Tock?"

"TikTok, Mum, are videos," I explained, handing her back her phone, not wanting to see my exploits. "Social media for kids."

"What's social media?" Mum asked.

"Margaret," snapped Dad, "you know what social media is."

"I do not," Mum answered.

"Then why," Dad asked, "do you keep posting pictures of owls on your Facebook page?"

We all turned to Mum.

"I do?" She was surprised.

"Yes," Dad answered. "Lots."

"Oh." Mum brightened up. "I must say, that does sound like me." And she squeezed Devon's hand. "They have honest eyes, and yours are—"

"What were you up to anyway, Mum?" Harry cried. "Skulking around other people's gardens at night!"

"You know what I was up to. We had some furry runaways."

"That's not what everyone else thinks," he spat.

"Okay… what does everyone else think I was doing?"

"They say you were trying to break into a house."

"Oh, come on, for goodness' sake."

But Harry was furious. "Do you want to know what they're calling you?"

"A caring mother?"

"No, The Mad Cat Burglar."

"Really?" It had a ring to it.

"And don't look so proud!" he yelled.

"By the way," I said sweetly, "I put your names down for the Maida Vale anniversary show next week. You'll be reading out that beautiful poem you both wrote. On stage."

"OH MY GOD!!!" Harry screamed.

Devon kissed me on the cheek, stifling a grin.

"Oh," I said, leading Devon to the door. "We wondered if you fancied a family dinner here tomorrow night. My parents will be out, so it will be just you, me, my brother, and sister."

"I can't wait," he announced warmly.

Here we go….

~ THEN ~

To: Minty Hutton

HM Prison Holloway
Parkhurst Road

London
N7 0NU

Dear Minty,

We have been so worried since your last letter. It's been a while now and we have heard nothing from you.

Have you been eating properly? I've read that prison food has a very high salt content. We do hope you're getting your five a day (this has become a big thing out here), although me and your father get all our vegetables we need from tins.

This week we had a lovely holiday in France with Tamsin and Thomas. They plan to marry soon after your release. Isn't that wonderful news?

That's all for now. Your father and I pray for you every night.

Do write to us if you get the chance.

Lots of love
Mum & Dad

CHAPTER THIRTEEN

THE NET CLOSES

~NOW~

The identity parade in Marylebone went very well, that is, if you were a member of the Met police. It did not go so well for me. My usual calm demeanour decided to take a holiday as the full weight of my predicament, which I had so far successfully boxed and stored away, burst free. As we filed into the room, the other women – of varying heights – smiled politely, but my eyes watered with dread, unable to mask my fear.

In that moment, panic took a firm grip of me. My eyes darted about, desperately searching for an excuse or a way out. I could almost hear the prison doors slamming shut once more.

Clickety-Clack-Lock-the-Latch

The security guard who had been working in Oleg's property during my stay stood somewhere behind the police's one-way mirror. He instantly picked me out of the lineup. However, as Michael wearily noted afterwards, there was only one woman in the row cackling with the whites of her eyes showing.

I liked the Inspector.

He had a nice way about him.

No arrest yet, which my father would call a 'good news

scene.'

'Emily' from Social Services arrived, prompted by the police report on my mother. They wanted to assess how I was coping with her, and whether the children were in a 'safe' environment.

Side-stepping over Paddington and Muffin, who were sprawled out like huge carpets on the floor, Emily took her seat in the corner. She opened her laptop, before being startled by the owls glaring down at her from the wall. "Goodness!"

"What's going on?" asked Mum.

"Emily's here to see how we're coping," I clarified.

"Espinacas!" Dad chuckled to himself.

"Dad," I said calmly, "it's time for your eye drops, and your egg is boiling nicely."

Harry appeared. "Mum, I need my gym kit."

"I've washed it, dried it. Check the dryer," I said with a flourish. "Harriet, shoes on!"

A few minutes later, Harry's voice groaned, "Granny's put my gym kit back in the wash."

I ushered Harry into the bathroom. "Let's check the dirty bin for any hidden gems," I whispered, winking, and we began sifting through the pile of stinky clothes.

Mum popped her head around the corner. "Oh dear. Do you two want to borrow some pants? I have some spare, but I'm not sure they're clean."

"No, Mum, that's not what we're searching for," I replied.

She considered this. "Also, I found some toast. Does it need buttering?"

"Leave it, Mum, I'll do it," I said.

"I'm quite capable of buttering toast," she responded curtly.

"Look," I whispered to Harry, finding a top and shorts. We gave them a quick spray of deodorant.

Back in the lounge, I strapped up Dad's arm to check his blood pressure, letting it inflate, while finishing my cereal.

"Don't forget the eye drops," Dad reminded me, adding a playful cluck-and-wink.

"Where's that toast, Mum?" I said, heading back into the kitchen.

"I think," she pondered, "I gave it to someone, didn't I?"

Dad's voice came from the lounge, "Can I take this thing off my arm yet? It feels like it's going to explode!"

In the background Emily's typing grew more frantic.

"Is anyone eating toast?" I hollered, marching back to Dad and unstrapping him from the machine, then scooping up a kitten which had entangled itself in Paddington's fur. I went back to the kitchen, pushed two more slices of bread into the toaster, filled a cat bowl, left the kitten in front of it, as the doorbell rang. I opened the front door to an excitable young man.

He babbled, "If you give us an exclusive for Sunday's paper, we will—"

"Nice hat," I pointed, "but no thank you." And I shut the door again. "Where was I?"

Mum was trying to give Dad his eye drops, while he was batting her away, undeterred by her resolve. "Come on, Barry," she pleaded. "Why won't you put these in your eyes?"

I took the bottle off her. "Because," I reluctantly admitted, "that's hearing-aid cleaning fluid and it would—"

"Blind him?" Emily suggested.

"Godfathers!" Dad exclaimed, lurching away from Mum's reach, eyeing her with a mixture of suspicion and fear.

In the background the clattering of Emily's fingers went supersonic.

Harriet appeared, thrilled. "I found the toast, Mummy. It was in the tumble dryer," she said, munching on a slice.

"Great," I said, before remembering Dad's egg. I ladled it out of the pan and onto a plate, only to find that there was no salt left. "Harriet!" I ranted. "Please stop emptying sea salt in your baths!"

"But I want to be a mermaid," she retorted. "The book says it works. And when Aunty Maxi was last here, she ordered sushi in a beautiful box, and she said we were eating like rich mermaids."

"Okay," I said, completely forgetting my line of thought, "just don't do it." Turning to our social worker, I asked, "We haven't lost any points yet, have we, Emily?"

Emily attempted to look reassuring. "Don't worry, it's really not about points, it's about…" Her voice trailed off as she was distracted by Fiddlesticks, who was licking Harriet's toast on the table.

Mum broke in by announcing proudly, "I've made something lovely here, for someone." Then she frowned, studying the glass of orange juice in her hand, with a hard-boiled floating object in it. "Although, I'm not sure what on earth that thing is." She looked up again. "Does anyone want it?"

"No thanks, Granny," we all answered.

Personally speaking, compared to our usual mornings, I

think we all coped famously.

Emily said she would be back in touch.

My parents, the dogs and I took a lovely walk in Regents Park, until a drunk man in a business suit began chasing geese. Paddington knew the park rules; and if he wasn't allowed to chase geese then neither should this man, so he bounded over and barked at him to tell him off.

"Good boy," Mum remarked.

"Not a good boy!" the man called out.

"Is a good boy!" Mum retorted.

"Not a good boy!" the man bellowed, his tone becoming nastily threatening.

To my utter astonishment, everyone in the park joined in, a chorus of "IS A GOOD BOY!"

The drunk man glared at us all, realising he was outnumbered, shrugged dismissively and wandered off, probably in search of good sleep. On my return home, waiting for us outside our basement flat door, was a new bin with a red bow around it.

My first present from Devon, and it was a bin. I liked that.

CHAPTER FOURTEEN

CONFRONTATION

~NOW~

Maxi had taken my parents and the twins out to dinner, leaving Tamsin, Rupert, and me at home. Our main table in the lounge was set with candles, faint chill-out lounge music playing in the background, and the comforting aroma of cottage pie cooking wafted in from the kitchen. It was a lovely, soothing scene, made more deceitful by what we were about to do.

Rupert was pacing nervously. "Driving along Oleg's road wasn't the normal route, and it would be one hell of a coincidence," he said.

"But," I countered, "I feel in my heart that Devon is who he says he is."

"Oh, that's fine then." Rupert scowled sarcastically. "If you know it in your heart, in your absolute heart of hearts."

Tamsin, ever the pragmatist, tried to keep the meeting on track. "Don't take the mickey, Rupes," she chided. "Listen, there's too much at stake. We can check him out, and if he passes, it will be over."

"Remember, Mints," Rupert added, "this is for your peace of mind too."

But it wasn't about my peace of mind, was it? It was for theirs. And if it all went wrong and Devon didn't forgive me… What then?

Tamsin was straightening the cutlery on the table. "Right, remember—"

I huffed, "Yes, yes, when you're both speaking, I say nothing, until he admits it, or you tell me it's okay."

"Correct," said Tamsin. "And even if he leaves?"

"I wait until you two give me the nod," I replied, "and then go after him and hope he comes back."

"He will," Rupert assured me. "And when he steps back through the door again, we'll all laugh and tease him for believing our prank and open the champagne."

"But…" Tamsin warned, "you can't open your mouth until we say."

That's when the dogs barked, signalling a friend was coming down the stairs. Devon was here. I skipped over, flung open the front door, and there he was, in a black dinner tuxedo, one hand in his pocket. I leapt up and threw my legs around him for a snog, hoping he'd remember this when things heated up, and whispered in his ear, "Thank you for my bin."

He laughed. Inside, he gave Tamsin a cheek kiss and shook Rupert's hand. "Minty's told me so much about you," he said.

"Has she?" Rupert tried to smile, but concern flickered across his face.

"Come and sit down." Tamsin ushered him to his seat, leaving me to apprehensively slide in next to him.

Once Rupert and Tamsin were positioned opposite us, the interrogation began.

"Minty said you work for an animal charity," Rupert started. "How long have you been doing that?"

Devon made a nonchalant gesture. "Oh, years."

"What was the charity again?" Tamsin enquired.

"AFA – Action for Animals," he answered.

"Right," said Rupert, pouring him some wine. "I saw the website; not a lot of content, is there?"

Devon took a sip. "Our funding is from private donors, so it can be kept low-key."

"Working there must be very rewarding," Tamsin said.

Devon nodded. "It is, but it's hard when you hear the stories," he began.

"Yes," Tamsin agreed, "and we all find it hard hearing stories too. You know, the ones people make up."

Devon's eyes hesitated. "I don't follow you," he said.

"I mean, when someone pretends they're someone, lies about it, just to get closer to the family."

Devon glanced at me, then back at them. "I'm lost."

"Look," Rupert interjected, "we know you don't work for a charity."

Devon's face fell. "I'm not sure what this is about."

"You don't work for a charity, Devon," Rupert said, his tone more condescending. "You made it up."

"Hey," Devon replied, "I can understand you all feeling a little paranoid, but this is crazy. If you want, I can give you the company number."

"We have it," Rupert said. "And you've been tracked and traced. Your car, for instance, has a device under it, bought online, which tells us where you are every minute of the day."

"What the fuck?" Devon spat.

"There's also one in your shoe," Tamsin added.

"And another in the lining of your jacket," Rupert continued.

"Funny." Devon's expression changed, and he laughed. "Good one."

But his laughter was solitary, fading as no one else joined in.

"We know where you live, sleep," Tamsin said sternly, "who you talk to…"

Rupert took the lead. "And even what time you take a dump. The game's up, and your name's not Devon."

"I—I don't know what you're all playing at…" Devon stuttered.

"It's not a game," Rupert interjected firmly, "and we're not playing. We'll tell you what you want to know, after you admit a few things. If you don't, you get nothing from us, and we'll never see you again."

"Minty?" Devon looked at me, his eyes searching.

"We protect our sister," Rupert added sternly.

My mouth opened and closed, but no words came out.

"I have nothing—" Devon began. "I'm off, I'm out of here. Minty? You coming?"

All I could manage was a squeal.

Devon stood, shaking his head. He started to put on his jacket, then grimaced, glared at it, and instead draped it over his arm. "Minty, I said are you with me?"

I shut my eyes and turned away. I heard the front door open, and when I opened my eyes, he was gone, leaving the door wide open.

Beneath the table, my legs were running in place.

"Patience, Minty," Tamsin advised.

I gave them a wide-eyed, pleading look.

"Hold it…" Rupert said softly. "One, two, three, four, five…" He slowly counted; our eyes fixed on the open door. Then I heard the metal gate above open and shut.

"Six, seven, eight, nine, ten!" I blurted out, unable to hold back any longer.

Leaping up, I fluttered to the door and outside, my bare feet on the paving. I could hear him on the phone above me, on the street, talking into his phone.

"They know," he went. "Don't know how, but they know."

His footsteps went and I stood, unable to move, sickened and confused. Could there have been another explanation? I started up toward our gate, to follow him, but a wave of nausea overwhelmed me, and I stopped.

He had lied. He had never loved me. It had all been an act. And I had believed him.

I retched, crouching over. After a few minutes, I straightened up and headed back inside our flat.

"You loser!" Rupert cheered triumphantly, champagne bottle in hand.

"Where's Devon?" Tamsin peered past me to the empty doorway.

Their silly grins vanished.

"Mints?" Rupert asked.

"You were right," I said quietly. "He's not who he said he is, he's been lying."

The champagne cork popped.

I was blank.

Back to where I had been before Devon.

A blank canvas, which was now slightly soiled, like one that once held a vibrant picture but had been wiped clean with white spirit, leaving only a faint outline of what could have been.

And a funky smell.

Fundamentally, my mood had taken a turn towards the darker side, and my commitment to personal hygiene was on an indefinite hiatus. Succumbing to my mother's insistence, I found myself draped in that grey cardigan she adored – my energy to resist had evaporated. Even the once amusing idea of cleaning in a fairy outfit now seemed utterly unappealing. Apathy had set in; I simply didn't care anymore. Tamsin and Rupert were frustrated; they wanted to discuss what I might or might not have told Devon the Deceiver, but I couldn't face any of it.

In the afternoon, Mum wanted to help: "Why don't you call Devon?" she suggested. "He'll cheer you up. We like Devon, don't we, Barry?"

"Margaret," Dad groaned, "that's why she's upset. They've split up."

"Oh, have they?" Mum pondered. "What did you do wrong?"

"It wasn't her fault," Dad explained.

"Oh?" Mum looked confused, and I kissed her cheek, seeing her struggle.

Well," she continued, "I've always said anyone who works with animals must have a good heart. Haven't I, Barry?"

Dad shook his head. "I'm not sure he works with animals, Margaret."

"Oh." Mum seemed to think deeply. "I know what we need to cheer us up, a lovely Sunday roast!"

I sighed. "I'm going to take the dogs out for a walk."

With Muffin and Paddington saddled up, off we went around Maida Vale.

So, who was Devon anyway?

A strange thought struck me. It would be ironic if my poor mum had been blamed by us for moving things into different drawers, when it was actually OUR fault, because Devon or someone else had been sneaking about at night, searching our home.

Outside, there were lots of people and vans, and that stupid man up a pole.

Were they fakes too?

Everyone, everywhere, fakes and liars.

When things went bad your dogs were often there to make you feel better. Like when Muffin kissed away Harriet's tears, it was beautiful. This would not be one of those times.

Up by a collection of posh cafés and restaurants, where people dined at tables in the sun, Paddington had come to a halt on the pavement and wouldn't budge. He was hunched over in his 'I need the toilet' position, the tip of his tongue held between his teeth in concentration. But nothing was happening. I waited patiently, offering a tight-lipped smile to those sitting nearby; a smile that said, 'Gosh, isn't it just my luck that this would happen here.' But nothing came from Paddington's rear.

Now… One problem with Old English sheepdogs they fail to mention on doggie-sites: their hair keeps growing all over their body until they look like a huge shaggy gonk, and if you don't keep their hair trimmed around their bum-bum area, it can get matted and next time they go, they can't. With Paddington's furry face, tongue stuck out, hunched over, unable to move forward or back, sad eyes asking Mummy for help, I knew what I had to do. He'd be frozen in that position until something was freed-up. Resigned, I put a bag over my hand.

My thoughts drifted to Devon. Was he working for Quinn? 'Get close to her,' they probably told my ex-lover. 'And find the truth!' 'Easy,' I imagined Devon saying, 'she'll fall in love with me, no problem.' What an idiot I'd been. Did he ever feel anything, or was it all lies? No, surely not. There must be something slightly attractive about me, something that might have ignited a spark in his heart…

While prodding around with my bagged hand in Paddington's rectum, I pondered whether Devon had ever truly loved me. Around me, the innocent laughter and chatter from the nearby tables seemed to mock my gullibility. And then a thought struck me: what if he was watching right now?

This thought made me burst into spontaneous laughter at the pathetic nature of my situation, as I felt more eyes turn to watch. My laughter turned to fever-pitched cackling as I continued my bag-work. My mother's grey cardigan got caught in the foray, and a passing mother tutted, and shielded her child's eyes, as if to protect her from a woman who clearly enjoyed poking her dog's bottom in front of people eating in restaurants. Like that was how I got my best kicks. Finally, as Paddington went, I cheered loudly in relief, feeling very much like someone you may change seats from, on the tube.

Bagging up Paddington's offering, I turned my head, and

saw the entire Meredith family sitting at a nearby table, staring in baffled bewilderment. I rolled my eyes theatrically and joked, "It was touch-and-go there for a bit, if you pardon the expression." They looked horrified, so I held up the bag and jangled it triumphantly and added, "But we got there in the end!"

All fine, except Arabella had been filming the whole scene with her mobile phone. Harry wouldn't be pleased. Maybe he wouldn't find out. We headed to the park to clear our heads and chase spaniels.

However, when we arrived back home, Harry was waiting for us.

Drat. This Tick-a-tock was incredibly fast.

"Mummy," he said, assuming a parental tone, "I think we need to talk, don't we?"

My parents hid their amusement at his seriousness.

"Oh-kay sweetie," I answered carefully. "In my bedroom?"

Harriet gave me various silent gestures which I interpreted as, 'Don't worry, Mummy, I'll be listening behind the door, ready to jump in, if things get tough.'

Inside my bedroom, Harry and I climbed onto the bed, and sat opposite each other, cross-legged.

I waited.

No one spoke.

He bit his lip.

I tried to hold his hand. He pulled away.

Well, this was strange.

I blew out some air and looked around the room. Behind him I could see the recently completed puzzle lay in a scattered heap beneath the wall, a testament to my mother's failed attempt to hang it up, mistaking it for a picture. Harry, opposite me, was formulating a word. Goodness, this was going to be a biggie.

"I'm not mad," I shot out of the blue. "I know you may wonder sometimes."

"I know, Mum. But you are sad," he replied.

I shook my head in denial.

"You are. You were sad when Granny first got Alzheimer's, you were sad a year ago when Dad died, and you were sad when you found out about him and that woman from the pub…"

"Okay, but your father was a wonderful man," I began, "and life is an adventure…"

"Stop it," he cut me off. "I wanted you to cry when he died, but you didn't." He took a deep breath, looking into my eyes. "And you're not crying now."

I shrugged, and stuck out my bottom lip, hoping that would help.

"And it made me cross, it was like you didn't care. But that's just the way you are," he said, and then suddenly hugged me tightly.

"Err." I tapped his head. "Talking of the way I am, you haven't been on the Tick-a-Tock today, have you, sweetie?"

I felt his head lift slowly and our eyes met. I grinned sheepishly.

In an instant, he leapt off the bed, and vanished.

Harriet bounced in. "What happened?"

I put my finger to her lips. "Shhh, wait for it…"

From the lounge an agonising scream erupted. "Oh… my… God… Mum… NO… NO… NO!"

I grimaced. "I got in a bit of a pickle with the dogs—" My

phone pinged with an encrypted message from Quinn:

IF YOU DON'T MEET ME TOMORROW – I WILL ARRIVE OUTSIDE YOUR FLAT WITH TWO VANS AND TAKE YOUR WHOLE FAMILY WITH US!!

Two vans seemed excessive. Was he planning on taking the cats and dogs too?

ME: But I really have little to show you yet :(

QUINN: Show me what you have, and it better be good!!

I'd always thought I had things under control as long as I had that painting, but there was still no answer when I tried to call the number again.

Had something happened?

~ THEN ~

From: Minty at HM Prison Holloway

To: Mum & Dad

144 Elgin Avenue
Maida Vale
W9 2NT

Dear Mum & Dad

Some good news!

Someone on our block, who'd seen my picture in the papers, confirmed my true identity. I did a few drawings for my cell mate Beth and she began to believe me. She liked them so much in fact everything changed overnight. For the next few days I was drawing other inmates' children, fathers, mothers and sometimes pets from photos given to me, and Beth was charging them tobacco. But the governor of Holloway Prison found out and was very cross about it and she removed our phone privileges, and all my pens and pencils. Since then, there has been an issue with me getting permission to even use a pen at all. Someone suggested with any kind of tool, I could be doing forgeries. The governor is worried about bad publicity, as this prison is one of those they want to close down. I had special permission to write today, but only while being watched. (In case I create a fake Picasso lol.)

Anyway, miss you both heaps.

Love,
Minty
xxxx

~ NOW ~

TUESDAY

I awoke realising today I would have to meet Quinn, the psychotic killer who liked to torture people. And I didn't like the sound of torture. But I was between a rock and a hard place.

And would Devon be there, sitting next to Quinn?

My stomach twisted into knots.

That horrible thought needed hiding.

Going there alone was a foolish, reckless idea, but some things didn't have the same importance they once did.

Quinn was very sure I was being watched, so he had me run all over town. Firstly, I got a number six bus to Kilburn, grabbed a slice of pizza in a café, then off we went again. I hopped on the number eight bus, but not the first one, the second one. In a swift move, I jumped off as the doors were closing and caught a tube to Oxford Street. From there I found my way to Chelsea

I was sitting on the top deck of the bus, watching London

unfold beneath me, when my phone buzzed. It was Devon, and we began a back-and-forth text exchange.

> ***DEVON:*** *Where are you?*
> ***ME:*** *None of your business.*
> ***DEVON:*** *It is my business. We lost you in Kilburn.*
> ***ME:*** *You following me?*
> ***DEVON:*** *WE were.*
> ***ME:*** *Who's we?*
> There was a silence before my phone buzzed again.
> ***DEVON:*** *MI5.*
> Another text followed soon after.
> ***DEVON:*** *What can I say… you created quite a stir.*
> Hmm, if it was MI5 I guess it was a notch better than working for Quinn. I texted back.
> ***ME:*** *You lied to me.*
> ***DEVON:*** *Where are you heading?*
> ***ME:*** *I trusted you.*

There was nothing coming back for a bit, just London passing by below. My phone buzzed again.

> ***DEVON:*** *You need to trust me now.*
> ***ME:*** *I trust you like I trust my dogs not to eat Jasmine's food.*
> After no immediate response, I added:
> ***ME:*** *Jasmine's the cat.*
> ***DEVON:*** *I got it. Thanks. But if you're meeting*

Quinn, you should worry this time, because we can't help you.

I turned off my phone and sighed.

Boys.

I needed to learn cartwheels instead.

The Everman Cinema on Kings Road was our designated meeting spot. Once I had bought a ticket, I went in search, along a corridor and through some double doors beneath a neon SCREEN 4 sign.

The small screening room boasted red velvet sofas and armchairs in each row. Quiet music played in the background, and because the adverts for the film hadn't even begun, the lighting was dim, creating an intimate but slightly eerie atmosphere. The room was almost empty, except at the back. There, taking up an entire sofa with his massive frame and clad in a black tracksuit, sat a very serious-looking Quinn. His body language radiated brooding fury, the kind I remembered could explode into force without warning.

Behind him on another row sat the huge man I had seen in the school fête. Both men had deep, lumpy furrows in their large chunky foreheads, brows so furrowed I imagined mice could launch canoes along them.

As I ascended the steps towards the back of the cinema, the air seemed to thicken with the weight of their threatening demeanours. Reaching their level, I navigated my way along the sofas, and squeezed down next to Quinn.

He smelt like he hadn't been to sleep.

Beside him, between us, was a bowl of fries. He grabbed a handful, dunking them into mayonnaise and stuffing them into his mouth, his breathing loud and laboured between bites.

"Minty."

"Yes, Quinn."

"Whaur is it?" he demanded. "Ye teld me ye'd bring it wi' ye."

"Oh, yes I did," I replied helpfully. "It's here, I hope you like it."

I reached into my shoulder satchel and pulled out the ceramic cat I had made that day, with my father.

He turned the piece over in his massive paws, puzzled. "Wha'?" He looked at me, then back at the object. "Wha' the fook is this?" His eyes straining, glancing back at his friend, who merely shrugged.

"I'm calling it… CAT," I said, hoping to clarify.

He examined it more closely, then his gaze snapped back to me, angry. "Aye, is this a fookin' joke?"

"It's not meant to be funny," I replied honestly, "but art is subjective. Does it make you laugh?"

"No. It disnae make me laugh. Tae be fair, it makes me fookin'… ragin'!" The beast came out, and he repeatedly smashed the cat on the seat in front, reducing it to shards, sending pieces flying all around us until there was nothing left. He didn't look at me, he concentrated on cleaning his dusty hands. "Where's my new fookin' forgery, Minty?"

"Oh no… I can't paint anymore," I said as politely as possible. "That judge told me I had to wait ten years before I could ever sell my work and definitely, no… more… fraud."

"Do aye look like aye give a fook?" he snarled. "The police 'ave bin all over me, took everything, and the French stole tha' *Teacher* from us. Aye need this fookin' thing, and ye three gobshites fooked me over. And now ye owes me. Get back to wha' ye do, or I'll remove yer fookin' hands."

"Then definitely, 100 percent I won't be able to paint again."

"No. Ye fookin' won't."

We sat there in heavy silence. Bit of a stalemate. Or something.

Him glaring at me in the dark, and me just pondering over his words.

"That's not very nice," I pointed out eventually.

"I'm not a nice fookin' man!" he growled. "Wh d'you think this is, fookin' friends reunited? Ye 'ave exactly 'til Thursday before ye find out just how unfriendly I canna be."

Then we all left, we didn't even get to see the film.

CHAPTER FIFTEEN

RUNNING AWAY

To: Minty Hutton

HM Prison Bronzefield,
Woodthorpe Rd
Ashford
TW15 3JZ

Dear Minty,

We are so pleased to hear that you've been moved to an open prison and are eagerly looking forward to visiting you next week. It's wonderful that you're taking your father's advice to use this time productively to learn new skills. However, we were a bit surprised to hear about the ARC welding – isn't that quite dangerous? What about doing some nice flower arranging? Or needlework?

Also, have you thought about writing to your sister yet? I'm sure she'd be delighted to receive a letter from you.

Sending you all our love,

Mum & Dad
xxxxxx

The Teacher, the painting I had crafted for Quinn, was

discovered in France around the time I was finishing my sentence. The forged ownership papers were lost during the whole messy discovery process. In an unfortunate twist of fate, the painting was mistakenly verified as an authentic Rousseau and hailed as one of the most significant art discoveries of the decade. Subsequently, it was claimed by France as national property, leaving Oleg and Quinn without a penny.

After my release, Maxi kindly gave me a room and an admin job at her recruitment agency. "Oh my God, that's Maxi's car!" her staff would scream when she arrived. A few minutes later, she would stride in, all heels and attitude, demanding, "Who's been sitting in my chair and hasn't lowered it back!" striking more fear into her staff than any Goldilocks-bear could, despite being so petite that her feet only touched the floor when the chair was at its lowest setting.

However, recruitment wasn't my thing and I soon left. I travelled to Scotland for the Edinburgh Art Festival and landed a job in an HGV repair garage, where I met Dustin. His soft Scottish accent, messy blond hair, strong forearms, brooding brow and shy demeanour were enough to hook me. As someone who found social situations challenging, his quiet nature was a blessing.

We fell in love, moved to Sussex, got married, and rented a secluded cottage near the sea. Together, we worked in a garage in town, transforming old, forgotten rust bucket cars into gleaming classics. When I became pregnant with the twins, it meant double the love, but only large and moody once: two birds, one stone, whoop-whoop. But a couple of screaming babies later and I realised it was not so much of a whoop-whoop but a boo-hoo. Because they never slept at the same time. Thankfully my mother came to our rescue, staying with us for three months, and I don't know what we would have done without her.

Dustin, it turned out, wasn't shy at all, bless him, he just didn't like human beings. I mean really didn't like them. If he had been a toddler, he would have been called a 'Moody Mary.' I imagined he would soften with age like a tomato on the turn, but he didn't, and his dislike of conversation was only surpassed by his abhorrence for being asked questions, which meant I had to guess a lot and gauge from his expressions if I had it right.

Poached seabass with creamed spinach got a mild growl – he loved it. Vegetarian lasagna elicited raised eyebrows – maybe worth another try. Sauerkraut-stuffed cabbage rolls were met with a deep frown – what were you thinking, Minty?

Harry worshipped him and had miniature replicas of all the cars Dustin worked on and followed him around like a loyal lamb. We had an idyllic life with two bundles of joy. When the Harries started school, I wanted to return full-time to the garage but could sense Dustin needed his space (or as we now know, he needed a Spitfire). So, I bought my own tools and set up a forge outside in our garden, hammering, welding, and nattering to myself, keeping busy with the four Cs: cooking, cleaning, creating, and classes (teaching adults blacksmithing at home), and filling the garden with sculptures.

But my two paintings, the copy of *The Doctor* and the forged *The Teacher*, were never far from my thoughts, and I wondered what would happen if one day, they were linked back to me. I set up hashtag alerts on various social media sites, like #Oleg and

#Rousseau.

And nearly a year after Dustin died,

One day,

They all pinged together.

~NOW~

It was a half day at school, ending with a special church service. The vicar spoke with measured authority, the only other noise came from the congregation in the way of an occasional cough or shift in their pew. Mum and Dad watched intently, while nearby, heads nodded ever so slightly, in a valiant effort to appear attentive. Others let their gazes wander, seeking solace in the ornate details of the carved pulpit or flickering candles.

I studied that day's church service programme, which mentioned the Maida Vale Centenary at the bottom. Our plan was to head to Scotland in the morning for Tamsin's show and be back on Saturday in time for the twins to read their poem at the Centenary. They would be on stage directly after Meredith and Arabella.

Hmmm.

I had another look at the church pamphlet. There was a sentence at the bottom about Meredith Bain being… "a prominent member of St Dunstan's Church…"

A fiery heat rose in my chest.

And I felt strange.

So very strange.

Around us, the smell of wood and incense wafted through the air. The twins coloured in quietly beside me, surrounded by felt-tip pens; happy and oblivious to what was building inside me, and my jaw suddenly clenched shut.

Whoo-ballooooo…what was happening here?

Having wrapped up his sermon, the vicar stepped down from the pulpit. The organist was providing the intro for "Bread of Heaven," a rousing favourite hymn of my parents, and Dad sang louder than ever, but here, my heart raced uncontrollably – oh deary me.

The last verse had been belted out, and with the hymn over, the vicar moved to the front with only the gentle swishing of his cassock. At this point in the service, he liked to remind us about the upcoming parish events. "And I don't need to remind you," the vicar began, "that the school is giving you a holiday, not God! I expect a full church on Sunday, especially if you have a child at St Dunstan's enjoying our wonderful education," he winked, "and saving you a fortune on private school fees. And many of you, I suspect, will be racked with guilt…" There was some polite laughter. He carried on. "BUT God is on hand to help! And he will ease your conscience. We are passing along the pews some direct debit forms for you to quickly fill out, because…"

Adrenaline rushes were making me jittery, like when you drink too much coffee. Ahead of me, a choir boy handed the vicar a piece of paper.

"Right. What do we have this week?" the vicar boomed. "Oh yes, thank you, Christopher, the Maida Vale Centenary exhibition week showcasing our finest talent. It's an open-air event, and we are honoured to include our very own Meredith Bain, who not only is one of our most active mothers at the school and a world-renowned opera singer, but also of course, our most prominent member of our church community."

My hand shot up. "Never seen her," I called out, my voice echoing around the stone walls.

Every face in the church turned, with a collective rustling of scarves and coats.

The vicar paused. "Oh, well, err… you should go see her. Her voice is quite something—"

"In church," I called back, making everyone turn again. "I haven't seen her, here, in church." My hand dropped, fully aware my father was doing his cross-and-flabbergasted look.

The stone statues fell ever deeper into silence.

The vicar's face coloured. "Oh, but she usually attends every week and…"

"No," I cut in. "From what everyone says, no, she does not."

"Really?" He sounded surprised. "Are we sure?"

"One hundred percent, Vicar."

"But…" he began.

I shook my head. "My son will confirm I'm no good at maths…" Beneath me Harry clasped his hand over his mouth to stifle his massive boyish grin, "…But I can certainly add up the mothers who come here," I said. "And lovely Meredith is not one of them."

Maybe it was something Harry would like to have done in class or maybe it was something he did, but I'd never seen him look so happy with me.

The vicar nodded, somewhat flustered. "Oh, well yes, I haven't seen her recently, we'll look into it."

"Great!" I replied cheerfully, the anger dissipating as quickly as it had come. To lighten the mood I added, "But lovely stained-glass window you have." He turned to look up at the window as did everyone else, their coats rustling. I continued, "I think it's a Charles Kemp, isn't it? Dad?"

Everyone's head turned back to my father.

He didn't say anything.

He didn't have to.

I knew he was fuming.

"Your sister would never have done that," he uttered on the way out.

No, she would not.

But I did.

And very unusual for me.

I received an email a few hours later from the vicar saying something about not bellowing in church and suggestions in the suggestions box (now added beside the debit box). It turned out Christopher, the head choir boy, had been signing Meredith in each week, because he had a massive Meredith-crush, and once she had been told, she'd used this to her full advantage. After my outburst, Meredith received an email from the school telling her she would need to attend like everyone else. And word went around… she was not happy.

Meredith was gunning for me.

Whoops.

But where had my new-angry-me come from?

Another outburst came that evening, when miniature-labradoodle man stopped by our flat so his dog could try and bite Paddington's and Muffin's ankles under the gate.

"Oh dear, dear," he laughed. "Sir Barks-a-lot really doesn't like your sheepdogs one tiny bit!"

"If I open the gate, Paddington will like him though, for a late lunch-on-a-lead."

The man looked quite ill when he left. But the words had left my mouth without warning.

THURSDAY MORNING

Michael came around for a cup of tea in the morning, accompanied by a couple of officers, to take my passport and to let me know he thought it was time I got myself some 'legal representation.' As he left, he paused, turning back to me as he was closing the gate above. "It would look better to a judge if you helped us with this case, because very soon it will be too late."

"Okay, well, my door is always open, Inspector," I chirped.

His eyes turned sad. "I have asked you before, but do you want to admit anything else?"

I admitted I needed a dog-sitter.

"And…" he tried, "that's all you have to say?"

"Pretty much," I replied. "Unless you'd like to look after Paddington, Muffin and the kittens?"

He looked defeated and maybe a little broken. Emotional. It was odd. "No, Minty. I can't do that. But I will sort out those lights on Widley Road for your mum."

"Thank you, Inspector."

"Enjoy yourselves," he said. "Where you off to?"

"Oh, I'm sure you'll be following us, so you'll know soon

enough."

"Stay in touch, don't leave Britain. And I hope you're going somewhere nice."

What a kind thing to say.

At 10 a.m., while Quinn boiled with rage waiting for me to reply to his string of abusive messages about needing to meet him later, and Paddington was causing havoc at Maxi's place, over in Maida Vale, my parents, the twins and I fought through the pelting rain, the largest rainfall West London had ever witnessed, to climb soaking wet, into Dad's car, and begin our journey.

My father enjoyed driving as it was one of the few activities that didn't cause him any discomfort in his hip. It offered him a sense of freedom that he missed, since walking had become such a challenge. This was especially fortunate since we had a long journey ahead of us. We were going to Scotland. At one point, the rain was so heavy we could barely see out of the windscreen. When we did stop for a bite to eat, I noticed that the procession of cars following behind had gone, presumably lost in the rain and traffic.

Having received a few missed calls from Michael and Quinn, I turned off my phone. I also took out some cash, just in case they tracked or stopped my cards—a precaution I'd learned at Her Majesty's pleasure. Meanwhile, Rupert, Thomas, Tamsin, and their children were also en route to Edinburgh, flying first class. Tamsin and Thomas had kindly booked a lovely hotel for our family, and we arrived in the evening.

SCOTLAND

There was the football world cup, after that the Olympics, and right beneath them, for the most-visited event on earth, was the Edinburgh Festival.

"One hundred million people go each year!" Dad boomed at a family sitting near us during breakfast in the hotel. "Did you know that? I didn't. Did you? No? And our daughter has a show there."

"You must be very proud!" a member of the family responded.

My mother joined in, "And she paid for our stay here, which is very fancy, isn't it, Barry?"

"Trumpers-pumpers, Margie!" Dad exclaimed.

After a night of torrential rain, the world outside had transformed. The sun had risen, promising a hot day ahead. I tried THE number once more on my 'burner' mobile, and this time, it was answered. "Hello, this is Cynthia—"

~ THEN ~ (Going back a little to the night I took the painting)

I hopped out of the taxi and dumped the original Rousseau in the big black wheelie bin. My taxi had only gone about a hundred metres before I asked the driver to stop and turn around. About 10 minutes later, with the original in my hands, we pulled up outside Mum and Dad's flat. I dashed in, grabbed a pen, and scribbled 'To Cynthia and Kenny, lots of love, Minty' on the back of the canvas, where it was stapled over the frame. Then, I went back out, descended the steps into the basement next door to Cynthia's, and pressed her buzzer.

Kenny answered. I stayed for a cup of tea and gave them their 'present,' which I claimed to have painted because I knew how much Kenny loved Antoine Rousseau. We found a nice spot for it on their lounge wall, and up it went. Of course, they didn't know their flat was now worth perhaps 120 times what it had been ten minutes earlier. What a ridiculous world we live in.

Kenny was so grateful; he told me it was his favourite painting in the world. Later, Dad drove me back to where I was living with Tamsin and Rupert and dropped me off.

I was a bit giddy with what I had accomplished as I stood outside and dialled the one person whose opinion meant so much to me. "Hi, Maxi," I began. "You know how you thought my moral compass was broken? Well, I've corrected it now and done something much better."

"Oh, that's wonderful news," her voice tinged with cautious optimism. "I'm hoping you've stopped all this terrible nonsense. What did you do?"

"I stole a priceless painting from the Russian mafia and gave it to my babysitter."

There was silence on the other end of the line. Maxi didn't say anything. I guessed she was happy but didn't manage to find out. As I opened my front door, and switched on the light, I was suddenly surrounded by a circle of waiting police officers.

Chapter Sixteen

THE FESTIVAL

~NOW~

Since my arrival in Maida Vale a month ago, my plan had been to reveal the truth to Cynthia about her painting and ask for it back. Yet, I hadn't quite decided what to do with it, and considering I hadn't seen her since her husband's funeral, it seemed particularly callous to just show up and demand the return of her late husband's favourite painting. The painting, I imagined, which had served as a daily reminder of Kenny, especially with the anniversary of his passing looming. And then she'd gone missing. Our phone conversation continued. "Where have you been?" I exclaimed. "I've been so worried about you!"

"I went to Brighton for a few days," came Cynthia's voice, "where Kenny and I had spent our last holiday together. We'd had such a happy time there."

"Oh, thank God!"

"Well, I did wonder when you would be calling," she said. "I do watch the news, you know."

"You wondered? Why?" I asked, hit by a pang of guilt.

"Well, is it…?"

"Is it what?" I stalled, playing for time to ensure we were

speaking about the same thing.

"Do I have that painting on my wall?" She sounded both worried and upset. "Did you leave stolen property in our home? You said you painted it as a present for us, because you knew it was Kenny's favourite. Have you been lying all this time, putting us at risk?"

Now, please don't judge me any more than you have, but she sounded so hurt, and also I didn't want her having a heart attack, (and also, I am a coward, as you know).

"No, of course not," I quickly replied. "I painted you a copy. But people will think it's real, won't they? And I've been thinking a lot about this…"

"Oh, that's such a relief!" she cried out. "Thank goodness, and yes, they very well might. I keep expecting someone to rush in and snatch it."

"I don't want you to worry any further. I'll come over and pick it up this week. Although, I have a feeling I'm being watched."

"You are, dear. You're quite the celebrity now," she assured me.

"Really?"

"Yes, the whole of Maida Vale is talking about you, Minty. I wanted some pasta yesterday lunchtime, and Le Cochonnet was busier than I've ever seen it. There were no tables available, not one, and barely any faces I knew."

"Who are they all?"

"Some were reporters and tourists, but I heard there are also some treasure hunters, and some say even undercover police. Maida Vale has become a big attraction, and lots of Rousseau admirers, but some are certainly not fans of yours."

"Really? Why?"

"There was a man in there yesterday, who was demanding someone must know where you'd gone to."

"Did he have a Scottish accent?"

"He may well have done. Very tall and wide, apparently. I really can't remember the full story. What are your plans now, dear?"

"My plans are to pop past yours later this week, and get that painting, so you don't worry anymore."

I explained my idea.

Ambitious cultural events and projects had begun across Edinburgh, and one of the largest was the art festival, taking residence on one side of the 650-acre Holyrood Park. As we walked up, a vibrant mix of sights and sounds enveloped me. The feeling of anticipation was palpable, and the atmosphere teemed with creative energy. The festival grounds stretched out before us; a labyrinth of colourful tents, dotted about between trees and lush shrubbery, each housing its own unique display of artistic marvels. Everywhere I looked, there were vibrant paintings, sculptures, and installations adorning the stalls and open spaces. Each artwork seemed to tell a personal story, invoking emotions and inspiring imagination.

"Look at those massive tits!" Rupert gleefully screamed as we walked under art-deco breasts the size of houses.

"Grow up!" My father's hand came out, and he caught Rupert lightly around the back of the head. "You're upsetting your mother again."

Tamsin spotted us and led us over to her marquee, where Thomas and her children were waiting for us. Inside the white canvas opening, there were miniature models of all their award-winning homes, along with photos and drawings of properties they could build, were building, or had built. But Tamsin was hitting interstellar levels of stress never previously reached.

"I'm not making a big deal out of it," she fretted, "but our minuscule 'tent' is a long way from the action, and I was promised a top-20 spot." Opposite Tamsin's mini-marquee, there was a large digital flatscreen TV that showed live BBC highlights of the festival and things that were starting across the park.

"Come on," Dad said. "Let's get out of her hair." We left the Harries with Crispin and Clementine and their au pair while my parents, Rupert, and I walked up the hill, weaving in and out of the waves of people, passing more TV screens, and on towards the stage area at the very top. Dad managed to find a hospitality tent, which served cold beer, and while we had lunch, Rupert wandered off. He reappeared 10 minutes later, out of breath. "I've put your name down for something," he said with relish. "You'll love it, Minty, come on."

"What exactly is this?" asked Dad, immediately suspicious of his son's relish. "And how are you benefiting from it?"

Rupert gasped theatrically, one hand on his heart. "My own father doubts my honesty, well I never! I'm actually shocked."

"Be shocked," my father retorted. "What's in it for you?"

"Nothing. I wanted to help them out of the kindness of my heart. It's some welding metal thing, they had a no-show, I told them Minty could fill in."

And before I could say no, I was being led up to an area to the right of the stage, where there were assistants with high-viz festival jackets on. "Minty, you're slightly infamous, aren't you?" A very attractive woman, with dyed bright yellow hair and a clipboard, grinned.

"Am I?" I replied, glaring at Rupert, having found the answer to his 'kind gesture.'

"Yes, and we love infamous at the festival," she said. "We just need proof of certificates and the usual health and safety stuff." Mum and Dad found some seating nearby. I brought out my old phone and turned it back on for the first time since we'd left home. We went through the PDFs of any documents I had, while two assistants began dressing me in protective overalls.

After everything had been checked, the woman said, "Your equipment is all in there, and you'll get twenty minutes."

"That's barely enough time to fire up my torch," I said, putting a hand on the door handle.

"Not yet!" she screamed. "Only when the green light goes on!" Strange.

"So," I tried, "who'll be watching this?"

"Everyone."

A quick scan of the empty area behind me told me she was wrong.

"Have you met the others?" she asked, pointing to my right, where five burly men stood by similar doors. "You may recognise Big Ben Brighton."

Of course, I knew Big Ben. He was a successful international metal artist, standing six-foot-five and distinctively covered in tattoos from his bald head to his Doc Marten boots. He could even twist metal together with his bare hands.

"Jeees!" I exclaimed. "I have a whole shelf of books on him." I looked at Rupert. "He's like the Kurt Cobain of the welding world. Why's he here? Why am I here?"

Rupert clapped me on the back. "As long as you can get two bits of metal stuck together, I'll be proud. We can say it's minimalist." And he winked at Yellow-hair, who blushed.

I shook my head.

"Now listen," Yellow-hair was saying, "when the light goes green and the buzzer goes off, step through the door and go for it. The main pile of scrap is a free-for-all, but don't get in a fight." A fight? What free-for-all?

Rupert was in Dad's ear talking, and he looked thrilled, rubbing his hands together and leaning forward in his chair, giving me the thumbs up.

The TVs around us all changed, including the gigantic ones on either side of the main stage, which revealed a presenter. "Now for one of the main events of the day," she boomed. "The speed welding competition."

Shitty-sticks!

My phone had been buzzing constantly since I'd turned it back on. There was a message from Devon.

> **DEVON:** *We just discovered... The Doctor is yours. It's your fucking fake!*
> **ME:** *Oh. And why do you think that?*
> **DEVON:** *We don't think it!!! We know it!!!*
> **ME:** *Oh really.* (I added an emoji of my head exploding) *And how is that?*

DEVON: *Because... you signed it?!*

ME: *Oh.*

DEVON: *You're in the festival, aren't you?*

ME: *Maybe.*

DEVON: *So am I, and I need to reach you before the police do. The park is huge, where is Tamsin's stand?*

ME: *You know... I may have faked a little art. But you faked a relationship. Oh, and you wear too much aftershave.*

I turned off my phone, but my face must have betrayed my concern. Rupert came over. "What's wrong?" he asked.

"The police know I painted the fake Rousseau."

"Fuck!" Rupert screamed.

At that precise moment, Tamsin arrived. "We are dead down there," she grumbled. "No customers. A complete washout and…" She noticed our faces. "What?"

Rupert shut his eyes. "The police know she did Oleg's fake."

"How?!" Tamsin spat.

"Because I signed it," I admitted. Their eyes grew incredibly large, so I explained, "I did a pencil drawing of a mint-leaf under the oil paint, which I'd done on a few others."

"But…why?" Tamsin's words were clenched.

"It wasn't really my plan to swap them in the first place," I said. "That kind of happened on the hoof, so to speak."

"Well," she said, "you can't do this steel competition now!"

Rupert piped in. "No, you'll be on live TV, and they'll see you."

"I am going in there," I argued, "it actually looks fun."

Tamsin's frustration mounted, her hands clenched into fists. The hum of the festival, with its blend of music and chatter, seemed to fade into the background as our confrontation intensified. "Don't be ridiculous!" she fumed. "I know you've never forgiven us for what happened. But you can't go in there. And once they tie us all in with your bloody painting, everything Thomas and I have worked for could soon be gone. Why couldn't you do what we told you to do at the time!" Tamsin's face went from red to blue and then she exploded. "We said not to fake, but you never listen!"

"I did listen, but I wanted to do it, and maybe that was stupid," I conceded as the lamp above my head lit green, and I was pushed towards the door. "But there's one thing you should know."

"What?" Tamsin stammered.

I shrugged. "I still have the original." I handed my speechless brother my handbag, and my gob-smacked sister my phone, and went through the door.

The door shut behind me. I had stepped into an area about the size of our living room at home, flanked by black fireproof curtains on either side. In front of me was a large workbench equipped with better welding and cutting tools than I'd ever used before, along with my helmet/mask. Ahead, in an open space, lay a huge pile of scrap. While I attached my helmet, I could hear our introductions being announced over the speaker system: "…And our wild card, you may know her from her photo in the papers, is Minty Hutton."

The idea of a speed-welding competition was to find things

that went together to make a visual piece, but it was usually a daylong event. We had twenty minutes.

Already, the other competitors, clad in protective gear, had begun unleashing their skills in a fierce battle of creativity and speed. The sound of roaring torches filled the air. Over by the heap of scrap, the men were riffling through the steel with deep intensity. Cameras in each corner filmed our every move. I imagined my father watching from the other side, hoping I'd create something unique. Remember, Minty…

You could mould cow manure for all I care, as long as it's original.

Quite a bit was going on in my head, and it was hard to pack it all into drawers to get myself a clean work surface, so to speak, and to concentrate. To my right I could see Big Ben; a blister of activity, running around grabbing things and taking them back to his bench.

And the rest all burning and joining or choosing their next item.

Time was moving on, and yet I remained frozen.

Dad's words again…

But why don't you ever do your own work?

Because I don't want to.

Sparks showered like fireworks, illuminating the surroundings. The scent of burning metal, along with the rhythmic clinks and clanks of metal on metal, reverberated through the arena.

I had never wanted to do my own work. And that's just the way I felt.

When was the last time you did then, Minty?

I couldn't move, my legs were as if glued to the floor.

Were you ten? Twelve? No, it was younger than that.

Standing by the pile of scrap, I looked down. There was a dirty hubcap gripped tightly between my hands, my fingers wrapped around the steel, and my knuckles were white. Must have picked it out.

I squeezed my eyes shut. Maybe my old art teacher would be watching from first school. He was nice. He was nice.

I clung to that thought.

Why don't you ever do your own work?

The hubcap in my hands was from a Ford. A Ford, Mark 1 Escort. And I was stroking it. Tenderly. God, I missed him. I missed my husband so much. And I hated myself for feeling that. Why was I not good enough? And those pesky head-drawers were rattling, wanting to burst open, and I was holding them all shut, but the pressure behind them was building, and one exploded, its contents hitting me in the chest.

I knew he had been having that affair, and I'd shut it out, shut it down, locked it away. I didn't want to know he was unfaithful, because it would have confirmed what I'd always known: I was a poor imitation of what he really wanted.

Because there are so many beautiful artworks out there already. That's why.

No, that's not the reason though, is it? We all know why you won't.

Another drawer burst open; the way I dressed, what was I trying to say? Was this my attempt at being unique? Was this a lie?

Was I the fake?

Who the hell was I???

And the blinds on the windows unravelled and snapped

open and the drawers were all falling on the floor and the windows shattered and everything came at me at once.

I was scared and so I had always copied. Copied everything. Too frightened to ever try to be original. Never done it. Not since I could ever remember. And now it was too late, I was stuck. Petrified. Copying someone else's art held no fear and since college, it had given me the chance to live a different life. Not mine. I wasn't a good person. I knew that. What kind of mother would risk the lives of their children like I had?

Then more hit me. Everything I'd been too much of a coward to deal with since I'd learnt how to lock it up. Situations braver women could cope with every day, but I'd never faced.

And after that, things got a bit messy.

I remember a lot of screaming, tears, and cutting myself. And hands and voices and me shouting angrily to leave me be. The pounding in my head joined with hammering like a ketamine mushroom megamix. Memories hit me – humiliation, bitchy cliques, backstabbing, doubts about friendship, work bullies, sexual predators, barbed comments, unreturned calls.

And at the end. All I could think of was… What if my children were taken from me?

Devon was there too. Puke.

Exhausted.

I fell to the floor, sobbing, face in the earth. I hadn't moved, in twenty minutes.

The buzzer sounded, and the lights around us went green. I felt hands helping me up off the floor. Looking back at my empty workbench, dazed, I clambered out of my protective gear.

Stood, twisted my hair into its bun and stuffed my trusty paintbrush through it. Opened the door to the exit, outside, there were lots and lots of people, all with blank faces, staring at me.

A huge crowd of silent people.

Suddenly, they burst into cheers, jumping and clapping, their excitement building into a crescendo of jubilation. Behind the jostling horde, Dad, supported by Rupert, reached me. With a hand on my shoulder, my father rasped into my ear, "The world has at last seen a 'Minty'." Then he kissed my head.

My mother double-squeezed my hand, to convey a message without words: 'Dad liking your art… wonders will never cease.'

"But…" I shouted above the din, "I did nothing!"

Then I saw it. Being carried away. Flashes of feeling the metal smooth in my hands. Anger, love, fear, and blinding blue light. My sculpture was a smooth metal ball behind a jagged cage about a metre high, with what looked like a metal boot crushing it from above. All very odd.

I wish that moment of bonding with my father could have been savoured. An immense feeling of pride, at last recognition, and acceptance. Wasn't it funny, how a few words like that could be everything you dreamed of? Strange. But the clamour of the crowd faded abruptly, giving way to a more ominous sound. Police sirens pierced the air, their wails echoing my new sense of dread. I went from riding a wave, to sinking in despair, as my life began crashing before my eyes. The game clearly up, I braced myself for the inevitable – capture, handcuffs, a cell and my children torn from my side. I was too tired to even escape mentally.

Then, through the chaos, I saw Devon striding towards me. Dressed in a crisp white shirt and a sleek suit jacket, he moved through the crowd, directing festival-goers from his path with calm, effortless determination (one chap eating a hot-dog found himself pushed into a rhododendron bush). Beside him, Tamsin, frantically shouting with the twins in tow.

Rupert stayed with my parents, while the Harries and I were ferried through a labyrinth of tents until we arrived at a smaller one. There, we stood by the doorway, observing the crowds and the mayhem outside.

"You're going with Devon!" Tamsin bellowed.

"But that's not his name," I felt someone needed to point out.

Tamsin glared at me, then at him. "What's your real name?" she demanded.

"Does that matter at this time?!" came his terse reply.

We waited.

And he gave in. "Craig," he admitted.

I winced, repeating, "Craig? That's unfortunate. I can see why you changed it."

He barked, "Just tell me this isn't a wind-up, and tell me you really DO have this motherfucking original?!"

"I do," I replied, almost apologetically.

"YOU-FUCKING-REKA!" he exclaimed, grabbing my head between his hands and kissing the top of it. I wiped my forehead.

Tamsin butted in. "Craig's going to drive you and the Harries somewhere safe. You'll get the painting, and hopefully, he'll negotiate you out of all this mess. But don't give them a bloody thing until you've got something in writing, with charges dropped."

"I'm not going anywhere with a 'Craig,'" I argued.

Tamsin shouted, "The police are here, and it's possible everyone else that hates you is too. They won't play nice this time; they'll put you in some godforsaken hole to get you to talk. Is that what you want?"

In the distance, I could see more police cars arriving, shouting, and the heaving crowds now chanting rude things about the police. I glanced down at my children.

Harry shrugged. "This would never have happened in Sussex." Tamsin growled, "Shut up, Harry!" through clenched teeth.

I wasn't convinced. "How do we even know this Craig man is who he says he is?"

"I'm not stupid," Tamsin said. "He's shown me proof, and yes, he is 100 percent, stone-guaranteed, M.I. bloody five!"

"Filth," Harry explained to Harriet.

I clipped him around the top of the head.

"What about Mum and Dad?" I fretted. "Do you think they know the police are here for me?"

At that moment, a PA system boomed from a police car. "Minty Hutton, make your way towards us. We have your parents with us!"

And faintly, Mum's voice. "I thought you'd given up smoking, Barry."

"I have, Margie, I have," came my father's reply.

Tamsin nodded. "They know, and Thomas is with them. Now go!" she shouted, and we moved to the back of the tent, where there was an opening.

"I'll do it," I said, "but I'm not happy!"

Devon-the-imposter's eyes narrowed. "Do you want to be handcuffed in the back of a van?"

"Oh, stop it, Craig!" I scolded.

His eyes scanned for escape routes as fleeing bodies and cut-up conversations passed us by. We dodged through the moving throng, me holding Harriet's hand, Craig/Devon holding Harry's hand, slightly bent over, picking up speed over the grass, running towards the carpark in the distance.

We found his car.

CHAPTER SEVENTEEN

THE CHASE

~NOW~

"All of you in, now!" he bellowed.

"Oh, how quickly things change!" I managed, climbing in next to him with the twins into the back.

Inside, he took a breath, revved the engine, and then we were skidding towards the exit of the carpark, where vehicles were being checked as they left the cordoned-off area, by police. Devon (sorry, I am NOT calling him Craig) pressed one of the switches on the dashboard, and a blue light began flashing from somewhere and a loud siren boomed from within the car.

"Cool!" screamed Harry.

"Where are my mobile phones?" I asked Devon, noticing they weren't in my bag anymore.

"We threw them away," he shouted, "now get down!" With his left hand, he pushed my head to the rubber mat on the floor.

"Rude!" I mumbled, my head between my legs.

He let go.

I sat up again. "And all that time, this car of yours was a police car? We could have reached the Lake District much quicker," I pointed out.

Devon pulled into the outside lane, passing a queue of cars. With the siren screeching, he navigated through Edinburgh's cityscape, and each time we approached a red traffic light or any police, we held our collective breaths. Onwards through the bustling streets, we manoeuvred our way, leaving the city limits and switching off the deafening siren as the landscape transitioned into rolling hills and lush green countryside. The engine's powerful hum resonated through the vehicle while we swung around each corner.

Devon's mobile phone seemed to be upsetting him. "Get lost!" he thundered. But his phone cheerily rang on, ignoring him, while he slammed the car into corners at breakneck speed, muttering to himself.

I broke the silence. "Devon."

He did a double-take. "It's Craig."

"Not to me," I continued. "And I know how much you love your car, so it will be sad to see my children redecorating it VERY soon…"

He snatched a glance in his mirror at their pale little faces next to me, and the car slowed down. "Now…" he began in a calm assertive tone, "where in London is it?"

I didn't answer.

He persisted. "You need to tell me. I'll get someone to go pick it up, and all this will be over."

"No thanks," I replied.

"But at this stage, it would just be easier for everyone if—"

"Not a chance," I interrupted. "We'll pick it up together."

He sounded irritated and almost sulky. "You better actually have it. But also…thinking…" He fought for words, "You're not likely to forget where you put it, are you?"

"Forget?"

He shrugged. "I'm not being funny, but the inside of your head is a bit of a jumble. Things may get lost in there, or hidden…" He glanced at my children. "No offence."

My jaw hung open. "I do NOT like this real-you. The pretend-you was so much nicer!"

"Yeah!" Harriet agreed, meaning it.

Harry piped up. "Mum, does this mean we won't have to read our poem anymore tomorrow?"

"You're still doing it," I replied.

Devon's phone rang again, and this time he took the call. "I'm here."

A man's angry voice boomed inside the car from its hands-free device; "Just tell me you have her?"

"Yes," Devon replied, "she's here in the car with me now."

I mouthed 'she' sarcastically to my children.

"Praise the lord," the man said. "Okay. Well, just take her in."

"In where?" I whispered.

The man on the phone said, "Drop her off at the nearest police station. Things have changed."

Devon said nothing.

The man on the phone spoke again. "I said drop her off. Are you there? Take her to the nearest police station."

Devon glanced at us all in his mirror, released a huge sigh. "No," he answered.

The man was incredulous. "What do you mean, 'no'?"

"I mean…" Devon said, "I have a better idea. We'll catch up

soon."

Devon cut his phone off as the man began to shout.

"Yay!" cheered the Harries.

"Isn't he going to be slightly miffed with you?" I asked.

Devon didn't answer, and the tension in the air was palpable. So, I filled it with some casual whistling.

"Please stop," Devon requested.

An hour from Edinburgh, we had picked up refreshments and were now heading towards London. Devon had disabled his GPS, he explained, opting to take the smaller back roads instead.

"So," Harry ventured, "are you like James Bond?"

"No. James Bond is MI6," Devon corrected. "We're MI5."

"Oh, very different," Harry replied sarcastically.

Devon added under his breath, "And he's fictional."

Seeking to lighten the mood, I suggested to Devon, "Let's play true or false."

"Oh, let's," he answered, his voice dripping with a lack of enthusiasm.

"Firstly," I said, "that woman in the gym was your sister. True or false?"

"False. She's a colleague."

"And your love for gluing cups to cardboard?"

"False, not my thing at all."

"You don't say," I mocked.

"I thought it was pretty good," he added.

"It was not good," I answered firmly, "and you said you were too boring for a drama-loving wife… was that true?"

"True."

He abruptly snapped on the radio and tuned into the news.

Our story quickly came through, sounding dramatic:

Radio: *"In the latest chapter of the Antoine Rousseau saga, and what people are calling the art heist of the decade, the Met Police arrived at the Edinburgh Festival to arrest Minty Hutton, a Maida Vale mother of two. They discovered she had entered a speed welding competition and, in a twist of fate, she came first in the competition, winning the prestigious Festival Newcomer Award…"*

"Hurray!" my children cheered.

Radio: *"But then the police arrived to arrest her…"*

"Boooo!" we all went (apart from Devon).

Radio: *"And although they arrived in force with countless cars, officers, and police dogs, setting up blockades around the city, she managed to slip through their net and is now officially on the run!"*

"Hurray!" we cheered.

Then someone came on to discuss how this painting had become the most reproduced artwork in the country, with quality forgers selling fakes in every pub in every city, pretending they had the original. It had all been quite fun to hear, until they delved into depth and detail about me and my past. Afterwards, we switched it off, and no one spoke.

The weight of this newfound information lingered in the air, and I imagined their young minds were churning with questions and emotions. "So," I said, "does anyone have any questions about any of that?"

The twins shot their arms up in the back. Devon glanced in his mirror, then at me, twice, realising I meant him too, and he shook his head.

"Nothing?" I asked him. "Oh yes, I forgot when we met, you'd already had the benefit of a file on my life. All I had to go on was two dimples and a dodgy vest-top."

Harry piped up. "The man on the news said you've been to prison, Mum."

"Indeed."

"Why didn't you ever tell us?" Harry enquired from the back.

"You never asked," I answered truthfully.

He threw his arms in the air. "I didn't think I had to! So, have you ever killed anyone, Mum?"

"No."

He wasn't finished. "Have you blown anything up?"

"When I was young," I remembered, "a few party balloons, bad for the ecosystem. Oh, and one Christmas I inflated two full-size Mutant Teenage Ninja Turtles."

While driving, Devon took a sip of his coffee. "Which ones?"

"Leonardo and Michelangelo."

"Bad choices," he replied.

I let out an indignant huff. "What would you know about Ninja Turtles?"

"Enough to know they weren't great," he said, "but you probably liked them as painters."

"No, I chose them because they were great turtles. Tell me, who should I have had then?"

"Raphael," he answered definitively. "People said he was a little dull because he was so sensible, but he simply cared about people, wanted to protect his team, and was concerned about their safety. I related to him."

After pondering for a moment, I replied, "No, I think he

was just very… very… dull."

Devon choked on his coffee.

Harriet's voice came from the back. "What's prison like, Mummy?"

"It's like a boarding school," I considered, "for convicts."

"I am NOT going to boarding school!" Harriet stamped.

"Anyway," I assured them, "that's all in the past."

"Yeah," Harry replied. "Now we're just being hunted by all the police in England, Scotland, and Wales, unless I'm missing anything?"

Devon sighed. "Probably the French and Americans too."

"Great!" Harry sulked.

"Don't be upset," I said. "Life's an adventure—"

"Not helpful!" Harry spat.

Devon tried to regain control of the narrative. "We should be back in London around midnight, and we could get the painting and—"

"No," I interrupted.

"No?" he echoed, imitating my voice.

"It will be too late to pick it up," I said.

"Too late?"

"Too late," I repeated. "We can go in the morning."

"Why?!"

"It won't be open."

"Where have you stored it? A bakery?! What time in the morning?"

"Nine."

He wasn't pleased. "I should drop you off at the nearest police station. That's what I should do." He checked his mirror.

"Hey, Harry."

"Yes?" my son replied.

Devon winked. "Today, you did well, son, you're a tough kid."

"Thanks." Harry nodded sincerely.

"And in answer to that question of yours earlier… I guess it is a bit like being James Bond."

"Sick!" Harry gasped. "Have you ever shot anyone?"

I glared back at my son.

Devon tilted his rearview mirror to fix him with a disapproving fatherly expression. Harry shrank in his seat. After a moment, the man I had once trusted opened the glovebox, and with a voice that knew he would be winning on a bet, said, "But there's something you will like though, Harry…"

"Yeah?" Harry sat up.

"You wanna see some of the agent gadgets we get?" Devon smiled.

"Yes please!" Harry fawned.

"If you tell me where this painting is…"

I drew a breath.

"OKAY!" Harry squealed. "This is SO cool but show me one first."

"Right…" Devon handed something back. "That rather stylish, metallic gadget may look like a pen—"

Harry pulled it apart in under three seconds. "Yeah, it is a pen." Reaching forward, my son sprinkled the decapitated pieces into the centre tray. "And Mum never told us where she put it."

Devon cast a forlorn glance at his dismantled possession.

I added, "But he can probably superglue it to your finger if that helps?"

"Great," Devon mumbled.

I enthused, "They'd call you 'Double-O Pen-Finger.'"

"Funny," he said blandly. "So where are we staying tonight?"

"Yours?" I offered.

"Can't. It'll be watched."

"A hotel?"

"Too risky, we would need to pay on a card, they'll track us."

"You don't have a fake passport?"

"All out of them today, unfortunately," he replied. "And we need to find somewhere safe to go, where you won't be recognised. Any other suggestions?"

Harriet broke the silence. "We could go to the coast."

"Why the coast?" Devon asked, his voice serious.

"We could camp on the beach," Harriet replied, "and—"

Devon cut her off. "No, we can't, unfortunately that's not a good idea."

"Oh, please hear her out," I implored. "You never know. Go on, darling."

"…and, if we did…" suggested Harriet, "all the mermaids would swim up and help us. They would take us back to the sea to their water-palace and we could hide, and they'd teach us to breathe underwater, and we could stay there forever and ever, only coming up to solve mysteries and help drowning sailors."

Harry leant to one side and farted, making Devon put his window down.

"Or…" I said hopefully, wafting the air, "we could stay the night in Nathaniel's old barn?"

Harriet shrugged. "Okay."

I also put my window down, happy in the knowledge we had a plan.

It was dark by the time we got deep into the Oxfordshire countryside, our car bouncing happily around a series of tight bends along a beaten track, blissfully unaware of what would befall it later. At last Nathaniel's huge barn, with its flaking wooden exterior and muddy pools highlighted against the moon, loomed in the distance. This was where he sometimes went to sew clothing, build things, or paint, and in years gone by, we'd hang out there together, telling stories and smoking weed.

We parked up and got out.

That's when Devon shrieked. "Jesus! Something's attacking me!"

"What is?" I replied.

"I don't know," he wailed, "but it's biting me from all sides, what the fuck is it?"

My children giggled.

"It's not one thing," I explained, "it's a number of things, and they're not biting, they're guard chickens."

"What in God's name are guard chickens?!" he cried.

"It's kind of self-explanatory." I found the key under the mat, and we let ourselves into Nathaniel's old barn. Pitch-black inside, my hand moved around the wall until I found the light switch, half expecting to see a hundred police waiting in the darkness. There were none. Just the musty smell of old material, wood, and lots of mess. We found a torch and turned off the main light to attract less attention. There were blankets and sunbeds, and I put my very sleepy children to bed, while Devon and I chatted.

"You definitely have the original?" he rambled on. "Because I stuck my neck out for you, and this better not be a wild goose chase."

"It's not."

"Good, and forgive me if I sometimes doubt your state of mind."

"Slightly insulting," I commented.

"What with those tiny paper animals you'd hide in my car with secret messages."

"They were nice messages," I mumbled. "You won't get them ever again."

"I'm just saying, not to mention every time I went back to MI5 HQ, I had glitter all over my face, which I must say is a bad look for an agent, and now everyone thinks I'm dating a fairy."

"Not anymore," I muttered.

"And why didn't you give it back when you first got arrested?"

"I was still thinking."

"Thinking about what?"

"Where the painting would go if I gave it back."

"What does it matter? In some gallery in the US probably."

"It's a lot of money just sitting on a wall when it could do so much good. That money could change people's lives," I pointed out. "Especially at the moment."

He shook his head. "People like you piss me off. No offence."

"We do, do we?"

"Yeah. Save the world. Save the planet. Save the people. You can't save everything because, news flash... people kind of ruin the planet." He chuckled before spotting the microwave and a freezer. "Double eureka!" he exclaimed happily. "Looks like there's food here."

"People don't HAVE to ruin the planet," I huffed quietly.

"Preaching to everyone about their lives, it winds me up. I'm just being honest."

"Makes a change."

"Hey, you know I've found us frozen homemade pies," he called from the freezer. "A package here says 'A1'. What do you think that means?"

I made a nonchalant gesture. "A1 is the best of that batch of his pies."

"Nice." And he threw it in the microwave.

"None of this ever concerns you?" I asked.

"What?"

"Did you know four million children go to school without any breakfast in their tummies? And it's people like you who don't care..."

"I don't care? I fight for my country. You're just a thief who got caught. And then you sit there in your posh flat," he clearly wasn't finished, "pretending you're going to make a difference but doing fuck-all about it. People like you who change their social media status during a disaster, to show everyone they 'care'. The same ones who send 'thoughts and prayers' to a situation, instead of money. It's so funny."

"I make you laugh?"

The microwave pinged, and he put his fork in it and began eating.

"Yeah, you kind of do."

"I'm not that person you're painting. But you are right about one thing, I need to do more to help."

"See," he mumbled between mouthfuls, "just speaking my mind."

"Thanks," I said, before adding, "Oh, and just speaking MY mind, the A1 is also a road." I pointed out.

"Yeah, of course. So?" He shrugged, shovelling in more pie.

"Check the freezer, I think the A41 and B465 are there too."

He was processing this information, while his chewing slowed down.

I explained, "After Screechthud, Nathaniel takes the poor things home—"

"Sorry, what is Screechthud?"

"Screech…Thud," I clenched my teeth awkwardly, "it's what he calls them. He finds the poor things dead in the road, takes them home, removes the fur for clothing, and pops what's left in a pie." I took a big breath, dropping my shoulders. "Am I still making you laugh, honey?"

He ran out to retch.

I finished the pie. Delicious and organic.

Devon was annoyingly right, though. I was a thief and nothing more. But now I had a chance to make a big difference. And how often does anyone get that one chance?

The next morning, I awoke to their hushed voices.

"Does your car even have an ejector seat?" came Harry's disappointed voice.

"Sorry," Devon replied.

I tilted my head on my pillow to see their reflection in a dusty old mirror Nathaniel used when measuring jumpers. The twins were sitting side by side on the floor, backs against the wall. Devon was propped up against an old cupboard on the floor opposite them. It was a lovely picture.

Harriet asked, "Have you ever met the Queen?"

"No," he replied.

She pushed, "Do you want to?"

"No."

"Why?"

"She's dead," he answered honestly.

They both nodded, considering this.

Harry breathed into his hand. "Do you have a toothbrush?"

"No," he replied.

Harry's eyes lit up. "Okay, have you ever fought ninjas?"

"No," Devon answered.

"But," Harry pursued, "you can do karate, surely?"

"I know some martial arts."

"Sick." Harry was impressed. "And have you ever saved the world?"

"From what?"

"Ending."

"No. But I did save some of that pie from last night if you want any?"

They looked disgusted.

"Tough crowd," he said.

Harriet was next. "And are you married?"

"Not anymore."

"Do you have a girlfriend?"

"No."

"Are you telling the truth?" she said, pointing her finger from her eye level, as if Devon was prone to lying.

"Yes."

Harriet's questioning was becoming more interesting.

Harry's turn next. "You think robots will rule the world one day?"

"Maybe."

Harriet wasn't finished. "Would you ever get married again?"

"Ignore her," Harry jumped in. "Have you taken a bullet for the president?"

"No, Harry, I haven't. And he's American. Harriet, to answer your question, yes, if I found the right woman, and was in love."

"If you had to kneecap someone," Harry asked, "would you choose a gun? Because a hammer would make more mess." He made blood squirting sounds to illustrate his point.

"Jesus, Harry!" Devon exclaimed, visibly disturbed. "Harriet, your question."

"Do you like Mummy?" she probed.

"Yes," Devon replied.

She raised her eyebrows. "Do you love her?"

"My breath is really bad," Harry announced, changing the subject abruptly. "Is yours okay?"

"As it happens," Devon replied, "yes."

But I never got to find out whether he loved me or had fresh breath, because at that moment, a car pulled up outside and two doors slammed shut. I sat up and Devon sprang up like a cat and went over to the grubby window. He turned back to us with his finger over his lips, signalling for silence.

"What?" I mouthed.

"Trouble," he whispered.

Two men were talking quietly by their car, and I could only hear the gist of it. But they were angry about having to be there and didn't like the smell of the place and one of them called the other an inbred hick.

Devon seemed to think they were CIA and seriously bad news.

And then they were both attacked by chickens and ran off screaming to their car. After a standoff, with chickens all over their car's bonnet and roof, one of the men left at a trot towards a huge bag of grain. The flurry of chickens quickly caught up with him, swarming over his body, flapping and pecking with such fervour that he was momentarily lost in a whirlwind of feathers and squawking. Once he got to the bag, he cut it open and his attackers lost interest, to eat the feed instead.

"I'd better go and talk to them," sighed Devon, "tell them the truth."

"Which is?" I asked.

"That you're taking me to the picture, and we'll hand it over to the authorities and everything will be fine. We just need some breathing space, but," he continued, "they'll probably want to take you in. And when they do, they'll say THEY found you and THEY saved the day to get THEIR brownie points, and they may even take the picture back to the US.

"Oh," I said. "And you don't like that."

"No."

"Because you want your brownie points."

He looked at me and shrugged. "I guess."

"When everyone gets their points," I said, "what will happen to me?"

"If we get *The Doctor* back, and it's not damaged at all…"

"It may be slightly damaged."

He spun around. "Slightly? Why? I thought you said it was safe?"

"Well, I hope so."

"You hope?!"

"I'm just not sure the person who has it will have known not to spray it with Mr. Muscle."

"Jesus, who the fuck has it?"

"You'll see," I said, looking away, then adding, "hopefully." Just to throw in some doubt because I was still angry with him.

"Right," he said. "Go get the twins, get them out the back and into the car, quietly. And start the engine."

"Start it, from the driver's seat?" I asked.

"Exactly, where you would be driving it from. You can drive?"

"Hmmm, I can, but—"

"Good. Then watch me from the corner." He said all this while still peering through the barn slits. "And if I scratch my head, that's our signal. You drive out fast and pick me up on the way past."

"Is this going to be a car chase?"

"We're not in a movie. You just drive out and pick me up. It will give us a head start, and at some point, we'll lose them."

"Not sure this is a good idea," I began. "The last time I drove…"

"Just do what I say, it's a great idea."

"Why is it?"

"Because it's my idea." His confidence was never in question. He sighed. "And I honestly don't know what will happen to you. I'll do my best, but it's such a high-profile case, and you've given them quite the run-around. They will want you to pay a penalty…" He shook his head.

"A fine?"

He sighed. "No, I mean like…"

"Oh. I see."

Prison.

But before I could dwell on that image, Devon cursed. "Oh, fuck it, wish me luck." And then he was striding out into the yard, greeting them. "Howdy partners!"

The back door led out into the field, where we had parked the car behind the barn the night before. The twins got in the back, with me in the front. I started its engine, then quietly I stepped back out, and tip-toed over to peer around the corner of the barn to scan the horizon for any head-scratching.

Well, that was what was meant to happen.

But I didn't get a chance to check for our secret signal. Because as soon as I stuck my head out, one of the men spotted me and shouted, "That's her!"

I darted back, tip-toed again over to the car (not sure why), got in the driving seat, and tried to drive away, but instead, I steered the car out into the yard about 20 feet from them and then began skidding in the wet mud, doing circles on the spot, while the three men watched on, curiously. As we spun past them a third time, Harry said from the back, "Mummy, I think you're meant to be driving forward.

"I'm well aware, thank you, Harry."

At last, I stopped the car by Devon. He shook his head, looked down at his wet mud-soaked jeans and got in.

"That was quite something," he said. "They're CIA and not playing ball."

"Oh."

"Drive then, Minty drive!" he urged.

The two men were already running back to their car.

And off we went.

Now, I was trying to steer Devon's car along a very unused bumpy gravel and grass path, while behind us the CIA followed. I had the windscreen wipers going, plus both indicators, and now the car's siren had begun from beneath us.

"What are you doing?!" Devon bellowed.

"I don't know!" I bellowed back. (There was a lot of bellowing going on.)

"Mum…" Harry whined from the back.

"Yes?" I snapped. "What is it?"

"Does this mean…" he said, "we won't have to read our poem anymore?"

"NO! You're still doing it!" I shouted. "And if I were you, I'd start practising!"

Ahead, a tractor was narrowly avoided, while our car bounced over puddles and grass, the siren blaring. The vehicle jerked and jostled like a bull in a rodeo, with Harry's wavering voice adding to the frenzy, "The canal… in the thick morning mist… barges move peacefully by…" To help the fun, Harriet began singing at the top of her lungs.

Devon was finding all this difficult to cope with. I knew, by the way he was biting his fist and rocking.

Harry continued, "And in the clear reflection of the wateeeeeeer!"

Directly around a tight to the right, then one to the left, our wheels lost traction, and we slid sideways through a bush and down an embankment. Everyone screamed as we plummeted sideways into a stream at the bottom, wheels spinning in the mud.

"Fuck fuck fuck!" Devon exclaimed.

The car with those two American chaps drove past us.

We waited with bated breath.

Nothing happened.

It dawned on us they had not seen us disappear through a hedge. We clambered out and up the grassy bank to stand, looking down on his beloved car. Devon, his jacket slung over one shoulder, white shirt untucked, mud on those blue jeans, was visibly heartbroken. "You were saying," he said with a despondent sigh, his eyes never leaving his unfortunate vehicle, "something about the last time you drove?"

"Ah yes. I ended up in a pond." I shrugged.

"Oh." He nodded. "Should have listened."

CHAPTER EIGHTEEN

THE PLAN

~NOW~

A rugged 4x4 jostled its way through, its tyres crunching over the rough grass nestled between towering cornfields. It came to a halt beside us, and a man with a broad West Country accent leant out of the window. He chuckled warmly. "Guess you're not locals, eh? Seen plenty of vehicles stuck down there over the years. Whose car was it?"

"Mine," Devon admitted.

"Lovely engine," the man observed, "but it's the wrong choice of car for these roads, sonny."

"Yes, but," Devon began patiently, "I didn't intend to…" He trailed off, shaking his head in resignation.

The man then enquired, "Where you off to?"

"London," I responded.

"Hop in then," he offered, a twinkle in his eye. "I'm heading there myself."

As it turned out, he was on his way to the farmers' markets in West London.

Two strokes of luck in one day. But the thing with that kind of luck, you know life will rebalance the scales again soon.

Harry had already climbed into the front seat before we could protest. Devon, Harriet, and I squeezed into the back. The journey was surprisingly pleasant. We didn't use our real names (for obvious reasons). I called myself Dorothy, because I assumed we had been saved by a kind of friendly scarecrow from *The Wizard of Oz*, albeit one in a Land Rover. We engaged our rescuer with questions, to distract him from putting on the radio (in case the news blasted out).

Fred told us about his farm and his wife, who he'd been married to for thirty years, and amusing stories about the couples from London who had moved to Oxford to set up their own farms, but who'd come unstuck. And the women from London who'd totter around the village in muddy heels.

"You two planning to buy land?" he asked.

"Oh, no," Devon corrected him, "we aren't a couple. Just friends."

Oh, like that, is it? Not even for pretend?

I spoke rapidly. "No, we certainly aren't a couple, Fred. He goes for the type of women you mentioned before."

Fred laughed. "You beware of them, Devon, they'll be your downfall!"

"I tell him that," I said, nudging him playfully. "I say they'll be your downfall, but…will he listen? No. Never. He chases them around like a lost sheep."

The man roared with laughter, while Devon tapped his fingers on the door handle impatiently.

But I wasn't finished.

My blood was boiling. "And to be honest, it's not all his fault. When he was a baby, he got lost in the country for a week."

"No!" exclaimed Fred.

"You'll never guess how he survived," I said. "Do you want to carry on the story, sweetie?"

Devon forced a smile. "No, why don't you fill in the ending?"

"Fine," I said. "They found him in a barn, curled up in the hay with a cow."

"Oh, that's so incredible." Fred sighed.

"Suckling," I said, barely able to contain myself, "on a huge udder, and that's why years later, he only goes for women with enormous breasts." I grinned smugly. "Which of course, I'm sorely lacking."

I was proud of that.

We drove in silence. Although, Harriet, I noticed, had shifted further away from Devon, with a look of utter revulsion on her little face.

Devon released the gloves-are-coming-off-chuckle from his lips, which sounded like a near replica of the one John Travolta did in the film *Grease* when he was lost for words after being challenged by Sandy in the diner.

Long description of chuckle. Sorry.

Fred dropped us off on the High Street in Paddington. He told me to look after myself while patting my shoulder and fixed me with his eyes, as if he knew who we really were.

Paddington High Street on a Thursday lunchtime was a hum of activity, with the lively chatter of locals and tourists blending with the melodies of street performers, creating a mesh of urban sounds.

I hid my face and pretended to look at shop windows, while around me there was the sound of the occasional clatter of shopping carts or the jingle of a bicycle bell.

Devon bought a white hoodie from a sports shop and handed it to me. It went nicely with my jean-shorts.

He also gave me a pair of snazzy sunglasses.

Off Devon went again to buy a pay-as-you-go phone while the twins and I waited in a greasy spoon café for him. Inside, the aroma of coffee mingled with the sound of frothing milk and clinking cups. We found a clean table and ordered some drinks. Devon arrived, his face shadowed under a new hoodie, looking distinctly out of sorts. "I'm not happy," he said, confirming my suspicions.

"Why's that, sweetie?" I asked.

"Because of this!" He passed a copy of the *Sun* newspaper.

There was a photo of the two of us on the front page. It was slightly blurred, taken from the festival as we ran to his car, with the headline, 'Who Is Minty's Mysterious Man?'

"And don't you look sweet!" I exclaimed gaily. "But I have a question."

"Yes?"

"How do you run without them falling off?"

"Without what falling off?" He glanced down at the newspaper, his eyebrows energetically knitting together in a mix of anger and frustration.

"Your sunglasses? I have trouble just keeping my shoes on."

His grumpy face was clearly unhappy. Around us, the hum of the café continued, people immersed in their own worlds, oblivious to our tense exchange which continued like this: "What have I done now?" I prodded.

He took a deep, slow, patient breath. "You have no idea why this is bad for me, do you?"

"No, Dimples, I do not."

"Funny girl," he said, without humour. "This photo is bad for business."

"Why?"

"How many famous people do you think do undercover work?"

"Haven't given it much thought," I answered honestly.

"There aren't any!"

"Oh. But Steven Seagal used to."

"He's about twenty stone and six-foot-three…"

"And?"

"He did NOT work undercover."

"I saw him working undercover."

"Where?" he demanded.

"On TV."

"If you saw him on TV," he snarled, "he wasn't undercover!"

"But…"

"That's the whole point, MINTY, if he was on TV he was NOT fucking-under-fucking-cover!"

"Is there any need for that much swearing?" I reminded him.

He took a breath. "That was reality TV. Nothing more."

"You don't seem to like Mr Seagal very much."

He whispered, "I don't give a fuck about Steven Seagal, Jason Bourne or Dwayne the fucking Rock Johnson. I care about my career, which at the present moment, since I met you… has been slowly disappearing down the toilet!"

At that moment the waitress appeared with a polite smile, asking us what we wanted to eat.

Speaking in the lowest voice possible, I murmured, "Four full English breakfasts, please."

After she had left Devon asked, "What are you doing?"

"Ordering breakfast."

"Why the stupid voice?"

"Shhh…" I rasped. "I'm undercover."

"Oh, God help us," he breathed.

Devon had emailed Maxi from a made-up account, requesting a meeting to discuss the hiring of a few receptionists for a new tech firm. The address of the property we had given her was in a busy street nearby, with cars passing and people going about their day. Crouching behind a parked car, we waited, and at last Maxi's car arrived. She was quickly out, checking the house number, then strutting up their drive, disappearing momentarily before reappearing, visibly bewildered. I'm guessing because the owners of the place told her they did not need four receptionists. However, by that time the twins were on their mission and popped up to greet her, throwing their arms around her shoulders, and with their deftness of practised conspirators, had slipped a phone into Maxi's hands.

We didn't see much more of her because we were already walking in the opposite direction. We rang her phone…

"Where are you?" she answered, in her usual curt tone.

"Can you take the twins to the Maida Vale Centenary show?" I said.

"Of course."

"And can you tell my parents I love them, and look after them?"

"I WAS looking after them, before you called—" she began, but we had gone into the bustling station, and as we entered, the sounds and the tube-line-people swallowed her voice, cutting our connection. We were on our way to Maida Vale, and things were about to get sticky.

We took the Bakerloo line, and left at Warwick Avenue, the stop before Maida Vale, walked through some arches, breathing in the musty air, and stepped onto the escalator. We stood one in front of the other in our hoodies and shades, passing posters for theatre shows and watches. But I couldn't shake off the feeling that the police might be waiting for us at the tube exit, adding a thrilling edge to an otherwise dreary journey. No police there though, but lots of them in the distance, towards the Maida Vale tube. We took a turn down various backstreets, edging closer to our goal at every step.

I had told Devon where the painting was, and that Cynthia thought it was my artwork. And we had a plan for Jenny at Jenny's Crafty Kids. Devon was going to pretend he'd arrested me. We would walk through the shop to the back alley, find Cynthia's garden-gate, and hope she was in, then grab the painting before all hell descended.

We arrived at the Crafty Kids shop door.

The bell pinged, letting her know guests had arrived.

We entered.

Chaos reigned inside. Jenny was in the midst of a colourful

battlefield, with children in smocks brandishing paintbrushes like swords, and the air filled with their joyous shrieks and laughter. Jenny was crouched on the floor, moving a pool of blue paint into a dustpan with a large cloth, while above her they mainly threw paint at each other across large oblong tables covered in white plastic.

We stood awkwardly for a bit.

Devon was ready to flash his card, but without looking up, Jenny bellowed over the din, "Yes, yes, yes, sit over there and I'll be with you!"

Devon and I shrugged, and he beckoned me.

We snuck through to the back, along the corridor, and found the door unlocked.

Jenny was still battling to control the mayhem.

The door led us outside to a small, enclosed concrete area. We pushed open the wooden gate and passing through, it was like stepping into another world. The stark concrete gave way to the lushness of a garden with the blooms and the gentle trickling sound of water. And there was Cynthia, absorbed in her peaceful task of watering her flowers.

Her basement flat offered a welcome cool respite from the summer heat outside, and was an instant reminder of my treasured memories, transporting me to my childhood where Rupert, Tamsin, and I were huddled on her sofa watching *Emmerdale Farm* or *Last of the Summer Wine*. The nostalgia smelled comforting and peaceful.

Her living room was adorned with antique furniture, each piece for me bringing back memories.

Delicate porcelain figurines and mementos filled a glass case. A blend of old wood and polished brass filled the air, whilst a grandfather clock ticked quietly on, to mark the passage of time.

Time, which Devon didn't think we had much of… "Would you both like tea?" Cynthia enquired politely.

"Thank you," I replied. Although I noticed my response irritated Devon.

"How do you like it?" she asked.

Devon huffed. "However it comes."

Devon's impatience was like a storm cloud ready to burst at any moment.

"Devon, is it?" Cynthia asked, pottering off to the kitchen.

I leapt in… "Not always. Depends on who he's with."

"Oh well," she called back, "you youngsters. Whatever the latest trend is, I guess. Did you meet on one of Minty's blind-walks?"

"Blind-walks?" said Devon.

I explained happily. "You take the dogs out for an hour and instead of you walking them, you let them walk you, take the tube, or bus, and just see where you end up an hour later." Devon blinked at me blankly. I carried on. "You can take photos of where you are, if you wanted, and keep them for—"

"I get it," he snapped.

Cynthia's voice drifted in from the kitchen: "Davina McCall met her husband dog-walking, did you know that, Devon?"

Devon blew out some air. "No, I did not know Davina met…." he trailed off.

"Dear, what is it you do?" Cynthia enquired of Devon.

I quietly uttered, "He was doing me for a bit, while lying."

Devon whispered back, "You lied to your eighty-year-old babysitter."

I hissed, "And apparently you saved a beached whale!" He pulled a face.

I pulled a worse one back.

He raised his voice. "Sorry, Cynthia, but we are in a bit of a hurry. Can I see the painting Minty gave you?"

She came in with a tray with a pot of tea and cups. "The one Minty painted for us?"

"Yes."

Setting the tray down on a coffee-table, she looked up. "The one she gave us years ago?"

"That's the one. *The Doctor*."

Her voice was tinged with kind concern. "I really didn't think you'd be able to get here, what with all the police and things, and I didn't want you worrying about it anymore. Anyway, you don't need to go through that now."

"Go through what?" Devon leant forward.

"Worrying about that painting," Cynthia said smartly.

"What?" Devon seemed unable to swallow. "What do you mean? Please, tell us quickly?" Words tumbled from his mouth.

"I mean Devon," she said, "it's fine. No need to worry, anymore."

I decided to help out: "We aren't, Cynthia. We would like to know where it is. It was on this wall before."

Devon's gaze snapped to the wall, then whirled back at me, then darted towards Cynthia, then back to the wall. His head began jutting and jolting as he took in every wall as if short-circuiting.

"I'll be honest, dear," she said, "I was never a fan. Kenny loved it. Anyway, it's gone."

"Gone? Where?!" Devon stood, his voice rising.

"Oh!" Cynthia exclaimed, finally grasping his concern. "I didn't think you would mind?"

"Cynthia, we mind." Devon's voice crescendoed into a roar. "EVERYONE MINDS, the WORLD MINDS, that painting was an ORIGINAL ROUSSEAU AND WHERE IS IT?!"

"He's kind of shouty, sometimes," I informed her. "But he doesn't mean to be."

"Oh my!" Oh my!' She fell back, supporting herself with one hand on the arm of her chair. The news heavily affected her balance, and she sat down. "No, not this one. It can't be, Minty wrote on the back, she wrote – *To Kenny & Cynthia, love, Minty*."

This stunned Devon. "You wrote on the back of a priceless painting?"

I shrugged. "You shoot people for a living."

"Oh…" cried Cynthia, her hand fluttering to her chest, her other hand gripping the chair, as the gravity of Devon's words hit home. "My, oh, dear. That painting, I always considered it quite depressing, morbid even, a doctor standing over someone old and sick."

"Where is it, Cynthia?" Devon demanded.

"In heaven, I guess now," she responded.

"Heaven?" he roared. "You've disposed of it?!"

"Oh no, no," she jittered, her voice trembling with uncertainty. "When I heard Minty was going to take it away, I asked Kenny if he wanted it with him, up there."

"Sorry." Devon, sounding now like he was going to cry,

stared at the ceiling. "Who is Kenny, is he on the next floor up? And can we speak to him now?" Devon rasped.

"There's only one floor," I clarified.

"Unfortunately," Cynthia explained, "he passed away eight years ago."

"OH FOR FUCK'S SAKE!" Devon cursed, his temper flaring uncontrollably. "Not for the first time, MINTY, being with you is making me feel slightly seasick while I'm sucked into THIS WORLD OF YOURS!"

"Just sitting next to you," I replied, "makes me feel the same way. And I would like it if you could refrain from any more shouting. Poor Cynthia doesn't need this, do you?"

Cynthia shook her head swiftly. "Let me explain," she said. "I write on a chalkboard outside, and once in a while Kenny replies to me. And I asked him if he wanted this picture and a couple of nights ago, he wrote 'yes.'"

"Did he?" Devon's voice hard and sceptical.

"So, I wrapped it up," she said, "and put it on the flowerbed last night, and it's gone."

I took Devon to one side and explained who had been replying on the blackboard. We went back into the living room to face Cynthia.

"So, you see," she said, "it's gone now."

"The stoner took it," said Devon definitively.

"Which stoner?" asked Cynthia, as if she knew quite a few.

I glared at him.

"The one living above you." Devon hunkered down, ignoring me so his head was level with hers. "Listen, it would be great if your late husband was writing on that board, really it would. And he very well may be watching us all now. But Minty is about to be arrested by a mountain of police and if we had that painting before this happens, we may get a chance to stop her returning to prison, so, do you have—" He halted as we heard sirens approaching. They then disappeared into the distance. "A ladder, Cynthia?"

"A small one behind the rose bushes."

A few minutes later, Devon had located the ladder, propped it against the wall and was climbing up, before he stopped, turning back to look at me. "What are you doing?" he asked.

"Following you." I threw him the widest grin I could. He shook his head. "Just wait here, keep the ladder steady." I stepped down, reluctantly. He continued up.

Crashing sounds and muffled voices from above sent a ripple of anxiety through me as I held the ladder. He reappeared again, descending with a look of newfound determination.

I spoke to his bottom, as it descended, "Was he up there?"

"Yeah." He arrived next to me. "And he told me where it is."

"Are you sure he told you the truth?"

"Oh yes." He nodded. "He paid off his weed guy with it. Lives close by, come on."

As we walked briskly back through Jenny's shop, her face registered pure surprise. She paused mid-task, with one child, her gaze from us to the back door. Devon put his finger to his lips as if to say it should be kept a secret. Then we were gone.

Out into the pavement, we located the Weed-Guy's flat two streets along and pressed his intercom. We lied and said we were friends of the stoner chap. He buzzed us through the door, and we climbed up three flights of stairs to his rather smart studio flat. Devon flashed his badge at the door, and we entered. This time, being on the third floor, the flat was super-hot and humid. Hoodies down, glasses off. Devon wasted no time, his tone sharp as he cut straight to the chase. "Where's the painting?"

"I don't know what you're talking about," Weed-Guy replied. "Hey, you're the *Maida Vale Mum*, the one that stole…"

"Yeah yeah," interrupted Devon, "so you do know, then."

We scoured the flat, every nook and cranny a potential hiding spot. My years of training searching the twins' room for missing items had honed my skills. Behind a set of drawers, my hands brushed against something unexpected. Pulling out a large stash of weed, I couldn't help but let out a triumphant, "Oh lookie lookie, I win!"

Devon cast a disapproving eye at me. "Put it down."

I huffed. "Don't look so righteous, you smoked it with me."

"I did a lot of things for my job," he retorted smartly.

"Oh!" My mouth was moving while my brain was catching up.

The Weed-Guy interjected, "Are you really police?" His voice sounded doubtful.

"Art!" I screamed, startling them both and taking a relieved breath. "Art isn't the only thing I can fake."

Devon laughed dismissively. "You're good, but not that good."

I provoked him further. "Feeling a little unsure, Mr Bond? Are we shhhhaken, not stirred?"

"Can you two both piss off now?" The man pulled out his

mobile phone and began punching in numbers. "This is harassment, and I know my rights."

"Sit down!" Devon barked, but while the man licked his lips, swallowed, he carried on with his phone. In one swift, calculated movement, Devon snatched Weed-Guy's phone and twisted his arm behind his back, slamming his face down on the table. Devon leant in. "We just want the picture, dickhead."

Weed-Guy squealed, "It's worthless anyway!"

I winced. "Is violence really necessary?"

Weed-Guy was adamant. "No, it is not necessary!"

"Then tell us!"

Weed-Guy wailed. "It's another fake, everyone from here to Holland Park has them!"

"How do you know it's fake?" Devon asked.

"Had it valued."

"By who?"

"Peter."

I stepped in. "Is Peter a fine arts valuer? And did he use X-rays and radiography?"

"No," he squealed, "he's a porn actor with a massive cock."

"Helpful," I replied without conviction.

Weed-Guy continued, "And has an evil parrot. He said the picture was a bad imitation, but he'd try and flog it down the pub, he works there, he said he'd pay me half of what he made."

Devon released him.

He shook his arm free. "So was it real then?"

Devon's eyes were dark. "Just call him."

Weed-Guy fumbled with his phone nervously, his fingers struggling to behave.

No one answered.

Devon took his phone with us and left the man handcuffed to the radiator with a bottle of water (and some honey sandwiches which I made in his kitchen).

Chapter Nineteen

THE FINAL STRAW

~NOW~

After getting the information from the pub manager, Devon and I found ourselves on the street outside, discussing our next move. We walked and talked in our hoodies.

"Peter Cramer," he said, "he's involved in the stage set for some production nearby."

"Yuck!" I exclaimed.

"It's not that type of thing," he said. "It's like an amateur charity theatre group."

"Where?" I asked.

"Up the road in Little Venice, big event."

"The Maida Vale Centenary?" I suggested.

"That's it. They've even got an opera singer, apparently," he added, handing me the programme.

I took the leaflet from his hands. "Meredith Bain," I announced theatrically.

"Who?" He handed over a Polaroid. "Here's a shot of the bar staff, he's on the right."

The Maida Vale Centenary Show was a week-long open-air event set in Little Venice, at Rembrandt Gardens. This area, a stretch of grass measuring 150 metres by 50 metres, was beautifully lined with lilies, roses, and lavender. It sat right above the T-junction of Regent's Canal, providing a perfect spot for the event. One canal off the junction leads to Paddington Basin, another towards Camden; the last takes you to the Grand Union which goes all the way to Birmingham. Close by is a triangle of marshland called Robert Browning Island, which we will come to later.

There were only two gated entrances to the gardens, each guarded by a police car parked outside the event. To reach our destination, we needed to pass between these cars. As we made our way, people bustled by on either side, hardly giving us a second glance. Devon pulled me to one side. "I need you to wait here."

"Okay," I said happily.

"And you'll be here when I return?"

"I think so," I answered.

He looked around then back at me, like he was dealing with an internal battle. "I'm trained to be able to look at someone, and know how they'd react to a situation, and I'm good at it," Devon explained, before he slowly lifted my glasses up. "But when I look into your eyes…"

I threw him a massive, innocent grin.

"I honestly…" He shook his head. "I don't know."

"Really?"

"Just tell me you won't run or something?"

"You want me to say I won't run?"

"No, I want you not to run."

"Okay. I won't run, mister." I laughed.

He didn't laugh. "What's so funny?"

"Just picturing what would happen if I did run," I said. "You chasing me around, like kids playing kiss-chase."

His gaze never left my eyes. "You see what you did just then. People in your situation should be panicking."

"I see."

"And I'm not trying to worry you, but if we can't find this fucking picture, you, me, and your children, it's all…"

"Not good?" I tried to help him.

"No, it's not good, it would be very much a major cluster fuck."

"Right."

He sighed, turning away. "Maybe you should come with me, just need to get you past those police."

Rembrandt Gardens, typically a sanctuary of tranquillity and beauty, had been transformed into a bustling hub of activity. Families mingled among food stands, their enticing aromas wafting through the air – the sweet scent of popcorn mixed with the smell of grilled chicken wings. Knickknack stalls added to the variety, with the subtle fragrance of handmade soaps and candles. The focus of the attention was a stage area; standing tall and proud, a vibrant centrepiece, with people gathered around and filling the seats in front of the platform. Large speakers flanked the stage, amplifying music, while a group of toddlers in ballet costumes finished their dance to muted applause.

The announcer, her voice brimming with enthusiasm, promised a day of truly stellar entertainment. However significantly, a large portion of that entertainment, about to unfold, was conspicuously absent from the Performance

Programmes being sold at a nearby stall.

A van which was parked down one side was unloading costumes and outfits from its rear.

"Wait there," Devon commanded, pointing to an exact spot on the kerb, and off he went. I took a side-step to fill the spot he'd pointed to. A few minutes later he was back, with a huge papier-mâché head and a tree costume. "Put this on," he urged.

"No," I replied.

"Why not?"

"It's awful. I think it's meant to be a tree and it's painted very badly."

He fixed me with a hard stare, to let me know there would be no choice in this matter.

"Fine," I told him, reluctantly pulling on the costume over my jean shorts and fitting the head on top, which was instantly hot inside. We headed to the Centenary, him dressed as he usually did, very cool, hood down now, but with shades, and me dressed like a complete idiot, in a badly painted tree-costume-thing.

The day had grown hotter as the afternoon wore on. The audience in front of the stage occupied every available seat and spilled around the edges, the crowd extending along the canal's edges. Many were leaning against barriers or finding spots to sit along the banks, with drinks, food, or ice creams in hand. We passed between the panda cars and merged with the people, slowly making our way along seats and families. I spotted Maxi, my parents, and the twins over towards the back with Mrs Belvedere, their form teacher.

I waved, but realised I was just a tree, waving.

Devon called his boss as we walked. And his side of the conversation went like this: "I didn't realise they were upset, and to be fair, we weren't aware they were chasing us. Hmm, now that I think about it, they were driving pretty close. No, I'm not trying to wind you up. I'm with her now, and if you stop shouting… listen, I'll call you back when I have it. Ten minutes max." And he hung up.

Up on the stage, a flurry of activity unfolded. Stagehands were busy moving scenery depicting Maida Vale's local landmarks. Among them were the iconic Abbey Road studios and its famous zebra crossing, a usual haunt for Beatles enthusiasts, cardboard churches, a canal backdrop, and what seemed like a part of Maida Vale Park (disappointingly without my 'Krays'). Amidst this, some actors were taking their final bows and exiting the stage. Watching and directing stagehands was Peter, who we so urgently needed to speak with. As Peter climbed down the steps towards us, Devon grabbed him, rather roughly (again) twisting his arm behind his back (once more).

"Who the fuck are you?" Peter almost gurgled.

"MI5, nob-head," replied Devon. "Where's the fucking painting?"

"What painting?" Peter gasped.

"I'm at the end of my patience with pricks like you," admitted Devon, quite candidly. "And you've been fighting with someone recently from the look of those scratches."

"That's my parrot!"

"Oh, well, get a dog. We spoke to your weed-guy, he told us you had the painting!"

Peter's face screwed up in desperation. "It was a rubbish

copy. I offered to value it for him. He turned me down. That was it."

"He said you have it!"

"And you believed him? He's a dealer, for fuck's sake! He was lying. He's probably sold it on by now."

Devon yanked him in very close, his voice low and threatening. "If you're bullshitting me, you'll spend a long time wishing you hadn't." He took a deep breath, looked at Peter's face once more before releasing him. "Damn it!" He turned back to me, hands on hips, and seemed to be weighing things up before shaking his head in deep frustration.

"What?" I asked.

He looked down, then slowly his eyes came up, level with mine.

"I'm going to call this in. I have to, Minty… it's time." I tried to nod inside my head-thing.

"Can you hear me…?" he asked.

I tried again to nod.

"And do you understand what I am saying?"

"I think so," I mumbled from within.

He was saying it was all over. And all the horrible things he had warned me about were now on their way, they would be happening to me and the Harries… and the world would go very bad. Awful, but inside my helmet I felt safer.

"Minty!" Devon shouted suddenly, cross. I heard his hands slap the sides of my papier-mâché head, yanking it off.

Innocently, I looked up into his eyes as the fresh air reached me. "Yes?" A drip of sweat trickled down the side of my face.

"This is it… We have reached the end." Then he did

something very strange; he put his hand tenderly on my cheek. "I'm so very sorry," he rasped; and kissed me tenderly on my lips.

I didn't respond. And I didn't kiss him back because I didn't know it was happening until it had happened.

I wish I had known. People were often confusing.

"I let you down," he said, gently.

I tried to speak, but couldn't, because he plonked my tree-head back on. We looked at each other through my homemade helmet. I could hear my breathing, loudly in my ears. I moved my head slightly, so the holes matched up with his eyes.

"What's going to happen next?" I asked.

"Sorry, honey." He shook his head.

Devon dragged his eyes away, turning to make that call, when I was hit by a number of very confused emotions and a barrage of coniferous trees. Each one was as badly painted as mine. I stumbled, pushed along to the back of the stage. Someone grasped my makeshift branches, sewn onto the costume, leading me. We ascended the steps, hidden behind a side curtain. Then, before I could gather my thoughts, we emerged – the five of us trees – onto the stage to a wave of rapturous applause. From where I stood, I could see the crowd extending all the way along the canal. People perched atop cars and lounged on canal boats, with the throng even spilling out beyond The Bridge pub. Below, in the front rows, sat the untouchables – Meredith, Karen, and their friends. It dawned on me then: the applause wasn't for us trees. It was for Meredith, now being introduced, gracefully making her way to the stage in a lavish white ballgown and opera gloves. As she passed by, a strong scent of perfume enveloped me. She approached a silver retro '50s-style microphone. Meanwhile, we trees started to sway our arm-branches, like there was a wind.

There was no wind.

We were plum trees. I was dressed up to look like a plum tree from her blooming garden.

Around us were brown boards overlapping in various shapes from the stage-set of Maida Vale, but now large fans sent red flamelike ribbons dancing in the air.

A string quartet began from the speakers, and Meredith sang.

And I must say, she sang very well indeed. As a string quartet resonated from the speakers, Meredith's voice soared, commanding the stage. Her performance was impeccable, her voice weaving through the melody with grace and power. Then, adding to the spectacle, Arabella burst onto the stage from the right. She somersaulted and cartwheeled among us, her acrobatics a dazzling display against the backdrop of Meredith's singing and the quartet's harmonious strings.

Initially, I mistook the distant sound of sirens for part of the orchestration. But as the sound grew clearer, it was unmistakable – the police were arriving, and a lot of them. Meredith, undeterred, continued her performance, her voice now competing with the growing clamour. The thumping of a helicopter's rotor blades overhead interwove with the music, helping to create a surreal and intense atmosphere. As the sirens encroached from every street leading to Little Venice, they drowned out much of the music. Meredith concluded her song to distracted and scattered applause, the audience's attention torn between the performance and the unfolding drama.

Inspector M.T. James had made his way through the crowd, arriving from the back. Devon, already deep in conversation with other officers, was introduced to him. Peering through the eyeholes of my costume, I could see their brief but animated discussion. They gestured towards the stage as they talked, eventually standing together, side by side. The helicopter above maintained its vigil, circling persistently, drawing the gaze of many spectators upward.

The sirens gradually quieted down.

Meredith had stormed off. The announcer, sounding hesitant, called my children's names. Maxi, with gentle encouragement, guided my twins, my pride and joy, up the steps. They appeared stage left, their little faces etched with apprehensive uncertainty. With hesitant steps, they passed my costume, oblivious to the closeness of where I was, and went up to the microphone, so they could begin with their poem. Everyone fell silent.

However, before they could utter a single word, they were interrupted by a police PA system blaring out, "Everyone on the stage, stop moving and the plum tree at the back, please remove your costume head!"

The twins looked back at us trees. Us trees exchanged looks with each other and one tree removed their head.

"Okay," came the Inspector's voice, this time from the PA system. And there was some muffled chatting, as he conferred with Devon.

"The tree on your right!"

Another tree pointed to themselves.

"No," the PA system said patiently, "next along."

Now everyone was looking at me. And from the holes in my costume, I could see my children also staring at my tree-costume thing. This had not gone to plan.

Tum-te-tum-te-tum.

My awkward humming echoed loudly inside the costume.

With a sigh, I removed my papier-mâché head, revealing myself to the crowd of 400, the police, Inspector James, the untouchables, Mrs. Belvedere, the Headmaster, Maxi, Devon, my parents, the helicopter, and finally, my children. A collective gasp swept through the audience, followed by a shriek: "That's her! That's the mad cat burglar!" A heavy silence descended over Maida Vale.

"Hi, kids," I said weakly.

Their mouths agape, the twins managed a stunned "Hi, Mum," before they ran to me, to hug my costume.

"I didn't want to miss your big moment," I said, trying to explain. "I guess you don't have to read your poem now, which is a shame. I really like it."

"We know," they replied in unison.

That's when I spotted it – the painting, swathed in bubble wrap and a patch of silver electrical tape, slotted into the corner of one of the scenery backdrops. Peter the porn king had been lying. He must have brought it here directly after his visit to the Weed-Guy. With no dressing room or proper backstage, as the producer, he had cunningly hidden it within his own set design.

Rushing forward, I reached it, and yanked it out of its housing, and frantically tore at the tape, unwrapping the bubble wrap. "It's here!" I exclaimed, lifting the painting for all to see. "Found it!" My voice resounded across the venue like I had just located a lost phone.

The crowd gasped as I slowly turned, displaying the Rousseau in my hands to every corner of Little Venice. On the back was my handwriting, still intact.

"KER-BANG!!!"

Cutting through the murmurs, a gunshot rang out.

Screams.

Three rows back from the stage, Quinn and one of his friends stood, menacingly brandishing shotguns. "Aye you be smart, or yee be wiping ye'guts off-the-florr!" Quinn bellowed in his usual ambiguous manner.

A man, possibly Karen's husband, paused, a look of bewildered confusion on his face. He seemed to consider asking for clarification but was barged out the way by Quinn and sent tumbling backwards over plastic chairs before he could utter a word.

So much for untouchable.

Below me, Quinn had arrived and heaved his massive frame onto the stage, an imposing sight. His accomplice continued to wave his shotgun threateningly. Quinn stood, towering above me, snatching the painting with one huge hand and gripping my wrist with the other. "Tyn-a-go," he snarled menacingly.

As Quinn's threats echoed through the air, the crowd scattered, a visible wave of fear rippling through them. The police, unarmed, seemed to be taken by surprise with the suddenness of it all. I was pulled/dragged off the stage, my knees banging into things as we went. Somewhere another gunshot went off, which kind of threw Quinn for a bit, then we were down the steps and out across the grass. General pandemonium spread before us. No sign of his friend, until Devon sprang back up, the shotgun now in his hands and Quinn's accomplice on the ground.

Quinn swore and glared at the distant exits, which were blocked by a wall of police cars. His gaze shifted to the canal next to us, where a narrowboat was slowly moving away from the dock. With one powerful stride, Quinn was on the barge, dragging me with him.

Now it all became a little strange.

There we were, standing at the rear of a barge, accompanied by its owner – an old man with an impressive flowing beard, who steered the vessel slowly into the central pathway of the canal. On the banks, people were either fleeing or rushing towards us with their mobile phones out, filming the spectacle.

And once everyone had found their preferred distance from us either stopped running away or had arrived on the banks, it became very peaceful. The canal boat we were on barely made a ripple as we floated gently along in the sun, and it was beautiful and would have been perfect, but for the shotgun held to my head, and Quinn's gasping, farting and grunting. Quinn reminded me a lot of a St Bernard, crossed with a Chow Chow. This would give you something giant and slobbery, that grunted a lot. "Ya fookin twat," he grumbled at me, "yee shud-a-dun wha' I tolđ-ja." He then turned to the barge owner. "Can-a-the piece-ashyte nay-git-fookin-faster?"

The beardy barge owner shook his head. "She takes her time but will get there in the end."

We were moving exceedingly slowly; so much so, even my father managed to keep pace. Supported by my mother, he walked along the bank just behind Devon and some officers. They were four or five metres away. Dad's voice carrying over the water as he shouted encouragement. "Minty, don't worry, we'll have you out of there soon!"

"Thanks, Dad," I replied.

"Maybe ask him if he'll let you go," he suggested.

I spoke quietly to Quinn's angry face. "Will you let me go?"

"Nae, you'd be lucky ta keep ye life."

I relayed to my parents over the water, "He says it's looking doubtful, Dad."

Quinn was a bundle of nerves, his gun waving at anything that irked him.

Mum called politely across, "Will you be coming back for dinner this evening, dear?"

I asked Quinn, "Will I be back for dinner this evening?"

Over his shoulder I could see my parents' expectant hopeful faces on the bank.

"Na," said Quinn. "An if you ask me another dafty fookin question, I'll blow off one a ya legs," he growled.

I slowly shook my head at my parents.

But Mum wasn't finished. "Shall I defrost a pizza then for the twins and your father?"

I gave her a thumbs up. Dad shook his head. And I wondered if maybe Quinn would try and shoot my mother from where he was, and I considered whether shotguns, which were that short, shot that far. I had no idea. One of those things you wished you had looked up beforehand.

We passed Robert Browning Island in the middle of the water, where the three stretches of canals met.

On one of the banks, TV crews had arrived, and all kinds of people were setting up to film on every side of our lethargic route. Quinn, though, was acting more and more like a caged animal, pacing the length of the boat and waving his gun wildly. Each time he did so, everyone ducked and screamed.

Whilst he seemed busy on the far side of the barge, and as we glided past the final edge of Robert Browning Island, I seized my chance. Clutching the painting, I took a leap onto the island. One foot splashed into the water, and I stumbled, landing heavily on my back at the water's edge, still gripping the painting tightly. Twisting my head, I watched the barge's rear drift further away. Seizing the same opportunity, the old man leaped from the barge, causing a great splash as he hit the water.

Quinn, alerted by the noise, discovered he was now alone on the barge, travelling very slowly, towards Camden. The crowd on the bank erupted with a cacophony of cheers, whistles and applause. But just as quickly as it had arrived, the cheering finished, while Quinn lumbered around the boat to my side, muttering, swearing, and threatening. A hush fell over everyone, who took a collective breath, but Quinn was now too far away to jump. He glared at me with exploding red-faced hate-filled venom as the boat drew further along the waterway.

He raised his gun. "Na one will 'av yee or yee fookin paintin th'n," he bellowed.

Devon's voice rang out from the bank. "NO!" People screamed.

In that moment of chaos, Quinn pulled the trigger. But, as he did, he stumbled forward, accidentally firing both barrels through the bottom of the barge, opening a dark shattered hole in the stern. A profound silence enveloped the canal, broken only by the quiet chugging of the barge's engine while Quinn, now on his knees, looked back at me.

Piercing the stillness came my father's relieved voice. "Espinacas!"

The final glimpse I caught before the barge disappeared from view was of Quinn staring back curiously at my father, as if a man shouting "Spinach!" in Spanish was the bizarre final straw in Quinn's unravelling world.

"Minty, we've got a boat on its way to you," Devon called from his position next to my parents.

"Devon," Dad said, "you're a good chap."

Devon seemed momentarily disarmed, hearing my father get his name right (although not unfortunately his real name).

"No rush, I'm safe," I called. "I have *The Doctor* with me."

"Excellent. Is it damaged at all?" Devon enquired.

"No, looks fine to me." I nodded. "Although…" Aware I was being watched and filmed by a lot of people, I pulled the paintbrush from my hair. "It could do with a slight improvement here or there," I called back, happily.

He laughed nervously. "What you up to, honey?" His voice edged with panic.

Sitting on the bank, with Rousseau's masterpiece facing me, I dabbed my brush in some of the mud, and pretended to brush it over *The Doctor*.

"NO!!!!!!!" Devon shouted, his outcry echoed by gasps from our audience.

I looked up. "What is it, dear?"

"Are you mad?" he exclaimed.

I swivelled the painting around, revealing that my brush had never actually made contact.

"Very funny," Devon managed to say, relief in his voice. "Maybe prop it up over there, honey, so it's nice and safe."

He clutched his chest as if my prank had given him a mini heart attack.

"Actually," I mused aloud, "you know what even half the value of this thing could do for a lot of families."

"Yes, but that's not how this works," Devon countered, his voice firm. "You know that."

"Oh, well then, what's the point?" I retorted. Standing up, I held the painting precariously over the water.

It took quite a bit of persuasion that day while holding the painting over the water's edge. Despite initial reluctance, the government eventually conceded, under media pressure, that at least £40M would be allocated for good causes.

And as for legal matters, my friend, the Inspector, assured me, I didn't have to go to prison again, because the painting had been the property of the Russian mafia, so it didn't seem justified.

We celebrated at the Pig & Parrot, with Rupert, Faith, Maxi and Paulie, Tamsin and Thomas, their children, and our whole family. Dad cradled my Edinburgh Festival trophy, eagerly showing it to anyone who did or did not want to see it, and Nathaniel's band entertained us, with Nathaniel, of course, playing the acoustic toaster. At the end of the last song, the toast popped up to the beat, and Nathaniel caught both slices.

"Crickey!" my father exclaimed.

And a few days later, Devon and I walked the Krays together in the park and encountered a group of young school children with their teacher. The teacher crouched down next to Paddington, while he gathered his class around him. "Listen, children, this dog is very famous, does anyone know why?" They shook their heads. He announced proudly, "When you go home, you can tell your parents today was the day you met the Durex Dog."

"No," Devon corrected him. "That's not the right advert."

"Yes, it is!" the teacher insisted.

Devon gently helped him. "Wrong ad, buddy, you want the paint one."

The teacher's eyes at last widened, as realisation dawned on him. We left him to answer the barrage of questions from the curious children.

Social Services agreed to let the living arrangements carry on, if some of the kittens found new homes, which they did. Arabella took one of the kittens home too.

:)

CHAPTER TWENTY

SIX MONTHS LATER

~NOW~

Meredith's husband, Alistair, found himself embroiled in a scandal, prompting him to extend his ten-year plan to become prime minister to a more distant fifteen years or more. This shift was NOT to Meredith's liking, we had heard.

I had been competing in speed-welding competitions across Europe, winning some and losing others. One day, my parents, Tamsin, Thomas and their children, Rupert, Devon, the twins, and I were in Paris for a show I had that weekend. We arrived a few days early to give me time to prepare, and also for my father to fulfil his wish of visiting the Louvre.

Our whole family went.

The museum quietly buzzed with visitors from all corners of the globe, there to admire the works of art on display. The air was filled with whispered conversations and the occasional gasps of awe as people discovered the marvels that awaited them. One of the works was a huge oil painting of an owl.

"Look at that chap, isn't he glorious?" Mum enthused with delight.

"Yes, Margaret," Thomas responded dryly, "we all know you

love owls."

While most of us moved on, Mum stayed, captivated by the painting.

"Margaret," said Devon, who had held back to stay with her, "why do you love owls so much?"

"Oh," she shrugged, "they have these big, beautiful eyes that look at you, wanting."

"Wanting what?" he probed.

Her gaze turned distant. "There was an owl at my father's vicarage, belonged to my aunt, kept in a cage. He hated that horrid cage. And I did nothing. Nothing to help him!"

Devon nodded. "I think, Margaret, that owl will have been watching you, and knows you cared."

Her face lifted, and she squeezed his hand.

And so, there was a reason after all.

There often is for most things.

We went for a coffee.

That afternoon, we were all once again gazing up at more paintings. We were in one of the grand galleries and found ourselves looking up at my own painting: *The Teacher,* positioned behind a large gold rope and security. The very piece which I had created over a decade ago, which had since been 'discovered' in France, and although major news at the time, was never mentioned by my father. After a while, we were about to move on, when a cheery American fellow nearby exclaimed, "Folks, isn't it just knock-me-down-with-a-feather remarkable!"

"What is it, George?" Dad asked him.

The man continued, "Hey, come on, don't you see the resemblance?"

The painting depicted a classroom scene complete with a blackboard, desks, children, and, and closest to us, a striking, beautiful woman staring out of the picture, in deep thought.

We all turned to look back at my mother, who smiled.

"You know," Mum said proudly, "I was once a teacher… wasn't I?"

"That's right, Mum, you were," I responded warmly. "And all the children adored you."

If you enjoyed the story, I would be incredibly grateful if you could take a moment to leave a review. As a self-publishing author, your feedback means the world to me and helps others discover my work. Simply scan the QR code below or even please just head to Amazon. THANK YOU! Holly

Amazon Review

Goodreads review

See Holly's website Hollydenham-books.co.uk for photos of the real characters, and other titles including Holly's Inbox. *Meet the real Paddington & Muffin here - TikTok account paddingtonmaidavaledog.*

(Also thank you Steve for your anecdote.)

Printed in Great Britain
by Amazon

44191584R00178